PENGUIN CRIME FICTION

THE TRANSCENDENTAL MURDER

Jane Langton was born in Boston, Massachusetts in 1922. She received her B.A. in Astronomy from the University of Michigan and her M.A. in the History of Art from Radcliffe College. She is the author of several children's books and has written for *Children's Digest* and *The New York Times Book Review.* Her other novels of suspense include *The Memorial Hall Murder, Dark Nantucket Noon, Emily Dickinson Is Dead, Natural Enemy,* and *Murder at the Gardner*, all available from Penguin.

The Transcendental Murder

  JANE LANGTON

PENGUIN BOOKS

PENGUIN BOOKS
Published by the Penguin Group
Viking Penguin Inc., 40 West 23rd Street,
New York, New York 10010, U.S.A.
Penguin Books Ltd, 27 Wrights Lane,
London W8 5TZ, England
Penguin Books Australia Ltd, Ringwood,
Victoria, Australia
Penguin Books Canada Ltd, 2801 John Street,
Markham, Ontario, Canada L3R 1B4
Penguin Books (N.Z.) Ltd, 182-190 Wairau Road,
Auckland 10, New Zealand

Penguin Books Ltd, Registered Offices:
Harmondsworth, Middlesex, England

First published in the United States of America by
Harper & Row, Publishers, Inc. 1964
Published as *The Minuteman Murder* by Dell Publishing Co., Inc. 1976
Published in Penguin Books 1989

10 9 8 7 6 5 4 3 2 1

The Emily Dickinson material quoted in this book is from the following sources:
 The Complete Poems of Emily Dickinson, reprinted by permission of Little, Brown and Company.
Copyright 1929, © 1957 by Mary L. Hampson. Copyright 1935, © 1963 by Martha Dickinson
Bianchi.
 The Poems of Emily Dickinson, edited by Thomas H. Johnson, reprinted by permission of the
publishers and the Trustees of Amherst College, the Belknap Press of Harvard University Press,
Cambridge, Massachusetts. Copyright 1951, 1955 by the President and Fellows of Harvard College.
 The Letters of Emily Dickinson, edited by Thomas H. Johnson and Theodora Ward, reprinted by
permission of the publishers, the Belknap Press of Harvard University Press, Cambridge,
Massachusetts. Copyright © 1958 by the President and Fellows of Harvard College.
 Bolts of Melody by Emily Dickinson, edited by Mabel Loomis Todd and Millicent Todd Bingham,
reprinted by permission of Harper & Row, Publishers, Inc. Copyright 1945 by Millicent Todd
Bingham.

LIBRARY OF CONGRESS CATALOGING IN PUBLICATION DATA
Langton, Jane.
  The transcendental murder/ by Jane Langton.
    p.   cm.—(Penguin crime fiction)
  ISBN 0 14 01.1384 3 (pbk.)
  I. Title.
PS3562.A515T7   1989
813'.54—dc 19   88–22806

Printed in the United States of America
Set in Times Roman

For Grace Brown Gillson and Joseph Lincoln Gillson

Ruth Wheeler of Fairhaven Bay is in no way responsible for the wild idea behind this book, but her knowledge of Henry Thoreau in Concord was a great help in the writing of *The Transcendental Murder*.

CAST OF CHARACTERS

Homer Kelly . . . celebrated Emersonian scholar. (In his opinion Concord was a polite little suburban pest-hole, living on its picayune history. It made him sick.)

Mary Morgan . . . Concord? Mary would never have said as much out loud, but she felt herself walking on holy ground. (Looking at her, Homer found himself mumbling a phrase by Thoreau, "The eye is the jewel of the body.")

Arthur Furry . . . Honor Scout. (Practically a witness to the murder at the North Bridge on the anniversary of the celebrated Battle of April 19th, 1775.)

Alice Herpitude . . . Head Librarian, Concord Public Library.

(Because I could not stop for Death, He kindly stopped for me.)

Teddy Staples . . . stone mason, bird-watcher, modest reincarnation of Henry Thoreau.

Ernest Goss . . . owner of the letters that were "transcendental dynamite," father of Charley, Philip, Rowena and Edith.

Elizabeth Goss . . . wife of Ernest. (No real tears, no true laughter.)

Charley Goss . . . impersonator of Dr. Samuel Prescott, Concord hero of 1775 who sped Paul Revere's news to Concord and rallied the Minute Men. Charley's feet, alas, were clay.

Philip Goss . . . by contrast with his brother's, Philip's feet were of some noble material, surely, and set on rising ground.

Rowena Goss . . . beautiful sister of Charley and Philip. *(Neither do men light a candle, and put it under a bushel. . . .)*

Edith Goss . . . ugly sister of Charley and Philip.

Thomas Hand . . . farmer, chairman of April 19th celebrations.

Gwen Hand . . . wife of Tom, mother of Annie, John, Freddie, expectant mother of a fourth child. (But surely not now, as the wind rises?)

Mrs. Florence Hand . . . with her son, Tom, real "Old Concord," true squeezings from the Concord grape.

Howard Swan . . . chairman of the Alcott Association, Moderator of Town Meetings. (Nobly bald, like Bronson Alcott.)

Mrs. Bewley . . . maid-of-all-work. ("WHAT'S THAT YOU'VE GOT THERE, MRS. BEWLEY?" "MESSAGES FROM JESUS! TAKE THEM! TAKE THEM!")

Roland Granville-Galsworthy . . . self-styled Oxford don.

The Concord Independent Battery . . . good fellows all, guardians of the two historic cannon fired at the North Bridge.

James Flower . . . Chief of Concord Police. (Nine inches under the required minimum height, a failing counterbalanced by competence, personality and a special dispensation of the Legislature.)

The District Attorney of Middlesex County . . . (Frightened of cows.)

The Governor of Massachusetts . . . (Fond of Longfellow.)

. . . and not to be forgotten—the august wraiths of Ralph Waldo Emerson, Henry Thoreau, Bronson Alcott, Margaret Fuller, Louisa May Alcott and Emily Dickinson. . . .

Chapter 1

Those whom we can love, we can hate; to others we are indifferent.
HENRY THOREAU

There was a big man sitting at the other end of the table in the reference room of the Concord Library when Mary came in and put down her file. He had a safety pin on one side of his glasses and adhesive tape on the other. His necktie was allover butter-flies. He glanced up at her briefly. He had to look way up, because Mary was six feet tall. For a minute as she settled down with her book she thought about the sharp look of his small eye and the sawn piece of brown hair hanging across the top of his face. Then she got to work.

Memoirs of the Social Circle in Concord, 1895–1909. Read the memoir on Sam Staples, who locked up Henry Thoreau in 1846 for not paying any poll tax to a government that counten-anced the Fugitive Slave Law and war with Mexico. Read it and stop playing around. Look at Sam's chin-whiskery face. Look for references to your ladies. Did Sam know Elizabeth Hoar, Margaret Fuller, Lidian Emerson? Of course there was no hope that any of them knew Emily Dickinson, glorifying Amherst only one hundred miles away. Sam must have known Sophia

Peabody Hawthorne. (Peabody. Was the accent on the first syllable or should you come down hard on the penult, too? If a bag of salted penults costs five cents, how much for a bag of antepenults?)

Mary closed her book with a bang. Come now. It's just this sort of thing that keeps you from getting anything done. Concentrate. What about those female Norcross cousins that Emily Dickinson had in Concord? Did she ever come to visit them? Did the Norcross sisters have any male relatives in the *Social Circle?* Mary ran her finger down the list. No Norcrosses here. Try another volume. She got up and looked through Volumes I and II. No luck. Vaguely she looked around for Volume III.

"Here," said the man at the table, "what name are you looking for?"

Mary stared at him. He had it. "Norcross," she mumbled.

His big thumb flipped the book open at the list of memoirs in the front. "Not here," he said. Then he snapped the book shut and went back to his notes.

Well. That was that. Mary would have liked to look for herself. But she said, "Thank you," and turned to something else. She found Edward Emerson's book about his father and spent her morning on it. Her beautiful free morning. Even with her eyes on the page she was conscious of the way the stranger at the other end of the table used his books. It was a subject on which she was a connoisseur. All the other days of the week Mary stood behind the charging desk, a guardian of the books in the library rather than a reader. And so she knew them all— the magazine leafer, the morning-paper reader, the homework doer, the author of a talk on Concord gardens of yesteryear. This man knew what he was looking for, where to find it and how to take it away. He made notes in a rapid scrawl on a pad of lined paper. He hauled a sheaf of papers out of his briefcase, ran swiftly through them, extracted one and scribbled across the top. Once he snorted to himself. Something was funny.

Edward Emerson wasn't. He was reverent. No one who had known Ralph Waldo Emerson was ever anything else. Usually Mary felt reverent, too. But now she would have loved a breath of Emersonian scandal. She hung her feet in their big tennis shoes on the rung of her chair, and hunched her shoulders over her book. The man pushed back his chair and got up. He rose and rose and blotted out the window. Mary looked up in spite of herself. Tall enough, she thought, then checked herself savagely, and glared back at Edward Emerson. The man went out.

Mary got up, too, after a while, and left the reference room. She crossed the main room with its check-out desk, its balconies, its white busts of Henry Thoreau and Nathaniel Hawthorne and Louisa May Alcott and Bronson Alcott and Ebenezer Rockwood Hoar and its great seated statue of Emerson and went into her own office to eat her paperbag lunch. She left the door open and looked out at Nathaniel Hawthorne's naked classical collarbone. For Mary the Concord Public Library was a pleasure dome and palace of delight. The high dusty ceiling might have been a sultan's canopy, the stern Carrara Transcendentalists so many dancing girls. Mary had caught the transcendental fever long ago, and she planned never to recover. She was writing a book now about the women, taking her time, still reading at random. She had happy thoughts and rattled them out on her typewriter. Everything she wrote was covered over with a film of sweetness, and whenever she read it she licked the sugar. Later it would not be so. She knew how the sugary bits would not fit in, and the grandiose ideas would turn insubstantial. But now it was all sugar, sweet sugar. Mary stared at the wall, put down her sandwich, and turned to her typewriter—

Thoreau made glorious stabs at verse, near-misses. It took an Emily Dickinson to transfix the Transcendental Idea with the hard small shot of her poetry. But how alike are some of their images! Compare Emily's

     Split the Lark—and you'll find the Music—
     Bulb after Bulb, in Silver rolled—

with Henry Thoreau's

    The air over these fields is a foundry full of moulds
    for casting bluebirds' warbles.

Mary jumped. "What?" Someone was standing behind her. It was the big man from the reference room. Had he been reading over her shoulder? What was the big idea?

He stuck out a drawer from the card catalogue and pointed to a card. *Thoreau the Poet-Naturalist,* by Channing. "Where is it?"

He might have said please. Mary gave him her big kindly smile and pointed him in the right direction.

A moment later he was back. "Not there."

"Perhaps Miss Herpitude can help you," said Mary, wishing he would go away. Then she repented. How could he know it was her day off? "Do you know Jetsom's new book?" she said.

"Jetsom? Which Jetsom?"

Which Jetsom? Why didn't he look it up? Mary looked at her typewriter. "F.A. Jetsom," she said carefully.

He went out, but a moment later he was back, looking at her suspiciously. "You mean R.F. Jetsom, don't you? Ralph Framingham Jetsom, *Thoreau at Harvard?*"

"No," said Mary. "I mean that other Jetsom. F for Flotsam, A for And." She banged out a sentence of gibberish on her typewriter, then looked up to find him still there. She put her glasses on. "It's my day off," she said humbly.

She was like a big untidy flower, the man decided, one of those red and white striped carnations named after Mrs. Jocelyn Pope Hopewell or Mrs. Eisenhower Roosevelt Jones, or a sort of bouquet with a couple of fringed gentians in the middle, whatever a fringed gentian looked like, but probably like those black eyelashes hanging down like tassels over those blue eyes. "The eye is the jewel of the body," he murmured to himself, quoting Henry Thoreau.

"What's that?" said Mary. Some insult, no doubt.

"I said, all right for you." He turned on his heel and went out of the room.

Mary took the pickle out of her lunchbag and took a bite. She was surprised to find that what was shaping up in her mind was that tiresome triumphal arch again. It was part of the baggage that followed her around. There it was, with all its gear, the

colossal cornice and the coffered barrel vaults and the chan-
neled pilasters and the gesturing statuary and the streaked marble columns. And through the opening that same tedious
procession was passing, splendid with banners and horns and
horsemen in red and blue and gold. What was it for? Who were
they? Where were they going? The man on the biggest horse,
the one who was looking at her, had a face now, the face of the
man with the basso profundo voice. Hey, get out of there.
That's my private triumphal arch, my private horses and horns
and my red and blue outfits. Go away.

Chapter 2

I have travelled a good deal in Concord.
HENRY THOREAU

Outside it was March. Mary stood on the steps of the library looking up. A noisy flock of grackles had filled the elm trees like a convention of Shriners using up all the available hotels. The sky was blowing away like a silk scarf caught in the branches. High up in the blue air there was another flock of grackles, hovering over the shining ragged Y of the junction of the swollen rivers and over Walden Pond and over the hills named by the Indians—Punkatasset, Nashawtuc, Annursnac— and over the glistening dotted swamps and over the brown haze of elms and maples and buttonwoods that obscured the veering arrowheads of Concord's streets. The flock opened out, then collapsed and thickened and began to descend, wheeling over the bronze Minuteman at the North Bridge, flapping down on the rooftops of the Milldam stores that were slung sway-backed between their chimneys, screeching at each other from the gigantic white Woolworth false-front with its pseudo-Colonial urns, fluttering to the sidewalk momentarily between the Greek columns of the old bank building, then tossed up again like a blanket shaken out by a housewife to circle around the white belltower of the First Parish Church, banking sharply in alarm at the cracking of the tall-masted flag on the traffic island, and coming to rest at last for a screaming committee meeting on the Old Hill Burying Ground at the end of the street. Below the graveyard lay the Milldam with its stores, and Monument Square with its Civil War Memorial obelisk and its little temples devoted to Christian Science, the Knights of Columbus, the Masons and the Middlesex Fire Insurance Company. Running away out of sight were the tree-lined streets with their old wooden houses—to the southeast the simple ones with the small windows, and Emerson's place and the Alcotts' Orchard House and Hawthorne's Wayside and the Antiquarian Museum, and to the west beyond the Milldam on Main Street the bigger, finer houses with their broad flat pilasters and imposing doorways and their back yards sloping down to the river.

Mary walked down the library steps and started home, thinking about the movies. In the movies, when there was something energetic going on, the background music was "The Ride of the Valkyries." Or if there was something sad, they played sad music, exalting the action into poetry, so that you turned with tear-filled eyes to your neighbor, whispering, beautiful, isn't it. That was what living in Concord was like—the movies. Only instead of music you had historical association, or something pungent that Waldo or Henry had said. And if you were cursed with a photographic memory you couldn't even walk down the street without the drums and fifes starting up, or the transcendental jukebox. Here was the Milldam. In Thoreau's day the mill had already been long gone, replaced by a row of stores. Henry had called it Concord's Rialto. There by the bank had been one of the blockhouses during King Philip's War. Beside the bus stop was the place where old Simon Willard and Peter Bulkeley had bought the original six miles square from Squaw Sachem and the Indians of Musketaquid in an atmosphere of peace and concord in 1636. You couldn't cross the square without remembering that Emerson never crossed it without feeling a wild poetic delight, you couldn't look at the Catholic church without thinking of its start in life as a home for the Universalists, and of the handsome invitation they had issued to everybody in favor of the universal salvation of all mankind to meet at Bigelow's tavern to choose officers. You couldn't even glance down Monument Street without thinking of the red backs of the British Regulars filing down it on their way to the North Bridge and the beginning of all that important trouble in 1775. That April day had been the first occasion when history had shone her spotlight on Concord, when a scattering of balls from a few fowling pieces and Brown Bess muskets had left a hole in the fabric of things-as-they-were that wasn't to be sewn up again. Then in the forties and fifties history had aimed her burning glass at Concord again, and in simple houses noble as Doric temples there had flamed up a kind of rural American Athens, with Margaret Fuller for a visiting oracle, Emerson and Thoreau and Alcott for philosophers and Nathaniel Hawthorne for a weird kind of Sophocles. And so important to the general blaze of utterance had been each particular pond or wood lot or boulder field that Emerson had make a joke, once, about the poor blockheads who were not born in Concord, but had to do the best they could, considering they had never seen Bateman's Pond or Nine Acre Corner or Becky Stow's swamp.

The next generation had sugared down into a Louisa May Alcott, no Transcendentalist, and after that Concord had been content to live in the shadow. But it was still a lively and ravishing suburban town. Mary would never have said as much out loud, but she felt herself walking on holy ground.

Muddy ground. Wherever the grass was thin, spring was trying to exhale itself through the frozen earth, and there were glutinous footprints everywhere from yesterday's wallowing galoshes. Mary picked her way carefully. In the shadow of the curb, under the metallic platelike masses of ice, dirty with sand and gravel, below the hardened drifts yellowed by dogs, there ran a stream of clear water. If you could live through March, the old trick would happen again, and March would be transmogrified into April and May.

"Mary!" It was Charley Goss, pulling up to give her a ride.

Mary got into his car and accepted a jocular kiss. It was only half-jocular, she knew, because Charley was sweet on her. So was his older brother Philip. A year ago they had taken turns proposing to her. No, she had said—no. But it hadn't seemed to stick, and they were both still working on it. Mary had begun to feel like a sort of giant prize panda in a ring-the-bottle game. Charley and Philip took her out alternately. She was an official friend of the family. Part of the official position seemed to be that it was all right to maul her a bit, and Mary, apologetic for being hard-to-get, went along in a friendly spirit, but wished they wouldn't. Sometimes she wondered how long she could hold out.

"How are Emily and Margaret and Henry today? Still frustrated?" said Charley, getting a rise. Mary always took the bait.

"Don't forget, they lived before Freud and so they didn't know they were, if they were."

"Well, I sometimes wonder if they didn't have their fun after all. Did it ever strike you as kind of funny that Henry Thoreau kept the home fires burning for Lidian Emerson while Waldo was away? And what about old Waldo and little Margie Fuller?"

"I don't suppose you'll believe it, but there was a time when men and women could be friends with each other."

"Listen, girly, men and women have only one kind of relation to each other, and that's all they've ever had or ever will have. Don't kid yourself."

"Any luck in finding a job yet?" (Change the subject.)

"Why, certainly, certainly. Lots of them. Did you hear about my spin with the Acme Cement Company? I was supposed to straighten out their accounts. Perfectly simple, nothing to it, I was going great. But then they got a big contract with the highway department and all of a sudden they didn't want their accounts straightened out any more. Well, that was all right with me because I walked right into a jim-dandy job at Madame LaZarga's Superfluous Hair Removal Salon. And I was doing fine there, too, getting in on the ground floor with all kinds of opportunities for advancement and a glorious future, and Madame LaZarga had turned out to be a really great woman, truly noble. But then my father got wind of it and that was the end of that. He just couldn't see the dignity in the removal of superfluous hair. The whole world panting for it, too. Think of it—millions of hairy people with whiskers sprouting out all over, and idealistic Madame LaZarga devoting her life to them. I don't understand why, but my father couldn't see it at all."

"Well, I'll bet the right thing will turn up yet." Mary looked at Charley and wondered for the thousandth time why her heart refused to leap over the stile for him, or for his brother Philip either. They were attractive, surely, with their red heads? And tall enough to look her in the eye? What was wrong? Charley's forehead, perhaps, was against him—that empty expanse of bland pinkish skin, crowning his cherubic face. And of course his feet were clay—Charley was the black sheep, the ne'er-do-well. But there was nothing wrong with Philip Goss at all. His brow was high and thoughtful like some furrowed promontory, and his feet were anything but clay. Some noble material, rather, and set on rising ground.

Of course the difference between them was their father's fault, the old blowhard. Ernest Goss showed an outrageous favoritism for his successful son. No wonder Philip was a promising lawyer, going places, doing well at everything he tried, while Charley just went from failure to failure. Poor Charley. Philip's success was like a kind of standard and plumb line for him, demonstrating what he might have been, a sort of perpetual I.O.U.

Mary looked out the car window. They were crossing the Red Bridge over the Concord River. The river had risen with the spring thaw and it was spread out for hundreds of yards in its broad bed. There had been a girl Henry Thoreau had loved, and he had taken her out rowing on the river. She had turned him down soon after she had turned down his brother John. That was what Mary herself had done—she had refused two brothers, too. Mary imagined herself sitting in Henry's boat, gliding under the shadow of the bridge, with Henry's great burning eyes on her. Suppose Henry had asked *her?* Henry Thoreau—

Charley pulled up in front of Mary's house. It was her brother-in-law's house, really, and her sister Gwen's. There were signs all over it. On the post of the mailbox on a shirt-board Mary's niece Annie was advertising KITTENS FREE FREE. Across Barrett's Mill Road on the produce-stand was a big sign that said SWEET CIDER, HONK YOUR HORN. And attached to the house itself was an engraved bronze plaque—

HOUSE AND FARM OF
COLONEL JAMES BARRETT
COMMANDING OFFICER OF THE MIDDLESEX MILITIA

ON THE MORNING OF APRIL 19TH, 1775, THE BRITISH MARCH
FROM BOSTON WHICH RESULTED IN THE OUTBREAK OF
THE REVOLUTIONARY WAR ENDED HERE WITH A SEARCH
FOR MILITARY STORES. GUN CARRIAGES FOUND BY THE
LIGHT INFANTRY WERE BURNED IN FRONT OF THE HOUSE.
OTHER WEAPONS AND SUPPLIES WERE SUCCESSFULLY
CONCEALED IN THE ATTIC OF THE HOUSE, IN FURROWS
PLOWED NEAR THE FARMYARD AND IN SPRUCE
HOLLOW BEHIND THE HOUSE.

"Come on in," said Mary.

There were bicycles tangled beside the door. It was Gwen's Girl Scout day. Three of the Girl Scouts were skipping rope on the dry ground beside the house. Two of them turned the two ends of the rope, and Annie stood leaning in, her thin body throbbing with the rhythm, getting ready to jump. Ready—ready—almost—almost—*now.* She jumped. She was in, jumping and jumping, chanting a jumping rhyme, breathlessly sucking in every other syllable—

> *Teddy bear, teddy bear, go upstairs,*
> *Teddy bear, teddy bear, say your prayers,*
> *Teddy bear, teddy bear, turn off the light,*
> *Teddy bear, teddy bear, say good night.*

Mary stopped to watch, fascinated. That was lovely—the way Annie had looked when she was leaning in, getting ready. Then when she jumped, she had to keep jumping and jumping. Jump, Annie, jump.

Down by the river where the green grass grows,
There sat Annie, as pretty as a rose
Along came Frank (giggles) and kissed her on the cheek.
How many kisses did she get that week?
One, two, three, four, five, six, seven . . .

Chapter 3

Bulkeley, Hunt, Willard, Hosmer, Meriam, Flint,
Possessed the land which rendered to their toil
Hay, corn, roots, hemp, flax, apples, wool and wood . . .
RALPH WALDO EMERSON

Tom Hand had hornswoggled his wife Gwen and her Girl Scouts into helping him. They were walking around the round oak table in the dining room under the big picture of the Angelus, assembling the pages of his *Preliminary Report of the Committee on Public Ceremonies and Celebrations Relative to the 19th of April Ceremony.* Tom was general chairman of the April 19th parade. "As if raising apples, asparagus, corn, cabbages and kids wasn't enough for me to do," he said. He was in high spirits. He snatched up a toppling pile of stapled reports, juggled it into a cube and dumped it into a cardboard box. "Is that you, Charley? Say, look here, we tried to get hold of you when we were typing this thing up. Are you going to ride again this year, or not? You sure as hell better, because it says in here you are."

"What, me ride for Dr. Sam Prescott? You bet I am. Dolly's raring to go. I'm already putting vitamins in her hay."

Tom's mother whammed the stapler on a pile of pages. "Now, Charley, you look out. If Sam Prescott hadn't got away when Paul Revere was captured, and if he hadn't brought the news to Concord, where would we all be right now, I ask you? Don't you go making a fool of him on that big horse of yours."

"Don't you worry your head, Mrs. Hand. And I promise not to trample on anybody either, unless they call me Paul Revere." Charley slapped his side and galloped around the room, while the Girl Scouts giggled. One of them naturally said, "Hello there, Paul Revere," and got spanked.

"Here now, Dr. Prescott, you behave yourself," said Tom. "My mother's a sensitive old lady."

Charley skipped out the door, then he yelled back in, "Sensitive old ladies like your mother know what a fool I am anyway. Don't you, Mrs. Hand?"

Mrs. Hand yelled back, "You just bet I do. When is Mary going to make an honest Christian fella out of you?"

"Whenever she'll have me. Put in a good word for me, will you, Mrs. Hand?" He disappeared. Mary watched him drive past Tom's cornfield and turn left into the driveway behind the long row of hemlocks that led to his house, the big impressive Goss house on the river side of the road.

"Of course, Philip is the sensible one, Mary dear," said Mrs. Hand. "That Charley, he's still sowing his wild oats. Though he may snap out of it, that's what I tell his father. Ernie says Charley is going straight to the dogs. I keep telling him he's wrong."

"Now, Mother," said Gwen, "let my poor sister alone. She's not going to marry either one of them if she can help it."

"Besides, I'm already madly, head-over-heels in love," said Mary, throwing her eyes up at the ceiling.

"Who with, Mary, who with?" said Mrs. Hand.

"Henry David Thoreau," said Mary.

"Oh, go along with you."

John, the first-grader, came in then, after loitering home from school. He blew up his lunchbag and popped it with a sharp bang. "I'm hungry," he said.

Chapter 4

=⧸ *I accept the universe*
MARGARET FULLER

Egad, she'd better.
THOMAS CARLYLE

Mary picked up the two gallons of good clouded Hand cider and slammed the door of the pickup truck with her knee. Then she stood for a minute in the small parking lot in front of Orchard House, looking across the dark fields, letting the hurdy-gurdy grind. Henry had walked here, calling on Alcott (his ally against the arch-enemy). Louisa May Alcott had written part of *Little Women* here, and Bronson had cultivated his vegetable garden without benefit of foul ordures, and conducted his School of Philosophy. And here on this very patch of ground Emerson must have stood, many times, listening to Alcott's never-failing fountain of eloquence. Wearying of it, perhaps, sometimes, and walking home to confide as much to his journal. But Bronson had been his Plato in the flesh. Or Apollo in disguise, the god of poetry himself, forced to do the plowing for King Admetus. But that was what they had all called themselves, struggling to earn the bread that would sustain their colossal souls—they had all been Apollos, gripping the plow handle for King Admetus, tilling the harsh fields of Thessaly, their eyes lifted to Mount Olympus.

"Come on in, Mary dear," said Mrs. Hand, bustling ahead. "We don't want the whole Alcott Assocation to have to wait for us." Mary followed her up the walk. In the front hall they ran into Ernest Goss, Charley's father. He was lighting candles, making a hash of it. Alice Herpitude was fluttering about, arranging little bowls of crocuses.

"Hello, Mr. Goss," said Mary. She towered over him genially, balancing her jugs of cider, passing the time of day, thinking cheerfully at the same time how much she disliked him. He was as "Old Concord" as anybody could be, but somehow he didn't ring true. Or he had lost the spirit of the forefathers, or something. He wasn't the only one who had. There were plenty of others like him, well-meaning people with money, living in housees that looked like Christmas cards, spending the summer on the Cape, getting tan, playing tennis, driving around in convertibles, living what was supposed to be the good life. But hollow somehow. Ernest Goss had a handsome wife, four handsome children (well, three anyhow), he talked with an exaggerated nasal Yankee twang, he was a graduate of Exeter and Harvard, he wore tweedy jackets from the Country Store and he kept up the general impression of being the superbly appointed country gentleman. But there was something wrong somewhere. He was like a paper pattern that had been cut out very carefully on the black line. His wife was even more so. Together they bored Mary exceedingly. What she liked to think of as real "Old Concord" was Grandmaw Hand and her son Tom, and a lot of others like them. They were true squeezings from the Concord grape. The old Barrett place was still a working New England farm, and the Mission armchair and the roll-top desk with the stuffed duck and the plastic globe and the feathery egg-boxes stacked on it and the spindly geraniums in coffee cans and the calendars and the Angelus and the linoleum on the dining room floor—they were not there to be part of a certain kind of setting, they were just there. And Tom himself, in his overalls, and Mrs. Hand in her husband's old hat . . . But of course it wasn't just a matter of living in the past. Those new families in Henry's Conantum woods seemed to have soaked up the spirit of plain living and high thinking that had always been the best of

Concord, like something given off by the soil, or breathed in the air. It occurred to Mary that Concord's aboriginal Indians had probably been just another flock of egregious individuals with a passion for sunsets and a taste for abstraction.

She lugged her cider into the little kitchen, ducking under the lintel of the door. And there she ran into the gorilla of the morning. He was leaning gigantically against the hutch-back bench, going over a handful of notes. "Excuse me," said Mary. She set her cider down on the black stove and opened the door of the cupboard where the paper cups were.

"So you're one of them, too," he said.

Mary looked up at him, and felt her cheeks flare. She knew what his "one of them" meant. (One of those little provincial biddies who play dolls with *Little Women*.)

"Yes," she said shortly. He lifted his notes again, and Mary started pouring cider. It felt odd to be in such close quarters with someone bigger than she was. Carefully she poured out twenty-four cups of cider, exerting all her attention so as not to spill any. She turned politely to nod to the gorilla as she finished. The darn man wasn't reading his notes at all. He was looking at her with eyes that were little barbs of concentrated curiosity. She might be some new species of woodchuck or pit viper or something. Mary's cheeks went back on her again. She turned away, ducked her head grimly under the door and went out to sit in the dining room beside Mrs. Hand. Homer Kelly looked at the blank back of the door. Too bad he didn't know one flower from another. Carnations, was it? Peonies, maybe.

Grandmaw Hand was being outrageously charming, chuckling girlishly with Alice Herpitude, recalling the old days, remembering the Chinese laundry and Pierce's Shoe Store and the meat-market with the carcasses hanging out back. "Ooh, I used to be so scared to go back there," said Grandmaw. "Remember, Alice?"

"Well, no, Florence dear. Don't forget, I'm practically a newcomer. I've only been here twenty-five years this fall."

"Oh, of course, I was forgetting."

Someone was sitting down in the empty chair on the other side of Mary. "Oh, hello, Teddy," said Mary.

Teddy Staples started to say hello, then he changed it halfway to how are you, and it came out, "Hew, hew! How, how!" One of the staples that held his shirt together popped into Mary's lap. Mary liked Teddy, and she put her hand affectionately on his arm.

"Have you seen any more of Henry's birds?" she said.

"I-I-I-I saw a pied-bill g-grebe the other day," said Teddy, his melancholy face brightening. Then it fell again. "But I've seen plenty of them before. There's just one I've really got to-to . . ." He started to cough, and couldn't stop. Mary slapped him on the back. Poor Teddy. His life was a simple, rounded eccentricity, a charming obsession, founded on two facts. One fact was that Teddy was the remote descendant of that same Samuel Staples who had locked up Henry Thoreau in the Town Jail. The other was the oddity that he had been born on the same day in 1917 that Thoreau had been born in 1817. Adding these two giant facts together, Teddy had come to believe that his life must be dedicated to Henry Thoreau's memory, and to the reliving of Henry's life as far as he was able. By some absurd sense of fitness, Teddy Staples mended his clothes with a Woolworth stapler, ka-snap, ka-snap. His one set of loose garments was a sort of masterpiece or tour de force of stapling, glittering at stress points with little silver dashes. Like Thoreau at Walden Pond, Teddy lived alone on the shores of the Sudbury River, where it opened out into Fairhaven Bay. Thoreau had made pencils and surveyed lot lines—Teddy won a narrow living as a stonemason. "M-M-Mary," he said, "I wonder if I-I-I . . ." Then the meeting was called to order.

Howard Swan did it with his usual grace. He was an all-round good fellow, and aside from Miss Herpitude and Mary and Teddy Staples, the only member of the Alcott Association remotely resembling a scholar. The rest were Louisa Alcott enthusiasts, proud of their responsibility for preserving the shrine to the memory of Meg, Jo, Beth and Amy. Howard stood up tall with the candlelight reflecting softly from his head (so nobly bald, with a light fringe of hair like Bronson Alcott's) and begged the officers of the association to be brief. The officers tried heroically, but failed. Old Mr. Pusey was already asleep on Jo's bolster. Mary glanced at Ernest Goss, sitting beside Mr. Pusey on the sofa. He was anything but sleepy, nervously drumming his fingers on his briefcase. What was he impatient for? The speaker?

Homer Kelly was introduced at last. He reared up in front of the niche Bronson had built for his bust of Socrates and put his notes on the table beside the plaster Rogers Group ("Taking the Oath"). His cowlick grazed the ceiling and the butterflies shone crassly on his tie. He began to talk about Margaret Fuller.

Mary listened soberly, smiling slightly when he was witty at poor Margaret's expense, disagreeing inside. Poor wretched Margaret. Mary had to admit that there was something vaguely repellent about the miserable woman, but this was hardly fair. She was too easy and quivering a target, and Homer Kelly wasn't the first to take pot-shots at her. "Bulgy-eyed spinster"—oh, that was mean. He diagrammed cleverly the greasy little pigtails Margaret had looped in front of her ears. He imitated hilariously the famous serpentine motions of her long neck. He sneered at her belief in animal magnetism and mesmerism. He pictured her reclining on a sofa and crying, "Let women be sea-captains if they will!" Then he stopped being funny and began to talk about her study of Goethe, the influence of her periodical *The Dial* on American letters, and the mutual inspiration she and Emerson had been to each other. Grudgingly Mary had to admit that he knew what he was talking about. But she hated him. He was one of those condescending professors who will amuse a class any time by destroying the dignity of some illustrious name with gleeful exposés of old privacies, old scandals and senilities. Homer Kelly finished by returning to the attack. With a pyrotechnical flashing of his snickersnee he skewered old Margaret to the wall. Then he sat down, while his audience tittered and clapped. (It was all right. After all, Margaret Fuller wasn't really *Concord*.)

Howard Swan called for questions. Alice Herpitude asked one timidly. Homer Kelly answered it carefully. Then Mary heard herself speaking up. "Don't you think it's a little unfair to judge the manners of one time by the standards of another?" Everyone turned to look at her, and she hurried on, explaining. "I mean, what might be neurotic or even psychotic now doesn't seem to have bothered her contemporaries at all. She was courageous, really, and a sympathetic friend to younger people, and of course she was one of the first to speak up for women's rights. It's easy to laugh at p-prophets . . ." Now she was stuttering like Teddy. She stopped. Homer Kelly looked at her with a broad smile, a kindly delighted look (as though a pet dog had rolled over or a horse talked.) Everyone was looking at her the same way. "Dear Mary," she knew they were thinking, "such a sweet girl."

Homer Kelly opened his mouth to speak. But before he could get a word out, Ernest Goss was on his feet. He got up off the sofa so quickly he bounced old Mr. Pusey, who snorted and rolled his head about. Ernest was waving some papers over his head. "I have something," he said, "of the most profound . . ." He brushed importantly past Alice Herpitude and then tripped on the braided rug and lunged against the piano, smashing his way up the keyboard in a series of accidental arpeggios. The papers in his hand spilled all over the floor. Mary leaned forward to pick up one that had drifted under her chair. It was an old letter, the paper thin and yellow, the ink brown and faded, the writing bold. Across the top there was a crude drawing of a daisy. Then Ernest Goss snatched the letter from her. He gathered the rest hastily and stood up in the small crowded parlor right in front of Homer Kelly, who had no choice but to sit down.

Howard Swan frowned. "The Chair recognizes you, Ernest," he said.

Ernest had collected himself. He lifted his papers and began to make a speech. "Here in my hand I have the most amazing transcendental documents that have come to light since the death of Emerson. The only word to describe them is sensational. After they have been published, not one shred of present-day scholarship, no matter how eminent its authorship, will remain valid." He gave a meaningful glance at Homer Kelly, who politely looked stupid. "These letters, which I intend to call the Ernest Goss Collection, will demand a completely new look at the nature of transcendental friendship and the relations between the sexes in what we used to regard as proper and puritanical New England . . ."

Mrs. Hand looked big-eyed at Mary and whispered at her.

"Did he say the relations between the *sexes?*"

Teddy Staples leaned forward, bursting a seam across the back of his coat. "What in God's name are you g-g-getting at, Ernie?"

"Just listen to this," said Ernest Goss. He put on his glasses and began to read, hemming and hawing a little at first, for effect. The letter was a shocker.

My dear Waldo,

Oh, thou, other half of my thought, other chamber of my heart! Thou the castle's King, I the Queen! Long have I waited in the dust to behold thy golden litter! At first I feared thou wert cold, but now thou hast raised me to reign in full-orbed glory beside thy infinite majesty! That thou shouldst have worshipped poor Mignon's body as well as her soul transports her humanity to heaven's height. O, what rapture in Mrs. O'Flannigan's back sitting-room! O, divine divan! I am chosen among women! And thou, O sage, hast a Queen for thy Soul-wife!

Lilacs perfume the air with ecstasy.

Margaret

But what of Lidian, who shares thy earthly home? Would a more transcendent honesty veil from her the dazzling light of Truth, lest it bring pain upon her lower nature?

Ernest Goss looked up, shook his head and made a ticking sound with his tongue. He looked around at a roomful of blinking eyes and drooping mouths.

"Who did you say that l-l-letter was written to?" mumbled Teddy Staples, looking sidewise at Mary.

"I said Emerson. Ralph Waldo Emerson."

"You mean, our Ralph Waldo Emerson?" quavered Miss Herpitude.

"Of course I do. What other Ralph Waldo Emerson is there?"

Chapter 5

⤹ *Miss B——, a mantuamaker in Concord, became a 'Medium,' and gave up her old trade for this new one; and is to charge a pistareen a spasm, and nine dollars for a fit. This is the Rat-revelation, the gospel that comes by taps in the wall, and thumps in the table-drawer.*
RALPH WALDO EMERSON

Homer Kelly suddenly started laughing. He put his hand over his big ugly face and tried to mould it back into shape, shaking silently in his small chair.

Ernest Goss glared at him, and read the next letter stiffly. It was addressed to "My dear Henry," and it was written in the oblique language of transcendentalist correspondence. But in it the writer gave Henry leave to love her, begging only that he lift his regard for her to the same level of lofty and contemplative affection with which he regarded the stars and the moon and the sun. It was signed, "Your loving friend, Lidian Jackson Emerson." Breaths were sucked in.

But that wasn't all. There was a trashy bit of sentimental hero worship from Louisa May Alcott to Henry Thoreau. (Mrs. Hand said distinctly, "That's preposterous.") And there was a glorious elliptical impassioned transfigured love message, half broken poetry, which Ernest described as a letter from Henry Thoreau to one Miss Emily Dickinson at Amherst. "I love thee not as something private and personal, which is your own, but as something universal and worthy of love, which I have found . . ."

Homer Kelly listened to them all tensely, trying not to shake. But Mary seized on the idea of Henry and Emily, and thought it over. Was it, after all, so preposterous? The two of them had been alike in some ways—both had found satisfaction in seclusion, they had been tuned with the same rapt alertness to the symbolic lessons of nature, and now their two reputations overshadowed all the rest—Longfellow's, Lowell's, even Emerson's. And Emily had been in the habit of writing to at least one literary mentor for guidance—might she not have seen Henry's contributions to Margaret Fuller's *Dial?* She had read *Walden!* Might she not have written to him, might they not then have found one another out? What if they had!

Ernest Goss had still one more letter. Homer Kelly listened to it all the way through, doubting his ears, and then, looking at the stupefied faces of the members of the Alcott Association, sitting bolt upright at attention in Mrs. Alcott's chairs, he lost control of himself altogether and had to leave the room, ducking out into the hall and gasping behind the stairs. Margaret Fuller was scribbling away again, throwing her somewhat frayed bonnet full force at Nathaniel Hawthorne. He was her winged sphinx, his stories reminded her of her own deepest mood—they were moonlit, mesmeric. She wished him to know that she was high priestess of a secret cult called the *Exaltadas,* harbingers of a new era of mystic spiritual discovery and glorious bodily health through psychodunamy, the science of drawing pain from the limbs by the power of the soul. It had been her constant observation, ever since that day when she had reclined with Nathaniel in Sleepy Hollow cemetery, that her electric fluid flowed more freely into him than into any other person of the opposite sex. Ever since he had permitted her to make a phrenological examination of his skull, she had known that they were kin. Those colossal protuberances! Amativeness, Ideality, Adhesiveness, Intellect! So like her own! Should not two such natures, mutually magnetized, become One?

"Oh, really, that's going too far." Miss Herpitude looked intensely distressed.

It was the end. There was a terrible silence.

"Is that all, Ernie, or do you have a b-b-billy doo from Mary Magdalene to Jesus Christ?"

Howard Swan rose to his feet. "All right, Ernie, I'm going to ask you to resign the floor now. We appreciate your sense of humor. It was very funny indeed. Where in heaven's name did you get all that trash?"

Ernest Goss was wounded. He bristled with pomposity. "I am not at liberty to reveal the source of my discoveries. I have kept these letters to myself until now so that you people could have the honor of hearing them first, before I prepare them for publication. It's obvious to me that the Alcott Association doesn't appreciate the honor. Very well, I won't bore you with them any longer."

"Oh, for God's sake, Ernie, you know they're forgeries. I can't believe you can be taken in by such tripe. Here, let me see them."

Huffily, Goss held the letters behind his back. "I tell you they are genuine." He picked up his briefcase from the floor, stuffed the papers into it, snapped the fastenings and buckled the straps.

"Ernie, be reasonable." Most of the Alcott Association was standing up, arguing with him. Mary sat in her chair thinking up headlines. (FREE LOVE IN CONCORD. SCANDALOUS DOCUMENTS INVOLVE CONCORD SAGE.)

"At least you'll submit them to some sort of expert opinion before you put them in print," urged Howard Swan. "Someone at the Houghton Library, a handwriting expert, *somebody?*" He appealed to Homer Kelly, who had come back, wiping his eyes. "Come now, Professor Kelly, give us your opinion."

"My God," said Homer Kelly. "The language, the high-flown tone! O divine divan!" He burst into guffaws again, and slapped his knee.

Howard Swan made a gesture of annoyance, and started to shout. He was angry, very angry. And then suddenly the whole room was in an uproar. Teddy Staples had had enough. What was needed was a-a-action. He walked up to Ernie and snatched at his briefcase. It was an old one, and one end of the handle came off in his hand. Ernie jerked it away again. "You can't do it, Ernie!" yelled Teddy. He attached himself to one of the straps and yanked on it with all his might. Alice Herpitude pitched in. She put her arms around Teddy's waist, dug her heels in the rug and pulled. It was a tug of war. But then the other end of the handle broke, the rug went *swoop* and the briefcase socked Teddy in the jaw. He went reeling back on Miss Herpitude, who staggered to the rear, bristling with Teddy's popped staples. She sat down on old Mr. Pusey, who woke up and barked. Ernest Goss fell backward into the piano again, fortissimo. He regained his balance with an E-flat chord and lunged at Teddy. Teddy was half-stunned, and without too much trouble Ernie extricated his briefcase from Teddy's limp fingers and scrambled out of the house. Howard Swan hurried out after him. The meeting broke up in a shambles.

Chapter 6

Hosmer is overhauling a vast heap of manure in the rear of his barn, turning the ice within it up to the light; yet he asks despairingly what life is for.
HENRY THOREAU

Spring seemed grudgingly held behind Winter's back. Mary woke up on Saturday to a world of Venetian glass. The temperature had hovered around 32 for a week, and the rain had frozen in a crystal casing on everything. The least twig of every tree was reproduced in ice. Instead of flinging out their arms in the irregular wild gesture Mary loved, the tall pines across Barrett's Mill Road drooped their heavily burdened branches. The river below Tom's fields was buckled and pock-marked, useless for skating. The driving was a scandal. But the ground was beginning to soften up under the frozen slush, and Tom, anxious to get his corn and cabbages in at the earliest possible moment, was spending his days in the tractor shed taking his machines apart. He was the kind of mechanic who usually had his vehicles dismembered when they were most needed, and both his wife and his mother had nagged him into an orgy of greasy diagnosis and surgery. Around eleven o'clock the Goss brothers stopped by to talk to him, firming up plans for the April 19th celebration. Mary picked up Gwen's youngest boy, Freddy, and slid across the road to the tractor shed with a thermos of coffee. "Don't let him stop working while he talks," said Gwen.

"Tom, you haven't got both engines out, not again?" said Charley.

Tom, his hairy chest showing at the top of his union suit, wrestled with the last intestinal connection, then hauled on the winch. The engine of the John Deere sailed up into the gloom. "Needs an overhaul," he said. He lowered it gently to the floor and detached the giant hook. Freddy wanted to play with the engine, but Mary wouldn't let him.

"Concord Independent Battery going to be up to its old tricks, Philip?" said Tom.

"The usual thing, I guess," said Philip.

"You know the old saying," said Charley. "It's a wet cell, not a dry battery, whaddaya say, Philip?"

"We'll do our duty anyway, I guess," said Philip.

Tom reviewed the order of events. "Battery cannon fire sunrise salute at the North Bridge. Then the Battery leads off the parade at 9 A.M., fires a salute again during the Bridge ceremony at 10:30, then you fellas are off to the Rod and Gun Club to drink lunch. Right? Got your cannons shined up? Hired your horses yet?" Mary loved the way Tom talked. He said "hosses" for "horses."

"It gets harder every year," said Philip. "We've got promises from a couple of retired icemen and a garbage-collecting outfit."

"I always expect every year you're going to blow each other up," said Tom cheerfully.

"You sound as though you hope we will," said Philip.

"It'd sure put some pep in it," said Tom. "Your father still on the active list?"

"Father?" said Charley, with some sarcasm. "He wouldn't miss a chance to strut for the world. He's the rammer on Philip's gun."

"What does the rammer do?" said Mary.

"He rams the powder bag down the barrel," said Philip. "And the lanyard man pulls the string."

"Kaboom," explained Charley."

Tom looked curiously at Charley. "How come you're not a member of the Battery, Charley? I thought these honorary things ran in families? Your dad's been in for years, and now Philip's in it . . . I thought it went from father to son?"

"Oh, I guess they thought I was too busy impersonating Sam Prescott. I do it so damn well, you know."

"Oh, sure," said Tom. It was plain he had brought up a distressing point. Mary suspected Ernest Goss's own personal spite against Charley, and hated him for it. She wondered if Philip and Charley knew about the Ernest Goss collection of letters, and asked them about it.

They looked at her, their faces two blanks. "Letters?" they said together. "What letters?"

"Didn't he tell you? He was very disappointed in the Alcott Association, because they didn't believe in them at all. But Howard asked us not to talk about them. Maybe I'd better not say any more about it. I thought you knew."

There was an awkward silence. Then Freddy started for the tractor engine again, and Mary chased him back. She gave him a piece of chain to play with.

"Well, we're on our way home anyhow," said Charley. "Don't forget, girly, it's my turn to squire you to the square dance." He folded his arms and did a do-si-do. Philip turned away without speaking and started up the road. Charley made a horrible face at Philip's back and ran after him, with a long running slide along the ice. Mary went back to the house to help Gwen with lunch.

In the kitchen Gwen was buttering hot dog buns. She moaned in comic despair. "How am I going to tell Tom?" She had finally gone to Dr. Cosgro and discovered that she was, indeed, pregnant again.

"Just tell him," said Grandmaw. "You know he'll be pleased."

Tom came in and washed off his grease, while the women exchanged glances behind his back. "Go ahead," said Grandmaw. "Tell him now."

Tom pulled his face out of the roller towel and looked at them. "Tell me what?"

Mary started to laugh, and he guessed right away.

"No," he said.

"Yes," said Gwen.

"Ye gods," said Tom. But he took hold of himself manfully and kissed his wife. "This calls for a drink."

They were halfway through the drink when they remembered Freddy. "Oh, Lord," said Tom, and he ran across the road without his coat. He found Freddy on his hands and knees beside the tractor engine. His snowsuit was black grease from head to foot. Tom picked him up, gave him a whack and took him home to be cleaned up. Freddy bawled very loud.

Chapter 7

This Saturday evening dance is a regular thing, and it is thought something strange if you don't attend. They take it for granted that you want society!
HENRY THOREAU

The square dance was the week before the April 19th festivities. The freezing rain had given way to warm, and it poured steadily, as from a pitcher tipped smoothly in a firm hand. Mary ran from Charley's car into Girl Scout Hall on Walden Street, head down, with Charley whooping behind her. Inside the hall the fiddles were reeling, the feet stamping. Mary swung her wet hair out. Charley got spray in his eye. "Hey," he said, "you've got an awfully superfluous amount of that stuff. Why don't you let me go to work on it?" He whirled her around on the sidelines, with her coat still on. Charley was a bouncing square-dancer, not a very good one. Mary didn't mind. She adored it, and would have danced with a chimpanzee, as long as the fiddles played "The Crooked Stovepipe" and "Golden Slippers."

Oh, damn, that gorilla was here (speaking of chimpanzees). There he was, that Homer Kelly again, leaning against the wall, giving her that pit-viper look. Homer was with Rowena Goss, one of Charley's younger sisters. The pretty one. Pretty wasn't the word. Rowena had a brilliant smile and a splendid figure and the vibrant carrying voice of an actress, which she was, off and on. Rowena brought her prize over and introduced him. "We've met," said Mary. She began to get that drab, washed-out feeing that Rowena seemed to hand out all the time like so many upended bushel baskets, muffling the opposition. Usually Mary put her light under Rowena's bushel cheerfully. But this time she found herself thinking about Annie, and the way she had looked the other day, playing jump rope—the way she had leaned in, getting ready. Jump, Mary, jump. Off with the basket!

Then the fiddles struck up. Charley took Mary's hand and she abandoned care. The caller set up a whine. "Active couples down the hall, four in line, ladies chain with the one below! Swing! Swing! Allemand left and around we go!" Mary progressed down the dance, curtseying to new partners, swinging with the shorter ones as gently as she could, trying not to lift them off the floor. Here came Kelly. He took her in his arms and swung her. Swung her and swung her. Her next partner collided with him, and Homer broke away, his craggy face flushed, making a stab at the figures he had missed. Mary went on, bowing and whirling and bobbing like a monkey on a stick, telling herself how little physical things mattered, like being gloriously in rhythm with a big oaf of a man. It was meetings of minds that mattered, meetings of minds. Yes, sir.

Next day the sun came out again, and the yellow grass flushed green. It was Sunday. Late in the afternoon there was a honk in front of the house, and Mary went out to the roadside stand. Rowena Goss was behind the wheel of her car, with Homer Kelly sitting silently beside her in the front seat, his long arm slung up on the back. "Hello," mumbled Mary.

Rowena asked for a gallon of cider and handed out her bushel basket, free of charge. Mary took the basket and rammed it over her head, and went behind the counter to the freezer that preserved the cider out of season. She took out a jug, carried it back to the car, hunched down to the car window and handed it in.

"How much is it, Mary dear?" said Rowena.

"A buck," said Mary gruffly. Oh, for heaven's sake, why didn't she say yup or nope while she was about it?

They drove away. Mary caught Homer's little pig eyes looking back at her, and she heard Rowena say something about a character. Damn. That's just what she was, a big bumbling character that you stared at to see what queer erratic thing it would do next. Damn, damn.

Chapter 8

They congregate in sitting-rooms, and feebly fabulate and paddle in the social slush.
HENRY THOREAU

Preliminary report of the Committee on Public Ceremonies and Celebrations Relative to the 19th of April Ceremony. Chairman, Thomas S. Hand.

18 April, 8 P.M.	Military Ball at State Armory, Everett Street, sponsored by Company D, First Medium Tank Battalion 110th Armored Regiment Massachusetts National Guard.
10 P.M.	Grand March.

Before the Military Ball Ernest and Elizabeth Goss were giving a dinner party. Mary and Gwen and Tom were invited, but at the last minute the phone began to ring again, and Tom found himself bogged down. He sat by the telephone with the receiver pressed against his ear, bobbing Annie's yo-yo up and down, listening to a purist.

"Mr. Hand! I just want to know if you're planning to have

those dreadful drum majorettes again in the parade? It's bad enough with those Highland Pipers—what they have to do with 1775 is beyond *me*. Why doesn't everybody just dress up like Mickey *Mouse*?"

"Hello, Tom? Harold Quested here. Say, you know that kid in my bunch of Cubs, Julius Spooner? Well, he came to the last pack meeting with spots all over him and guess what? Yup, I'm afraid so. Every last one of 'em. Chicken pox. Except Julius, of course. He's radiant with good health."

"Well, let Julius carry the flag," said Tom.

"Mr. Hand? This is Mrs. Shuttle, you know, the little boy that's going to play the piccolo's mother, in the Spirit of '76? With the bandages? Well, Howie's sick. No, not chicken pox. He fell on the ice and skinned his face, and his embouchure is all swoll up. But Jimmy, that's his little brother, he'd just love to help out. What? No, not the piccolo, the bongos. You know, like a drum? Would that do?"

"No," said Tom. "But the drummer boy is sick, too. Maybe we can work something out." Gwen, her mouth bristling with pins, came up behind him with his old Navy jacket, and struggled him into it. She hummed with horror when she saw how far the buttons would have to be moved over, and stuck a pin viciously in the right place.

"*Ow!*" yelled Tom. He put his hand over the phone and told Gwen to go ahead, he'd come along later. Besides, he had the pickup to fix because somebody had decided they needed it for a float. "I'll see you at the ball," he said.

It was a fine night, so Mary and Gwen walked up the road and down the driveway that led to the big house by the Assabet River. Mrs. Bewley met them at the kitchen door and set up a cheerful shout. Mrs. Bewley was the maid of all work, a large, gaunt woman so nearly stone-deaf that one had to really holler to make her hear. She always hollered right back. She pulled Mary across the doorstep. "NOW, DON'T YOU LOOK PRETTY? I ALWAYS DID GO FOR PINK CHEEKS."

Mrs. Goss came hurrying into the kitchen to greet them. When she said, "How charming to see you," it didn't necessarily mean it was charming at all. It was just what she always said. Her command of any social situation was so stylized and flawless she might have been carrying it on in her sleep. Mary found it paralyzing. It wasn't too different from the effect of her daughter Rowena's bushel baskets. Mary sometimes wondered if that unshakable gentility could be jarred loose. What if she were to burst into tears and fall on Mrs. Goss's shoulder, and cry "Help me, Mrs. Goss, help me"? Nothing would happen, probably, except veils and swathes of formulae, wrapping themselves swiftly over the harsh real nature of the event. No tears, anywhere, no true laughter. Emily had said something about it—

> I like a look of Agony,
> Because I know it's true—
> Men do not sham Convulsion,
> Nor simulate, a Throe—

"Won't you take your things to my bedroom at the head of the stairs?" said Mrs. Goss. Mary agreeably started up the backstairs that led off the kitchen. "No, no," said Mrs. Goss sharply, "please don't go that way. I meant the front stairs."

But Mary was halfway up. "That's all right," she said. "I don't mind not being grand." Gwen hesitated, then went along with Mrs. Goss, who looked disgruntled.

At the top of the backstairs Mary discovered why she had not been wanted in that part of the house, and she felt a little ashamed of herself. There was an argument going on behind a closed door. She tiptoed past, trying not to listen. But she couldn't help hearing Ernest Goss's angry voice, talking rapidly. "I can take just so many of your threats, and no more. I'm not ashamed of my decision, I'm damned glad." There were sounds of a scuffle, and the heavy crash of overturning furniture. "Now, now, you get away from me. You lay one finger on me and I'll call the police. Get away from me, you hear?" Ernie's loud voice rose in a high frenzy. Mary paused and looked back at the door. Should she knock? Call for help? But then Ernest Goss started talking again in a normal tone, so low that she couldn't hear what he was saying. She didn't want to. Mary walked down the corridor and found Mrs. Goss's bedroom. Gwen was still downstairs, talking to new arrivals.

Pulling a comb through her hair, Mary waited for her and glanced around the room. Over Elizabeth Goss's bedroom fireplace hung a copy of the old Doolittle print of the Concord fight. There was another just like it in the Concord Library, with the same rows of little British soldiers, their backs straight as red-coated grasshoppers, and the same pretty patterns of smoke puffing out of the muskets. Then she turned to the bookcase and ran her eyes over the shelves. Except for a dutiful shelf devoted to Concord authors it contained a dull miscellany. Why, hello, wasn't that Volume I of Johnson's edition of Emily Dickinson's poetry? It couldn't be the Volume I that was missing from the library? Mary pulled out the grey book and looked inside the front cover. It must be the missing volume. The card pocket was mostly scraped off, but she could still see where the edge had been pasted. Mary riffled the pages. Why would anyone steal one volume from a set of three? Then she found the answer. The book had been defaced. One page appeared to have been roughly torn out. It was page 123. Why, Mrs. Goss, you old so-and-so.

Gwen came in then and left her coat, and together they walked down the front stairs and into the living room. It was a large handsome room with the meaningless perfection that was the mark of the interior decorator. Mr. Goss hurried in behind them. He was almost aggressively hearty, the gay host. Charley wasn't there, but Philip was, with his sisters Edith and Rowena, and Howard Swan and Homer Kelly.

"Mary, dear," said Mrs. Goss, "have you met Mr. Kelly? Oh, Mr. Kelly, I must tell you a secret about Mary Morgan. Both my sons are simply mad about her. Did you know? I just wish there were two of her."

Oh, damn. This again. Mary's autonomic nervous system sent up a huge hot blush. Homer Kelly looked baleful and mumbled something. Then he asked her if she had read any of the works of Mr. Flotsam A. Jetsom lately. Rowena laughed dazzlingly, distributing bushel baskets, and Mary couldn't think of anything to say.

"Oh, Homer," said Rowena, "I forgot to introduce my sister Edith." Edith seemed accustomed to being forgotten. Mary thought once more how extraordinary it was that two sisters so similar in feature could be so different in total effect. Edith had Rowena's broad high forehead, her strong Goss eyebrows and narrow nose. But Rowena's strong brows were a charming accent, while Edith's were heavy and ugly. Rowena's narrow nose was aristocratic, Edith's was skimpy and queer. Rowena's red hair was Titian, Edith's was carrot. Both were as tall as their brothers, but Rowena's carriage was statuesque (present-bosom!), Edith's was stoop-shouldered and flat-chested. Already an old maid, Edith liked cats and romantic novels. Everyone was sorry for Edith, including Edith. It was hard to be fond of her. She was cloddish, tactless and dull.

Apologetic for thinking so, Mary sat down beside her with her martini. But Ernest Goss was not one for letting corner conversations get started. He had a new toy. "I thought you'd all want to see the new addition to my collection," he said. Mary winced. It wasn't those letters again? No, no, it was his gun collection he was talking about this time. Thank goodness. He might be in the dark about Margaret Fuller, but he seemed to know what he was talking about when it came to Indian artifacts and antique firearms. He flourished a little gun.

"Here you are, girls. Something to carry around with you on a dark night. A lady's pistol, 1750. Isn't it a cutie?" He passed it around. "See? It has a box lock. The barrel unscrews for loading. You use this special little wrench to undo it."

Homer Kelly professed interest. Ernest Goss was flattered. Nothing would do but Homer should be shown the entire collection. It was kept in a highboy built by Joseph Hosmer, one of Concord's original Minutemen. Ernest pulled open drawer after drawer. "Here's a pocket pistol of around the same time. See that pineapple design underneath? That means it's English. This flintlock here is a duelling pistol, one of a pair. Oh, HELLO

THERE, MRS. BEWLEY. HOW ABOUT BRINGING SOME
MORE MARTINIS? Now, Homer, I know what you want to
see, you don't need to tell me. You want to see the gun the
Minutemen used at the North Bridge. Well, I've got one. They
don't grow on trees, but I've got one. Had this cupboard built
into the wall specially. Nothing too good for my prize piece.
You should see what Philip can do with this to a tin can at 50
yards." Homer took the long gun in his hands with awe. "It's
a musket. Five feet two inches long, that one. The farmers
around here had 'em for getting small game, grouse, waterfowl,
and so on. So it's called a fowling piece. See, it's English, too.
There's the pineapple finial on the trigger guard. Here's the
flint, with the little piece of leather around it to hold it in. Say,
Philip, let's show Homer how it works. Make me up five or six
balls."

"Where's Charley?" said Howard Swan. "He's the sharp-
shooter, if I remember correctly."

Ernie paid no attention. Philip got to work, while his father
lectured. "That's the ticket. The bar lead goes in the dipper, and
the dipper goes over the fire. Doesn't take long to melt. There.
Now, here's the bullet mold that goes with this gun. Makes a
one-ounce ball. See, it's like scissors, with a ball-shaped mold
on the end. You just close the scissors, pour the lead in through
the hole, wait a second, open 'em up, and then, presto, see
there? You've got a musket ball. You go on and make me some
more, Philip, while I load up. Well, well, look who's here . . ."

It was Teddy Staples, looking ill at ease. "Crashing the party,
are you?" said Ernest Goss. "Well, come on in and have a
drink. What's up, Teddy? You look fit to be tied."

Teddy looked around nervously. "Ernie, I've got to talk to
you. I've been thinking about those l-l-l-l-letters, and the more I
think . . ."

"Not the time or place, Teddy. Sit down, here, make yourself
at home. Take a look at these guns. Pass 'em along there,
Homer." Ernest went out to yell at Mrs. Bewley for more
drinks, while Teddy fingered the pistols and the fowling piece,
frowning at them, hardly seeming to see them. When Ernie

came back, Teddy made another appeal. "Five minutes, Ernie. Just f-f-five minutes. Your guests will excuse you, I'll bet."

Howard Swan spoke up then. "Of course we'll excuse him. Go right ahead, Ernie. Take all the time you want."

Ernest Goss turned red in the face. He ignored Howard and glared at Teddy. "All right, Staples, if you can't join the party, why don't you just leave. Go on. Get out." Teddy stood up, looking uncertain. Then he rammed on his hat and faltered out the door.

No one knew what to say. But then Elizabeth Goss brought out her veils and began covering up. Rowena helped out by trying to pick up the musket (oooo, it was so heavy), and her father took down the big powder horn from over the mantel and got on with the business of loading. He unplugged the end and tipped it to pour out powder. Nothing came out. "Where in the Sam Hill is all the powder? That Charley. . ."

Philip stared at the powder horn, then hit his forehead. "Oh, I'm sorry, Father, I forgot. I used up all of it. I meant to fill the powder horn again, but I didn't get around to it."

"Is that so?" His father sounded suddenly mild. "Well, we've got a canful right here, so never mind." He poured a small amount of powder down the muzzle of the gun. "Now, in goes the ramrod to push in patch and ball—and what about a few buckshot for good measure?"

Mrs. Goss was tittering gently. "Of course, Ernest, you know perfectly well that Charley is sure to confess to using up the powder, too. You know these boys of ours." She leaned over to Gwen. "Double confessions, ever since they were children. You know how little children always deny everything they're accused of? Well, Charley and Philip always did just the opposite. Both of them always *confessed* to everything. They still do."

"Well, this sort of unreliability is more like Charley," grumbled Ernest Goss.

"Father," said Philip patiently, "I said it was I who used up the last of the black powder. Not Charley."

It sounded like an old argument. "Let's see how she fires," said Homer Kelly.

Ernest Goss turned to Mary. There was a glitter in his eye. She was elected. Sportingly she agreed. It turned out that Ernest had to help her a good bit, the wag, with one arm around here, the other one there. She was aiming out the window at a tree across the lawn, the heavy gun wobbling against her shoulder. Ernest peered past her into the dark. Then suddenly he whipped the gun out of her hands and gave it to Philip. "Here, Philip, quick, show her how. See the elm down the road. Right now, go ahead. *Fire!*"

Philip aimed and fired. The noise was terrible in the room. Rowena shrieked. But out of doors there was another kind of shout.

"Jesus God," said Philip. He dropped the gun and scrambled through the window. "I've killed him. Oh, God, I've killed him."

Chapter 9

It was Charley. He had been outside, walking up the drive, beyond the elm tree. One of the buckshot had hit him in the leg. Mary looked at Ernest Goss. She couldn't believe it. He had seen Charley out there. Of course he had seen Charley. The man must be mad. She caught the look on his face (ain't I a naughty boy?) before he made an effort to wipe it off and look concerned.

Charley came hobbling in, supported by his brother. Philip was nearly in tears. He looked at his father accusingly. "I might have killed him," he said.

Mr. Goss turned testy. "Nonsense. Of course not. The musket's only good for fifty yards or so. Goes wild farther than that. Buckshot can't hurt you much at that distance. Let me see there, Charley. Oh, that's nothing. Don't stand there getting blood on the Bokhara. Go take care of it." He picked up the fowling piece from the floor and fussily gave it his attention. He cleaned out the barrel, wiped it all over and put it away in its cupboard. Charley limped out without a word, leaning on his brother, while the other members of the party didn't know which way to look.

But the evening was by no means a failure. Miraculously Mr. Goss turned into the jovial host once more and swept them along to dinner, occasionally letting someone else talk. Charley came back just in time to sit down at the table. He seemed his old debonair self. He had dressed up in his Dr. Prescott outfit, wig and all, and he was hamming it up, using a cane with dashing effect. Philip came back, too, looking solemn. Gwen promptly started talking to him about a town matter in which he was taking an active part, and he began to relax. The food was excellent, the table was beautiful, the candlelight was lovely. Even Mrs. Bewley's attendance to their needs, although clumsy, was somehow baronial. She was a servant of the old school, eager to please. But she had one well-known flaw. Gwen beheld Mrs. Bewley sticking the sugar tongs coyly into her bosom, the dear old kleptomaniac. It was just a habit she had. She didn't mean anything by it. Mrs. Goss always frisked her sternly before she went home. Mrs. Bewley never seemed to mind at all. "WHY, HOW DID THAT GET THERE. OH, TAKE IT, TAKE IT," she would say nobly, when the frying pan turned up in her shirtfront.

There was no hurry to get to the ball. You just had to be traditional and be there for the Grand March. But at last it was time to go. Howard Swan excused himself. He had to go home and get a good night's sleep because he was taking an early plane for New York in the morning.

"What? And miss my great day?" said Charley Goss.

"Believe it or not, there are some states in this country that never even heard of Patriot's Day," said Howard ruefully. "They go right on conducting business as usual, in spite of Dr. Samuel Prescott's famous ride and the shot heard round the world."

Elizabeth accompanied Howard to the door. Mary, coming along to get her boots, could hear him murmuring to her politely. His voice had a gentle, pleading tone. Was this another attempt on Howard's part at the suppression of the letters, getting at Ernie through his wife?" But Elizabeth was shaking her head. She sounded tired. "It's been thirty years, Howard... told you that the first time..."

The rest of the party had to wait for Rowena. She had undertaken major repairs, so her father improvised a sure laugh-getter to while away the time. He rummaged up a damp cocktail napkin and a hard lead pencil with a point like a needle. "Now, Edith, I want you to place the paper on the back of your left hand and write on it your name, address and phone number. Go ahead, now! Go on!"

Edith, basking in attention, struggled with the sharp pencil on the wet napkin. "Oh," she said, giggling, "it hurts! And it's tearing! It's gone right through! Oh, this isn't any fun at all! Why do I have to do it? You're mean! Ouch, it hurts! Oh, I'm not doing it well at all! There, it's all finished! Can I stop now?"

Her father scribbled on an envelope while she talked, snickering. When she was done he told her he was going to tell her what she would say to her husband on her wedding night. He read her words back to her, guffawing so hard he couldn't finish. Edith tried to laugh, but she turned an ugly purplish-red. Rowena walked into the room, looking freshly smashing. "It'll be different with her, eh, Homer?" said Ernest. He winked at him. "And some lucky fellow!" Homer winked gallantly back.

"Ernest, you're impossible," said Mrs. Goss. She looked unhappy. This was her formula for husband-misbehaving-in-front-of-guests.

The ball was in full fling when they got to the Armory. Tom came rushing in just in time for the Grand March. Gwen pleaded her delicate condition, so he snatched up Mary and marched her off with the selectmen and their wives at the head of the line. Johnny McPhale's Orchestra brayed "Off We Go into the Wild Blue Yonder," the electric lights shone through the transparent red-white-and-blue bunting, and hundreds of pairs of feet shuffled rhythmically around the big room. The Captain of the National Guard with huge pointing gestures aimed the column left and right and soon had people marching four, then eight, then sixteen abreast. Mary found her arm

hooked into that of the Chief of the Concord Police, Jimmy
Flower. He was a small gnomelike man with a bald head who
looked like one of the Seven Dwarfs. She beamed down on his
five feet one-quarter inch and said hello to his wife Isabelle.

"Jimmy," she said, "when is Isabelle going to give you a
divorce so you can marry me?"

It was a joke they had. Jimmy craned his neck up at her.
"What's the matter, Mary? Haven't you got a boy friend yet?
When in heck are you going to get married anyhow?"

"When you get down on your knees, that's when. I'm just
waiting around, withering on the vine. What's the matter, aren't
I pretty enough for you?"

"It isn't that. I'm just scared I couldn't carry you across the
threshold, that's all."

"Well, what if I carry you?"

"Say, that's a good idea. How about it, Isabelle?"

"Sure," said Isabelle. "But only if you promise to take
Frankie and Roggie and Linda and Sharon and the baby. Espe-
cially the baby. Then I'll kick up my heels and be fancy free.
Who knows? I might find me another beau."

"Oh?" said Jimmy darkly. "Like *whom?*"

"I don't now. Some nice tall fella. Say, Mary, you know who
I think is cute? That Homer Kelly. Boy, he's my type! You
know, the Abraham Lincoln type? Say, Mary, he must be six
feet six, how about him for you? He's cute."

Mary lost interest in the conversation. It had taken a bad
turn. He was not either cute. "Well, he's not my type."

The bandleader spoke hugely into the microphone. "Ladeez
and gentlemeeeeen, if you willlll, the Graaaand Waaaaltzzzz!"
Tom obediently gave Mary a big dancing-school shove and pro-
pelled her strongly around the floor.

Isabelle Flower looked across her husband's head at Mary.
"She's stuck on him," she said.

"Mary? Stuck on Tom Hand?"

"No, stupid. Stuck on Homer Kelly."

"But she just said . . ."

"Take my word for it," said Isabelle. "She's nuts about him."

"Oh, go on. You women. You know who Homer Kelly is, don't you?"

"Some kind of a writer, isn't he?"

"No, I mean besides that." He told her.

"No kidding?" said Isabelle. "Well, I'll be darned."

Chapter 10

The Governor of Massachusetts turned off his alarm clock, groaned, rolled over and sat up. It was April 19th, Patriot's Day. There was that ceremony out in Concord. For Chris'sake, he hadn't written his speech yet. He punched his pillow, lay down again and shut his eyes, seeking inspiration from on high. Of course he could always gas away about the forefathers. He could do that at the drop of a hat. But perhaps something more was called for here. Some quotation, some noble scrap of poetry. The Governor lay flat on his back, absentmindedly stroking the stiff hairs of his grey mustache. Then inspiration came to him, and he opened his eyes gratefully. There was that old poem, why, he practically knew it by heart already. How did it go?

> Listen, my children, and you shall hear
> Of the midnight ride of Paul Revere . . .

A natural. He vowed to do it all by heart, so help him, God. After all, it was an election year. Why not razzle-dazzle those folks out in Concord?

Chapter 11

To me, away there in my bean-field at the other end of the town, the big guns sounded as if a puffball had burst; and when there was a military turnout . . . I have sometimes had a vague sense all the day of some sort of itching and disease in the horizon . . .

HENRY THOREAU

Preliminary report of the Committee on Public Ceremonies and Celebrations . . .

19 April, 5:30 A.M.   Sunrise salute by the Concord Independent Battery and flag raising by Company D at North Bridge.

Mary, who had gone to sleep at one A.M., pulled herself out of bed at five, woke up John and Annie, poured out cornflakes for the three of them and drove them to the North Bridge. She parked in the parking lot across Monument Street, and the children got out and ran down to the bridge. They came right back, to report nothing doing yet. "Maybe this is them," said Annie, as another car rolled up beside them.

It was just Homer Kelly. He got out of his car, looking ten feet tall in a big fur hat. "There's nobody here yet but us," said Annie, jumping up and down and slapping her arms. It was cold.

"Oh, hello there," said Homer, looking in at Mary.

"They say sunrise, but they don't really mean it," said Mary.

"The crows are all ready to go," he said, looking up.

"They'll be after Tom's corn," said Mary. "He always plants some on April 19th, because that's what the Barretts were doing that morning in 1775 when the British came."

Homer went around the car and climbed in companionably on the other side, to keep warm. Before long some boys on bicycles came charging up and raced down the path to the Minuteman monument in the half-light. It was a full twenty minutes before a couple of jeeps came along, pulling the gun carriages and the two gleaming brass cannon. The jeeps were bristling with khaki-clad members of the Concord Independent Battery. Philip hopped out of the first jeep, waved at Mary and undid the chain across the broad path to the bridge. Ernest Goss was driving, his World War One campaign hat pulled down over his forehead, looking like an aging Boy Scout. The two cannon jiggled backward down the little slope. Mary and Homer started after them with Annie and John. Someone set off a firecracker, BANG. The Concord River was high, flooded around trees and bushy yellow willows. There was hardly any green yet on the trees. Some small oaks still wore untidy wastebasketfuls of rubbishy brown leaves. There were a few canoeists on the river, paddling in close. More onlookers came hurrying up, half-running. Among them was a clot of teenage girls insanely dressed in shorts and knee socks. The Honor Guard arrived, pulling on white gloves. The members of the Battery bustled around, setting up the two cannon side by side, facing away from Daniel Chester French's statue of the Minuteman, aiming out over the marshy edge of the river. The Battery flag with the crossed cannon was pushed into the ground between them, the ammunition box set up behind it. Captain Harvey Finn turned on the crowd in his white puttees. He started yelling politely, then more and more firmly to stand back. At last he was satisfied, and the gun crews went into action. The powder monkeys ran forward with their bright red bags of black powder, the rammers thrust the bags down the barrels with their long ramrods, then took up positions facing away from the muzzles, hanging on to the near wheels, bending over. The lanyard men stuck their long pricks in the touchholes to free loose powder from the powder bags inside, and then the thumbers twisted their firing mechanisms in place and stepped aside so that the lanyard men could insert the small yoke collars that prevented the firing pins from falling on the 32-caliber blank cartridges. Then the lanyard men picked up the strings that were attached to the yokes.

"Number one gun ready," said Philip Goss.

"Number two gun ready," said Jerry Toplady.

"By battery," roared Harvey Finn, *"fire!"* The lanyard men jerked their strings and there was a colossal double BABOOM. Smoke and flame poured out of the guns. The gun carriages rolled back and forth. The bridge trembled. Three crows rose cawing from the top of a snagged old elm. Homer smiled at Mary, and picked up John so that he could see. Annie's skinny body tensed against Mary, and she kept her fingers jammed in her ears. The smoke billowed up around the Minuteman's knees and around his plow. His own musket seemed to smoke. The rammers turned their ramrods around and dipped the fleecy pompons on the other end into the water buckets. Then they shook off the excess water and swabbed out the barrels of their guns. The powder monkeys trotted back for more powder.

Getting into the spirit of the thing, Homer repeated Major Buttrick's famous words, "Fire, fellow-soldiers, for God's sake, fire!" And Mary, between booms, told him about the gigantic 150th anniversary celebration that had been broadcast to the entire nation, when a nervous descendant of Buttrick's had garbled his lines. *"Come on you guys!"* he had hollered, *"for Christ's sake, shoot!"*

BOOM. The two guns were firing in slow alternation. *"Number one gun—fire!"* BOOM. *"Number two gun—fire!"* BOOM . . . BOOM . . . BOOM. John was beside himself with joy. It was like a war, a real war.

What was the matter? The cannon had stopped firing, and the men were standing in one attitude, looking at someone. It was Philip they were looking at. Mary saw him turning his head stiffly from side to side, while the others stared at him. Ernest

Goss stood in front of the Number One gun, his ramrod still halfway down the barrel. He, too, stared at Philip. Harvey Finn strode over to Philip and gripped him by the shirt. "What are you trying to do, kill somebody?"

Philip said nothing. Then Harvey let go and went back to his post. Ernest Goss, looking shaken, pulled his ramrod out of the cannon and stepped to the side. Philip looked at his father, and then hesitantly at Harvey. "Well, Philip," bawled Harvey, "you ready or not?"

Philip stuttered something inaudible, and Harvey yelled, *"Number one gun—fire!"* BOOM. *"Number two gun—fire!"* BOOM. The regular rhythm began again, and the salute ended with another double firing of both guns together . . . BABOOM.

Then the Honor Guard stepped up stylishly and hoisted the flag. Annie, sagging down in Mary's arms, saluted patriotically with the Honor Guard. A clergyman came forward and called on God. His prayer was long, and the teenager's blue knees knocked together with the cold.

It was all over. Mary looked for Philip, but he avoided her and walked away across the field by the Old Manse, alone. Homer consulted his newspaper. "What's this about a Lions Club Pancake Breakfast?" he said.

The cornflakes were rattling around inside Annie and John. "Oh, yes," they shouted, "pancakes!"

"Well, just one apiece," said Mary. "We've got to go home so you children can get ready to march in the parade."

In Monument Hall the Lions were struggling heroically with a fantastic bottleneck in the shape of a tide of hungry people and one small grill. The line of would-be pancake eaters doubled across the hall, idly paddling the air with their paper plates, their insides clapping against their backbones. Apologetic Lions moved up and down the line, passing out cups of coffee. Annie chewed her fingernails. Homer told Mary about his Ugly Word Collection, which included pianola, bowlarama, oleomargarine and frenchified words like shaze lownge, brazeere and neglazhay.

"Your neckties must be an inspiration to you," said Mary,

admiring the phosphorescent diatoms he was wearing.

Homer looked down at his necktie proudly. "It glows in the dark," he said.

"I've got a word game, too," said Mary. "I look for words that sound alike and more or less rhyme. It's kind of a nuisance because you can't stop. I wandered around the house yesterday for five minutes with a saucer in my hand, going from bashful flyswatter to gasfitter's daughter, to tiptoe, please, the Antipodes, to noisy gales, glassy knees, gluey noise, noisome grails."

"Are you bragging or complaining?" said Homer, stepping on the flowers.

"Bragging, bragging. Banjo band, bangled hand, newfangled strand."

Homer picked up newfangled strand. "What stout Balboa said when he gazed at the Pacific. 'This ain't the Indies, by God, it's some newfangled strand.'"

"And Emerson, too. That's what he said. 'This is a newfangled strand, this country, and why doesn't some newfangled man come along to match it.'"

John began to whine. He was tired of waiting, and tears came easily. He had discovered in first grade that life was essentially tragic, and it had come as a blow. He pulled at Mary's skirt. Then Mary and Homer began to bicker. She had gone so far as to say that Emily Dickinson was the newfangled voice that Emerson was looking for. Homer bridled at that and took out his skewer. "There's another one of your women with electric fluid."

"Oh, for heaven's sake," said Mary. (Don't let him get away with it. Jump, Mary, jump.)

She began, halting and stuttering, defending Emily. She was the greatest, the best, she saw the supercharged significance in humble things, in natural objects . . .

"Oh, that old transcendental fallacy, that things seen are purposeful symbols of things unseen. I knew a man once who found enormous significance in people's license plates. He was crazy as a coot." Homer looked at Mary's flushed cheeks. What were those pinkish flowers like gramophone horns? Petunias?

"Look," said Mary, "you can't use a madman's ravings to dispose of a whole philosophical position."

"Calm down, for Pete's sake."

Mary took a new stand on higher ground. She began to reel off ribbons of Emily's sharp, bright verse. Homer listened. John and Annie at last got their pancakes, and they all sat down. Mary sang on, disdaining food.

"There now, listen to that," said Homer, waving his fork. "'Twere better far, or something like that, to fail with land in sight (how's it go?)

> . . . Than gain my blue peninsula
> To perish of delight. . . .

"You see? Always turning aside, withdrawing from the experience, afraid to get their feet dirty. And another thing. Here they were always swooning and perishing with delight over things, but they couldn't stand the sight of each other. Old Emily up in her chamber, refusing to come downstairs to see visitors. She knew she'd scare them with her electric fluid. And you know what Waldo said. 'We descend to meet.' And Henry Thoreau was the worst—exalting his solitariness into a kind of solipsism almost."

O, Blasphemy. And this was the so-called expert. "Solipsism! Oh, really, you just don't understand them at all."

"Thank you," said the expert in a pained tone, wounded to the quick. Mary felt around for her coat. Oh, good for you. Insulting the country's most celebrated Emersonian scholar. That was well done.

On the way out they got in another argument over who should pay, and Mary unfortunately won. She scuttled the children off to her car, and Homer strode off the other way, wrenching at his tie.

Chapter 12

⊰§ *These martial strains seemed as far away as Palestine,
and reminded me of a march of crusaders in the horizon,
with a slight tantivy and tremulous motion of the elm tree
tops which overhang the village. This was one of the* great
*days; though the sky had from my clearing only the same
everlastingly great look that it wears daily, and I saw no
difference in it.*

HENRY THOREAU

Preliminary report of the Committee on Public Ceremonies and
Celebrations . . .

> 19 April, 9 A.M.   Ceremonial parade leaves State Armory,
> Everett Street, for North Bridge.

The weather had turned out well. Everybody in the family
was marching in the parade except Mary and Freddy and
Grandmaw. They took up a position on the Milldam in front of
Vanderhoof's Hardware Store. American flags, like something
pretty invented by Grandma Moses, were stuck into special
holes in the sidewalks along Main Street. Jimmy Flower's policemen directed surges of traffic out of the parade route. There
were balloon men on the corner of Walden and Main, their arms
floating high with buoyant clusters of gas balloons and fans of
plastic pinwheels, blurry flags and feathery celluloid dolls on
sticks. The balloons were transparent, with polka dots and stars.
Mary bought a red one for Freddy, and tied it to his wrist. He

tossed his arm around to make it bounce up and down. He was too young to have had one before. Somebody else lost his and it went sailing up in the blue sky. There was a braying sound of a distant band, and everyone peered down the street. Hello, there was Homer Kelly in his fur hat, hurrying Rowena Goss across the street. He nodded distantly to Mary, and she smiled back her friendly smile, wishing he would go fly a kite.

The Independent Battery came first. Philip rode one of the two lead horses, carrying the Battery flag, his thoughtful forehead seamed, his body tense and erect. The horses that pulled the limbers were heavy old plugs, but they made a fine showing, with the clop-clop of their great hairy-ankled hooves and the unfamiliar noise of metal wheel-rims on the streets. Three members of the Battery sat on each limber, with linked arms. Mary remembered that in the good old days after a traditional whiskey breakfast the linked arms had been a necessary precaution. Now the Battery carefully discharged all its duties before toasting the military spirit of the forefathers. After the Battery there was a blur of marching units and noisy bands, the trombonists and trumpeters staring cross-eyed at the music clamped to their instruments. Freddy clapped his hands at the red chariots of the Fire Department and waved at Tom, who was stepping along with his parade staff, handsome in his let-out uniform. Gwen, struggling with morning sickness, walked beside her Girl Scouts, wearing a green uniform that matched her complexion. Grandmaw chuckled and pointed at The Spirit of '76. The bleeding, bandaged drummer boy was extremely small and obviously an amateur, but he was beating the tar out of his instrument. Next in line was the High School Band, with the controversial drum majorettes prancing sweetly to the fore, showing astonishing lengths of bare white leg. After the band there was a big open car containing the Governor of Massachusetts and his wife. The Governor nodded and waved his hat, but his lips were moving, distracted. He was trying to remember what in hell rhymed with Revere. (Hear, queer, beer, near, leer, fear . . . oh, sure, fear. "A-cry-of-defiance-and-not-of-fear-a-voice-in-the-darkness-a-knock-at-the-door-and-a-word-that-shall-echo-forever-more.")

"My dear," said his wife, beaming radiantly to right and left, "why in heaven's name didn't you write it out? I know you're trying to work up a reputation for old-fashioned eloquence, but you'll just make a fool of yourself, that's all you'll do."

The parade was over. The watching crowds closed in behind the last band and followed them down Monument Street. Gwen hurried back and picked up Freddy and started walking against the stream toward her car. Homer and Rowena caught up with Mary and old Mrs. Hand. "Those noisome grails of yours," he said. "I've figured out what they're for. Black Masses."

"What?" Well, at least he wasn't not speaking.

"Noisome grails. For witches to use at Black Masses."

Oh, that was good. Mary chuckled.

"What happens now?" he said.

"Now everybody gathers in the field beside the bridge, there next to the Old Manse, and there are speeches and so on."

"These military demonstrations, all this nationalistic flag-waving. Honestly," said Rowena.

"You got something against parades?" said Homer.

He had changed his tie. This one was patriotic with red, white and blue ballerinas.

Chapter 13

What is the price-current of an honest man and patriot to-day?

HENRY THOREAU

Preliminary report of the Committee on Public Ceremonies and Celebrations . . .

19 April, 10 A.M.	Main ceremony at North Bridge. Prayer. Music by General Radio Glee Club. Address by His Excellency, the Governor.
10:30 A.M.	On appropriate bugle signal, Boy Scout contingent from Acton will march across the field to the west to the tune of "The White Cockade" played by the Acton High School Band. Arrival of Dr. Samuel Prescott, impersonated by Charles Goss. Laying of wreaths. "The Star-Spangled Banner," Concord Band. Salute by Concord Independent Battery.

The amplified voices of the General Radio Glee Club sounded tinny, singing Emerson's hymn—

> *By the rude bridge that arched the flood,*
> *Their flag to April's breeze unfurled,*
> *Here once the embattled farmers stood*
> *And fired the shot heard round the world.*

It didn't matter much that the Governor forgot half of his poem. The instant he said, "Listen my children," everybody stopped listening, and smiled around and visited. Grandmaw couldn't hear, but she guessed. "It's not Longfellow again?"

"I'm afraid so," said Mary.

It was pleasant to stop one's ears and just watch. Around the speaker's platform the parade-marchers in their contrasting uniforms stood in orderly radiating clusters. Beyond them the disorderly citizens came in all shapes and sizes and moved here and there at will, pushing baby carriages over the bumpy ground, carrying infants on their shoulders. There were boys in the trees, there was the smell of spring, there were grandmothers sitting on the trampled grass, and somebody's dog that shouldn't have been let out nosing around and barking. There were jets going over, and now and then, thin occasional fragments of the Governor's proclamation. "Whereas . . . and . . . whereas . . . do hereby proclaim this Patriot's Day . . ." Below the Governor the color and confusion of the massed marchers reminded Mary of two paintings rolled into one, some grandiose Napoleonic battle scene and a picnic in the grass. There were the fringed flags lying at every angle, the dazzle of sunshine on a sousaphone, the glittering splendor of the glockenspiel rising out of the high school band like the standard of a Roman legion, and under the crossed flags the reclining figure of the dying general replaced by the tired pimply second trombonist eating a sandwich.

The Governor finished and sat down, to a splatter of applause. Then a long straggling line of Scouts from Acton arrived, with more flags, and there were mutual felicitations. At last it was time for Charley. Mary craned her neck. There he was, right on time, accompanied by a shout that gathered momentum along Monument Street and echoed around through the field, "Here he comes!" Charley's outfit had been scrounged from here and there, but he looked reasonably like an eighteenth century general practitioner arousing the countryside. His hair was hidden under an orange wig that was tied back with a ribbon, and he wore a skimpy purple tricorn, with cheap gold braid around the edges. He urged Dolly as fast as was safe through the parted crowd, giving an impression of speed, leaning forward, waving one arm, crying, "The Regulars are out!" Then he reined in and tipped his hat to the Governor. "In case you don't know it, Your Excellency," he said, handing him a scroll, "the British are coming."

Mary felt the old movie music grinding. It was queer the way a real event was apt to become lost in the pageantry that grew up around it. But there had been a real Dr. Sam, and for a moment Mary reveled in knowing it. "Put on," he had said to Paul Revere, there on the Battle Road where the British had stopped them, and his horse had jumped over a stone wall and carried him and his burden of news to Concord, and on to Acton and Carlisle. It was Prescott's ride that had helped to bring not only a few hundred Minutemen to the bridge but three or four thousand to the stone walls and hill slopes by the end of the day, ambushing the British retreat, turning it into a rout. A hero he had been, for sure, and a martyr before the war was over, dying in a British prison, so that he never got to marry the girl he had gone to Lexington to see in the first place.

The Governor was reading the scroll out loud. It began with a "Whereas," and went on with a rather tedious statement of general approval of the whole thing by the mayor of Boston. Mentally the Governor resolved to suggest to the Mayor that next year he include a few appropriate lines from some traditional verse. Then he shook hands with Charley, calling him Paul Revere, and congratulated him on the successful completion of his famous ride. Suddenly he remembered some of the lines he had forgotten, and hanging onto Charley's hand, he pumped it up and down and declaimed them into the microphone.

> Through all our history, to the last,
> In the hour of darkness and peril and need,
> The people will waken and listen to hear
> The hurrying hoof-beats of that steed,
> And the midnight message of Paul Revere.

He sat down smugly, feeling that he had positively outdone himself. The military units stared stonily ahead, there was a flutter of polite clapping, and one loyal Prescott supporter said Boo. "Not Revere, you ass," hissed the Governor's wife. "That's not Paul Revere."

The Governor was thoroughly disgruntled. "Well, for Chris'sake, who in hell is it?" Then he nearly jumped out of his skin. KABOOM. The Concord Independent Battery was firing again. B-B-B-BOOM went the echoes running around. Babies set up a howl all over the field, and small galvanized hands let go of gas balloons. The Concord Band started to play "The Star-Spangled Banner," the Governor and his wife left to open a supermarket in Needham, and everyone began trying to find lost members of his family. A few well-disciplined men and women veterans stood and saluted, or just stood at attention. Mary didn't, but she felt vaguely guilty, walking to the car with Mrs. Hand. April 19th always curiously stirred her. She wanted to fire a musket or pitch a box of tea in the harbor or somehow shout her defiance of colonial power. Down with the King anyhow.

Chapter 14

Dying is a wild Night and a new Road.
EMILY DICKINSON

Preliminary report of the Committee on Public Ceremonies and Celebrations . . .

19 April, 8:30 A.M.	Acton Boy Scouts' Flag raising ceremonies at Isaac Davis farmhouse preceding hike down the original trail to the North Bridge.
10:30 A.M.	On appropriate bugle signal the group will march down to and across the bridge to the tune of "The White Cockade."

Honor scout Arthur (Tubby) Furry puffed along the Isaac Davis trail in deep distress of mind. It was terrible, it was really terrible. Angry tears overflowed his eyes and ran down his cheeks. He brushed his sleeve, stiff with merit badges, across his runny nose. If nobody could see you it was okay to cry. He half-trotted, sobbing and puffing. He'd never catch up now. The ceremony would be all over, and the presentations. He looked at his watch, and sniffled in despair. Twelve forty-five! He was over two hours late! What would Mr. Palmer say? How could he possibly explain to Mr. Palmer? He couldn't say he was just a natural-born heavy sleeper and had slept right through his alarm, and then his darned old mother had made him clean up his stupid room, could he? Just because he'd more or less forgotten to clean it up yesterday, for crumb's sake. Here it was, the most important day in his life, and his *mother* had made him clean up his *room*. It was his *duty* to be there with the others. He'd tried to explain to his mother, but she wouldn't listen. Here he was, Arthur Furry, the one who had the honor to present the flag to the Governor of Massachusetts, the *Governor,* for crumb's sake. And then his mother had said something awful. I don't care if it's Almighty God, she had said, you're going to clean up this ghastly mess right now, from top to bottom. That wasn't even a nice thing to say, for crumb's sake. Most of the time his mother was nice, but sometimes she could be awful, like now.

The muster field was empty. He had just known it would be. Arthur struggled across it, climbed over the stone wall on one side of Liberty Street and then over the stone wall on the other side. It was all downhill now. This was the battleground, and there was the bridge, and the field where the speeches were supposed to be. Arthur's heart sank. He couldn't see a single soul. The whole darn thing must be all over and everybody gone home. Oh well, he'd do his duty and go right there where he was supposed to go, and at least Mr. Palmer would have to give him credit for trying. That was what he was always telling them, *try,* go ahead, *try,* do your best at all times. Well, this was the very best he could do because of his darned old mother. Arthur put the ends of his neckerchief in his mouth and sucked them. Then he used them to mop his cheeks, which must be streaky from crying.

He was nearly there. The little hillock where the Minuteman stood was nearly an island. The flooded river had left only a narrow causeway at the bottom of the field. Arthur picked his way carefully. The ground was mushy in places.

Well, say! Maybe he was wrong! Maybe everything wasn't
over! That was a shot! Maybe the Governor and everybody
were still there! His mother had told him parades were always
late! Arthur's sodden face plumped out in a hopeful smile. He
began to climb up the hill below the Minuteman. Then he
scrambled back and fell into the straggly cotoneaster bushes to
avoid a huge shape that came crashing at him. It was a horse, of
all things—an enormous brown horse, jumping over the iron
fence, and there was somebody falling off it. The man landed in
a scraping thump in the muddy part of the trail. It was that Paul
Revere fellow, that Dr. Sam somebody, all dressed up in his
outfit. Should Arthur run to help him? But the man was on his
feet almost instantly. Keeping his back to Arthur, he limped
after his horse and struggled back on. His tricorn hat lay where
it had fallen. The man wobbled his heels into the sides of the
horse and it started to canter up the hill.

Arthur watched it disappear through a gap in the stone wall.
Well, gee, this was swell. He must be almost on time after all,
because the horseman was supposed to ride up about the same
time the Scouts from Acton were supposed to present their
flags. Hopefully Arthur climbed the hill and heaved himself
over the iron fence. There was a place there, he remembered
from last year, where the prongs had been bent aside. Then he
hurried around the bushes and came out behind the Minuteman.
Oh, for crumb's sake, there was no one here after all, except
somebody making a funny noise somewhere. Deeply disappointed, Arthur wheezed across the wooden bridge. Maybe the
ceremonies were still going on in the field over there on the
other side. Maybe he'd find the crowd of fellow Scouts and Mr.
Palmer all lined up in front of the Governor, and if he marched
up smartly to the Color Guard, Tommy Wiley would hand over
the flag so he could present it to the Governor, and maybe Mr.
Palmer would say Good for you, Tub.

But there was no sign of anything going on up there in the
field. Where was everybody? In the end Arthur almost tripped
over the man who lay by the wall. If the man hadn't attempted

to get up on one elbow, if he hadn't thrown his head back and
looked at Arthur, Arthur might have walked right past him.
Arthur stopped stock-still and stared back at him.

The man lay on his side within the chained-off space where
the British soldiers were buried. He was wearing a Concord
Independent Battery uniform. His campaign hat lay by his side.
One leg hung over the chain. Under him was a stiff spray of red
gladiolas, red and white carnations and a blue ribbon with
words written on it in glitter. Arthur could read the words. They
said "British War Veterans." Some of the white carnations
weren't white any more. One of the man's hands was across his
stomach, purplish-red stuff all over it. His face was ashen. He
tried to speak, but a gout of blood came up out of his mouth,
and he fell back, the blood running down the side of his face
and falling in beaded drops on the ground.

Arthur Furry, Honor Scout, had a badge on his sleeve
awarded him for his knowledge of First Aid. He knew how to
give artificial respiration, he knew where the pressure points
were, he knew how to make and apply a tourniquet and how to
care for a broken leg. But the Boy Scout manual didn't say
anything about people with blood coming out of their stomach
or their mouth. The pictures just showed a well-built handsome
man in a white shirt with his sleeves rolled up lying down in a
sort of neat way, with a very calm Boy Scout kneeling neatly
beside him, winding bandages around his arms or legs or putting on a splint. The man in the pictures didn't look up at the
Boy Scout with horrible eyes and bubble blood at him. Panic-
stricken, Arthur knelt down like the Scout in the picture and
wondered what to do. Should he turn the man so that his head
was higher or lower than his feet? Which, higher or lower? Or
apply a tourniquet? But where? You couldn't put a tourniquet
on a person if their stomach was bleeding, could you?

"Musket . . ." gurgled the man at him. He tried to say something else.

"I beg your pardon?" said Arthur, politely bowing closer.
The man struggled to speak, with the blood coming up in
gushes. He choked, and went into a sort of spasm. Arthur,

horrified, could think of nothing to do but unknot his kerchief and use it to wipe at the man's mouth, so that he could speak better. But the man's strugglings ceased. He rolled his head to one side and lay still. Arthur got to his feet and ran. There was a house at the left of the walk to the bridge. He ran and pounded at the door and rang the bell. He started yelling, "Help, get a doctor, help!" There were people walking on Monument Street, a woman pushing a baby carriage. There was a bus unloading passengers over in the parking lot. A bunch of men in ten-gallon hats and cowboy boots were getting out. A policeman was talking to the driver. Arthur jumped off the porch of the house and ran across the road. "Help!" he said. "There's a man dying back there, get a doctor!"

Everyone turned to look at him. The policeman started to run toward him. "Where, sonny?" he said.

Chapter 15

There was an old woman walking along Liberty Street, carrying a basket with a pink balloon tied to it. It was the Gosses' housekeeper-cook, Mrs. Bewley, ambling home from the celebration. She had swiped the balloon nimbly from the balloon-man, but all the rest she had scavenged perfectly honestly: the half-pack of cigarettes, the three popsicle sticks, the wing from the plastic airplane, the nickel, the button, and, of course, innumerable messages from Jesus. She didn't know what Jesus said, since she could neither read nor write, but sooner or later she would get someone to shout it in her ear. Those yellow ones probably said Juicy Fruit. It had something to do with the Garden of Eden.

It would be such fun to add all these new things to her collection! It had been a grand morning. Mrs. Bewley looked down proudly at her dress and smiled. The dress was over thirty years old, but it was brand new to Mrs. Bewley. It had started its long and useful life as a second-hand article in 1932 when it was displayed for the first time in the Girl Scout Rummage

Sale. Over the next ten years it had been handed down and sold and resold at the same sale, and then it had taken a new lease on life during a Clothe the Naked campaign conducted by the Evangelical Free Church. Sent to the remotest reaches of the Himalayas the dress that now belonged to Mrs. Bewley had become a part of the ceremonial wardrobe of a succession of tribal chieftains—until around 1950, when a resourceful chieftain with a large wardrobe and a flat tire traded it for a bicycle pump and a yak's hair fetish to the native lady's maid of a missionary's wife. Years later it went along with the lady's maid and the missionary's wife and the missionary all the way back to Boston for an Evangelical Congress, and then it found its way back at last to the Concord Girl Scout Rummage Sale (the lady's maid had discovered Filene's Basement). At the Rummage Sale it was clawed off the rack by an eager Mrs. Bewley, who couldn't fail to notice how much the buttons down the front resembled the beady brown eyes of her squirrel neckpiece. There were squirrels, definitely, running around inside Mrs. Bewley's head. But her eyes were as sharp and scavenging as ever. They saw something lying on the ground across the field, something that looked out of place. Out of place, hopeful and lost, as if it didn't belong to a solitary human soul. Of course if anybody should happen to come to Mrs. Bewley and ask for it she would be very glad indeed to give it right back. Mrs. Bewley scrambled over the stone wall and scuttled down the sloping field . . .

Chapter 16

✑§ *Crisis is a Hair*
Toward which forces creep
Past which forces retrograde . . .
EMILY DICKINSON

One of the tourists from Texas had longer legs than Patrolman Vine. He brushed past him and bounded down the path. "I'm a doctor," he hollered over his shoulder. Ralph Chope was the representative of a floor machinery company in Houston, but he had been a medical corpsman in the Korean War, and if there was one thing he knew how to do in the medical line, it was tell if a poor devil was dead or not. By the time Patrolman Vine came pounding up, Chope had administered his tests on the body, and had rolled it over and was groping with his fingers in the wound.

"Is he dead?"

"He sure is. Jeez, look at that. The ball went all the way through him and out the other side, almost." The Texan held up something between two fingers. "Looky here. That's a regular old-fashioned musket ball. Say, this sure is some show you're puttin' on here."

Patrolman Vine didn't think that was funny. He took the musket ball and looked at it, then wrapped it up in a clean handkerchief and put it in his pocket. He stared at the corpse, then wheeled and looked sharply at a growing audience of Texas tourists, the bus driver and the woman with the baby carriage. *"Okay,"* he said loudly. "Get back, now. Don't anybody touch anything."

Chapter 17

The village appeared to me a great news room . . . These are the coarsest mills, in which all gossip is first rudely digested or cracked up before it is emptied into finer and more delicate hoppers . . .
HENRY THOREAU

Letitia Jellicoe, acting as a substitute guide for the holiday in the Old Manse, had arrived with a young couple at the upstairs room which both Emerson and Hawthorne had used as a study. She pointed to the window that looked down toward the bridge and started her spiel. "You will see written on the glass with Mrs. Hawthorne's diamond the words *'Man's accidents are GOD'S purposes.'*" The young couple drifted toward the window, but Mrs. Jellicoe, suddenly sharpening and lengthening her focus, pounced at the window and got there first. Wasn't that a policeman running down toward the bridge? Was he chasing that man? "Thief, thief!" twittered Mrs. Jellicoe, and abandoning her charges she ran downstairs and across the field, crying, "Stop, thief!" at the top of her lungs. Broadcasting exotic and shocking pieces of information was meat and potatoes to Mrs. Jellicoe. Coming up against a crowd of people she elbowed her way to the front, and sucked in the whole frightful scene.

"That's Ernest Goss, isn't it?" she said sharply. "Did somebody . . . ?"

Arthur Furry spoke up then, with the information that was trembling on his lips. "It was Paul Revere. I mean, you know, not Paul Revere but that other one, that rides up in the parade. I heard a shot as I was coming up back there behind the Minute-man, and this man on a horse with a costume on, you know, and a wig, he rode almost on top of me, jumping over the fence . . ."

Everybody stared at Arthur. "And he-he said 'musket,' I heard him myself . . ."

"Who?" said Patrolman Vine. "Who said 'musket'?"

Arthur pointed to the dead man. "Him. He did."

Patrolman Vine squinted at Arthur. Then he put his big hand on Arthur's arm and pulled him forward. Arthur, staring up at him respectfully, began to be aware for the first time of the glory that was to be his. But then the policeman looked away from Arthur and spoke to Mrs. Jellicoe. "You've got a phone in there at the Old Manse? Would you get the station on the line and ask them to send some more men down here and the District Medical Examiner? Tell them there's been an accident, it looks like someone's been shot. You know the number? Okay."

Mrs. Jellicoe was off like a hare. She ran all the way back to the house and breathlessly did as she was told. Then she hung up the phone and rolled her codfish eyes up at the ceiling. The officer hadn't told her she was *not* to telephone anybody else. Why shouldn't she notify poor Mrs. Goss? After all, someone should tell the poor woman, and she, Letitia Jellicoe, might as well have the painful task. Mrs. Jellicoe stared at the telephone. She loved its rubbery black feel. In her grasp it was an instrument of steel. Quickly she called up Elizabeth Goss, informed her tactfully that her son had murdered her husband with a mus-ket ball at the North Bridge, reduced her to hysterics, and hung up gently, clicking her tongue sympathetically against the top of her dentures. Now, should she run back to see what was happening? Or perhaps she should take the time to make one or two more calls. She mustn't be selfish, after all . . .

The crowd beside the grave of the British soldiers was increasing. Patrolman Vine had all he could do to keep them from pressing forward and trampling the ground around the body. Arthur Furry, standing patiently to one side, looked modestly at the ground. He, Arthur Furry, had practically witnessed a murder, a real murder. There would be pictures and headlines. BOY SCOUT DISCOVERS BODY! Arthur's eyes widened. Whatever happened, he mustn't forget to do his very best at all times. He mustn't forget that he would be representing Troop 296 of Acton, in fact the whole entire Boy Scout movement. It sure was lucky he'd been so late. It was funny, but yesterday when he was supposed to be cleaning up his room, it was almost like something had told him he shouldn't do it, he should watch TV instead. It was almost like a voice. Arthur glanced gratefully at the body of the man he had seen in the agony of death. But that was uncomfortable. His eyes slid up to the inscription set into the wall above the body. The inscription lamented with condescending sympathy the two British redcoats who had fallen at the bridge.

> THEY CAME THREE THOUSAND MILES, AND DIED,
> TO KEEP THE PAST UPON ITS THRONE;
> UNHEARD, BEYOND THE OCEAN TIDE,
> THEIR ENGLISH MOTHER MADE HER MOAN.

Chapter 18

Baptismal waters from the Head above
These babes I foster daily are to me;
I dip my pitcher in these living springs
And draw, from depths below, sincerity.
BRONSON ALCOTT

Freddy was looking for something that would be nice to play with, like a tractor engine or a big greasy battery. There was nothing in the barn where his father and John were tooling up the corn planter. Freddy had just learned to walk, so he toddled out the door and wandered down behind it toward the red-painted shed where the cider press was, sitting down occasionally with a plop and getting up again. The door of the shed was around on the other side, facing the river. Freddy, his balloon wobbling on the end of the string on his wrist, started around the shed. Then he stopped.

"Horsie," he said. There was a man sitting high up in the sky on a horse. A funny man. A funny lady? The top of the man was like a lady, a funny lady. The lady looked back at Freddy. Then the lady turned up the sides of her mouth, and beckoned with one finger. Freddy trotted forward. The lady reached out and snapped the string of Freddy's balloon. The balloon started to sail up into the sky. The rest of the string fell down over Freddy's arm to the ground. Freddy looked at the string, unbelieving. Then he looked up into the sky at his disappearing balloon. He reached up for it and started to cry.

Gwen, going out of the house with a basket of wet wash, saw a big red bird in the wrangle of elm branches below the barn. No, it was too big for a bird, and it was floating up out of the tree now into the sky. It was Freddy's balloon. Poor Freddy. She put the basket down, hearing the telephone ring, and ran across the road. Freddy wasn't hard to find. He had gotten away from Tom and was standing beside the door of the cider shed, hollering his heart out, pointing up into the sky at the little red dot that had been his balloon. The long string dangled from his wrist to the ground. Gwen picked him up. There was a good three feet of string left. How had Freddy managed to break the balloon off at the top? Perhaps he had caught it on the edge of the shed roof, or on a nail or something. He was bellowing about a horsie and a funny lady. Gwen tried to comfort him, but he was inconsolable. When Gwen got back to the house, Grandmaw met her at the door, her face strange.

"Ernest Gross is dead," she said. "He was shot."

"Who?" said Gwen idiotically. "I mean, who shot him?"

"Someone on a horse, they think, dressed like Sam Prescott."

"Funny lady," roared Freddy. "Horsie!"

Gwen looked at Freddy, her lips tight. Not Charley? Then she looked grimly at Grandmaw. "I'm not going to have him bothered. I don't care who . . ."

Freddy was sucking his thumb, his cranky head on his mother's shoulder. He would be asleep in a minute. "No, of course not," said Grandmaw.

Chapter 19

❧ Here lies an honest man,
Rear-Admiral Van.
*
Faith, then ye have
Two in one grave,
For in his favor,
Here too lies the Engraver.
HENRY THOREAU

In 1846 when Henry Thoreau spent the night in jail as the guest of Sam Staples, the Concord Town Jail was a modest boxlike affair standing on ground now occupied by a parking lot behind Vanderhoof's Hardware Store on Main Street. By the nineteen-sixties the police department had grown to a force of twenty men, with a new headquarters on Walden Street shared by the Fire Department. The police occupied the right half of the brick building, with their own laboratory, dark room, firing range, parking meter repair facility, three radio-equipped automobiles and one walking mobile unit. Both Fire and Police Departments shared the use of the short-wave radio antenna. It was a good group of men, displaying the discreet and iron virtue of the best class of blue-coated law enforcers in the land. All of them were great broad-chested men except their Chief, James Flower. Jimmy was nine inches under the required minimum height, and he had worked his way into the Force and up to his present position through personality, competence and a special dispensation of the Legislature.

Thirty seconds after Sergeant Luther Ordway had hung up on Mrs. Jellicoe, a small parade of cars was turning out onto Walden Street, with Jimmy Flower already ticking off on his fingers a list of things to do. At the bridge he took calm and swift control. Patrolman Harold Vine passed on to him Arthur Furry's information and described the examination of the body by Mr. Ralph Chope of Houston, Texas. Chief Flower asked a few questions of Arthur Furry and Ralph Chope. He looked at Arthur's bright eye and flabby, pale face and directed that he be sent home in a patrol car. Then, after examining the body of Ernest Goss, he walked along the shore, looking at the ground. He peered across the bridge to inspect the place where the horseman had jumped the fence. He climbed over the fence in another place and walked gingerly around the area where the footprints of several hundred Boy Scouts were overprinted with the marks of a horse's hooves. Then he came back again the same way and did a number of things very quickly. He gave directions to the photographers, he organized a search of the immediate area for the weapon or for anything else of interest, and he dispatched Sergeant Silverson with two men to drive around by way of Liberty Street and attempt to pick up the trail at the point where Arthur had indicated the rider had left the field. He directed Sergeant Ordway to take charge of the on-the-spot investigation. Then he took the arm of Sergeant Bernard Shrubsole. "Let's go up to Charley's," he said. "We'd better round up Philip, too. There was some sort of hanky-panky with the Battery cannon this morning." On the way to the car they passed District Medical Examiner Walter Allen, hurrying up with his bag. Dr. Allen nodded without speaking.

It was quarter of two as they drove up Barrett's Mill Road past the Hand place and turned into the long drive that curved around in front of the Goss house. "Look, there he is," said Sergeant Shrubsole. Charley Goss was walking up from the barn with a hurried, distorted, limping gait. He came hobbling to the car, looking distraught, and leaned down to the window.

"I know what you've come for," he said. "I'll come with you. My mother isn't well. I don't want her to see you."

"All right, Charley," said Chief Flower, his voice gruff. "Climb in. But some of my boys will be along shortly to look around. "Where's your brother?"

Charley climbed in the back seat and sat down by Bernard Shrubsole. He was wearing khaki trousers and a white shirt and a pair of dirty tennis shoes. He was shivering. "Philip? Oh, I suppose he's s-still at the Rod and Gun Club with the Battery, having lunch."

"Well, I'll get out there, Bernie, and you can go on and take Charley to the station. One of the boys will bring me back." He looked back at Charley. "Look, go in and get your coat."

"No," said Charley, "I'm all right."

"Now, Charley," said Jimmy Flower, "you know what your rights are, don't you? To an attorney, I mean. I just want to be sure you . . ."

"An attorney?" said Charley. He was shivering uncontrollably. "Why should I need an attorney? I'm perfectly willing to admit that I shot my f-f-father myself."

Chapter 20

*The station of the parties
Forbids publicity,
But Justice is sublimer
Than arms, or pedigree.*
EMILY DICKINSON

At the Rod and Gun Club on Strawberry Hill Road the pie à la mode had just been placed on the table, and the members of the Concord Independent Battery were attempting to launch it into a sea of whiskey in which fragments of spaghetti and meat balls and green salad were already bobbing uneasily around. Police Chief Jimmy Flower's sobriety was taken as a profound tragedy and a personal insult. Jimmy was well known as a good fellow and a worthy citizen—why the heck did he look so grim? Surely he was badly in need of a little refreshment. Refreshment was thrust upon him. Chief Flower refused refreshment. Then Harvey Finn, looking him over critically, took querulous exception to Chief Flower's rubbers. He had never, he said, seen a more teetotalling, puritanical pair of rubbers in his life. "Take 'em off," he commanded, weaving imperiously across the floor.

"Take 'em off, take 'em off, ree-move 'em," sang Jerry Toplady.

Chief Flower ignored Harvey Finn. He crossed the room in

his rubbers and sat down at the table beside Philip Goss. He put
his chin in his small hand and looked at Philip. Philip's face
was highly colored. He leaned back in his chair unsteadily, and
looked back at Chief Flower.

"Where is your father, Philip?" said Chief Flower.

"My father?" said Philip, seeming to think it over. He turned
his head around jerkily. "He wazh here a while 'go."

"He went out, that's right, a while ago, 'n 'e didn' even
come back, I guess." Jerry Toplady nodded and nodded. "See?
He didn't even eat his dinner."

"What time did he go out?"

"Jeez," said Jerry proudly. "I couldn' even see the clock. I
was unner the table half 'n hour awready."

Chief Flower turned back to Philip. "Your father is dead,
Philip. He was killed by someone with a musket ball at the
North Bridge a little while ago. A witness saw a man dressed
like Sam Prescott riding away on horseback immediately after
the shot was fired."

Philip Goss lost all his high color abruptly. He stood up suddenly and stooped over and started to run, his hand over his
mouth. Chief Flower started up out of his chair, then sat down
again. Philip was going to the bathroom to be sick. After a
while he came back and leaned weakly against the wall, looking
very white indeed. The members of the Battery looked at one
another in shocked silence.

"I don't know what you want with me," said Philip coldly. "I
know nothing about it. Nor will I answer any questions until I
can discuss the matter with George."

"George?" said Jimmy. "George who?"

"George Jarvis. My law partner."

Chapter 21

When everything that ticked—has stopped—
And Space stares all around—
EMILY DICKINSON

A bird in the lilac bushes beside the Gosses' front door creaked like a guilty bedspring. Mary hesitated, then rang the bell. She had to find out what was going on. She wasn't prying, was she? She wanted desperately to help.

Edith came to the door, her hair wild. She put out her hand and grasped Mary's arm. "Come in. I thought you were the doctor for mother. She's in such a dreadful state. Nobody can make anything of it. She doesn't make sense. Oh, isn't it dreadful? How could Charley? Poor Daddy! They're questioning us, Chief Flower and Homer Kelly. Rowena and Mother are in there now. It's my turn next. But I don't know anything. I don't know anything at all. I was out walking around Annursnac Hill, at the time."

"It must be awful for all of you. I'm sorry. Did you say Kelly, Homer Kelly?"

"Yes, you know he's a Lieutenant-Detective for Middlesex County from the District Attorney's office. Didn't you know? Writing books on Emerson is just his hobby, or something."

Mary didn't know. She was thunderstruck. "Where's Charley?"

"They're holding him for questioning at the Police Station. Do you think they'll put him in jail? They've got Philip there, too. But they say it was Charley that did it. Oh, isn't it dreadful? How could he have been so foolish? Always so much wilder than Philip. Oh, dear."

Mary looked at Edith, feeling a little dizzy. She had the odd suspicion that Edith was enjoying herself. Her eyes were big and woeful, her voice almost gleeful. Like those people who read headlines aloud with gloating melancholy: FATHER KILLS SELF, FIVE CHILDREN.

The door opened and Rowena came out. Homer Kelly held the door open, his hand on the knob. He saw Mary.

She blurted it out. "I-I didn't know you were a policeman."

Homer looked tired. He turned away and looked at nothing. "Even Apollo had to plow for King Admetus," he said. His voice was dry.

He meant, like Bronson Alcott. Jimmy Flower came out, rubbing his hand across his bald head. Invisible inside the room beyond, there was a woman laughing. It was a peculiar, babbling laugh. Rowena looked up at Homer. "Is there anything else I can do to help?" She was wearing black already. No lipstick. Just mascara. Lovely and tragic. Her father was dead, her brother under suspicion, her mother collapsed or something —but Rowena the actress was playing a part, just as Edith was in her clumsier way. Mary asked after Charley.

"He's confessed," said Homer shortly.

Confessed. Oh, oh, no. Mary put out an unbelieving hand. Her eyes filled with tears. She turned her back on them, pushed open the front door and stumbled out. The door closed after her, and she started home, her knuckles in her mouth, thinking wretched thoughts.

Chapter 22

*Let us settle ourselves, and work and wedge our feet
downward through the mud and slush of opinion . . . till
we come to a hard bottom and rocks in place, which we
can call* reality . . . *a place where you might found a
wall or a state.*
HENRY THOREAU

Jimmy Flower had dragged another desk into his office for
Homer Kelly. But Homer wasn't using it, he was leaning
against the wall. Jimmy sat on his swivel chair, screwed high up
with his feet off the floor. Philip Goss and his law partner,
George Jarvis, sat in the two hard-backed chairs. Harold Vine
took notes.

Philip answered most of the questions himself, calmly, in his
clear voice, progressing in polished sentences from subject to
predicate, adorning them with dependent clauses and participles
that never dangled. Now and then there was a gentle demur
from George Jarvis, uttered in the politest tone, with an air of
such extreme courtesy that one hardly knew that a question was
being parried and set aside. There was an atmosphere of extreme fair play.

No, Philip had not seen his father leave the Rod and Gun
Club. Yes, it was true that he himself had left for an interval.
No, he wasn't sure of the time, nor how long he had been out.
He had felt the need of fresh air to clear his head. Jerry To-

plady had mixed the drinks with a heavy hand and Philip had never been able to live up to the Battery's mighty reputation for stowing it away. Where had he gone? To Nicholson's Barn, by the old sawmill there. No, he didn't think anyone had seen him, he had kept away from the road.

Jimmy asked him point-blank if there had been time for him to have walked home, changed clothes, ridden Dolly to the bridge, shot his father, ridden back home, changed clothes again and come back to the Rod and Gun Club?

Philip frowned and hesitated. George Jarvis broke in softly. How long did Chief Flower think all those things would take?

Chief Flower thought it would be hard to squeeze 'em all in under an hour.

Perhaps, George Jarvis thought, it would be preferable if Chief Flower simply asked Philip whether or not he had been away for an hour.

Philip could not seem to remember. He thought not. Well, then again, maybe he had been.

Homer Kelly sat down on the edge of Jimmy's desk and folded his arms. "Philip, can you tell us what went wrong this morning when the Battery was firing the Sunrise Salute? You made some sort of mistake?"

"I was tired. It was the sheerest stupidity. I gave the order to fire when my father was still standing in front of the gun with his ramrod down inside the barrel. If the lanyard man had pulled the string in response to my order my father would have been killed."

George Jarvis corrected him. "I doubt he would have been killed. You remember, Philip, when this very thing happened in Acton, the unfortunate fellow lost an arm, but that was all."

Homer scowled. "Isn't the order to fire supposed to be the duty of the captain? That's Harvey Finn, isn't it?"

"Yes, you're absolutely right. I'm only the lieutenant for the number one gun. All I should have done was to inform the captain that the gun was ready, so that he could give the order to fire. I guess I was trigger happy, as they say. I was tired." Philip smiled. "I still am."

"Why were you tired?"

Philip explained it patiently. "I went to the Ball last night, and of course the Battery gets up before Dawn in order to be at the bridge before sunrise with the guns."

That was all for Philip. As he and George Jarvis were shown out, to wait in the front office, Charley was ushered in. Homer caught the look in Charley's eye as he glanced at his brother. It was a speaking glance, full of message and meaning. And something else—sympathy, affection? Philip seemed to avoid it. He spoke to Charley, his words rapid and businesslike. "You're going to have legal counsel, aren't you, Charley? Let me get John Frippen. He's the best there is." Charley said nothing. He looked back and forth between his brother and George Jarvis, and then moved on into the office and closed the door behind him. He looked uneasy.

"What did my brother say?" he wanted to know.

Homer Kelly looked at Jimmy. Then he directed Harold Vine to read the first part of Philip's statement.

Harold flipped over the pages of his notebook and found the words taken down by Jimmy Flower. "Philip Goss said, 'I don't know what you want with me. I know nothing whatever about it. Nor will I answer any questions until I can discuss the matter with George Jarvis, my law partner."

"I don't believe it," said Charley. "You're lying. No, of course you're not lying." His face was distorted. He was hit hard. He folded over in his chair, and clasped his hands behind his neck, struggling silently with himself. "What do you want to ask me?" he murmured, his face still hidden.

"You say that you killed your father. Did anyone see you? Speak louder, Charley, I didn't hear you."

"I said, someone may have."

"Was it a man or a woman?"

"I don't know. I didn't see anyone."

"What were you wearing when you killed your father?"

Charley paused. He was still staring at the floor. "I was wearing these pants and a khaki shirt."

"How did you get there? To the bridge and back?"

"Well—I walked to the Rod and Gun Club and took Philip's car. Mine was—out of gas. Then I left it at the Club afterwards, and walked home."

"You got to the bridge in a *car?* Charley, the witness says the presumed murderer was dressed like Samuel Prescott and riding a horse. Your story doesn't fit with that very well."

Charley lifted his head and stared at Homer. "Like me? He was dressed like me?" Then he stood up and gesticulated. "It's not true. It's a lie. He wouldn't do it to me . . ."

"Who wouldn't? The witness?"

Charley's eyes were red. He glanced around the room, then sat down with his head in his hands. "Oh—my—God," he said.

Chapter 23

He shrinks from me as far as I have shrunk from him; his eyes no longer seek mine; there is war between us; there is hate in him and fear in me.
RALPH WALDO EMERSON

Arthur Furry had been brought back from Acton. He bit his fingernails nervously and looked with popping eyes at Charley Goss.

"All I saw," he said piously, "was the man's back."

Charley grimly turned around and showed Arthur his back.

"What about his height, Arthur?" said Jimmy Flower. "Would you say the man was about that tall? Mr. Goss is fairly tall."

Arthur, thinking about the honor of the Boy Scouts, stared at Charley's back and then rolled his eyes up at the ceiling. Jimmy felt a twinge of irritation. "I think," said Arthur, "if he were dressed up the same way the man was, it might be easier to tell."

"Have you got the Prescott outfit, Jimmy?" said Homer Kelly.

"Sure," said Jimmy. "It was in the horse's stall, kind of stuck behind the hay." Sergeant Ordway brought out a cardboard box and displayed its .contents, piece by piece. There was a black coat, longish and flared in the skirt, streaked and caked with mud on the left side, a ruffled shirt (obviously a lady's blouse in a large size), a yellow vest, a pair of narrow riding pants, also stained, and a set of soft leather boots. There was an orange mohair wig tied back with a black ribbon.

"Is that all?" said Homer. "I thought he had a three-cornered hat."

"That hasn't turned up," said Jimmy. "Although Arthur swears he saw it fall off."

"Scouts' Honor," said Arthur.

"What about the gun? No sign of it, yet?"

"Nope," said Jimmy, "although I don't see how in the Sam Hill we could miss it, if it's there. You say the thing is five feet long."

"What about the river? You've had skin-divers out there?"

"Yes, they've been and gone. Didn't find a thing."

Charley emerged from Jimmy's office wearing the costume he had put on earlier in the day for his ceremonial ride. His shoulders slumped. The jaunty look was gone. His garments might have been a shroud. Arthur Furry stuck out his lower lip and looked doubtful.

"He only saw his back," said Jimmy under his breath to Homer. "It could have been almost anybody. Well, we might as well see Philip in that rig. Harold, would you take that suit up to Philip when Charley gets it off, and bring him down here? Luther, you keep Charley there in my office for a while."

Philip was a little taller and slighter than his brother, and the dirt-stained coat hung loosely on him, his bare wrists showing. But Arthur, still uncertain, let his lower lip sag and put his finger in his mouth. (He's grubbing around in his little mind for the Real Honest Boy Scout Type Truth, decided Jimmy Flower, who had taken a dislike to Arthur Furry.)

"I think," said Arthur, "I would have to see them on the horse, you know, right there at the scene of the crime."

"Oh, fer . . . ," said Jimmy Flower. "Well, all right. We'll try to do that, but not now. Harold, you can take Philip back upstairs. Now, look here, Arthur, Sergeant Ordway showed you the horse Mr. Charles Goss was riding, on your way over here this afternoon. And you said it was the same as the one you saw. Right?"

"I said," said Arthur carefully, "that it could have been. I mean it was about the same size and color and everything."

"Was the horse you saw a mare or a stallion? I mean, was it a boy horse or a girl horse?" said Jimmy. "I mean, you said it went right over you, so you could have seen . . ."

Arthur's round face went red, but he rolled up his eyes conscientiously and let his lower lip hang slack. In the interval Harold Vine happily recalled a funny if apocryphal story about the time the Concord Independent Battery, hard up for horses as usual, had located nine, one a stallion, and then they couldn't find any more until the last minute when three more had been rented from a local stable. These had turned out to be a trio of mares who (it was dramatically discovered) were all in heat.

Arthur finally decided he didn't know.

Homer Kelly showed him a small piece of flat brown rock. "This is a flint which we presume fell from the priming mechanism of the murder weapon. It was found on the ground near the body. Now, Arthur, you say you saw no gun, no big long musket, that you remember? There was nothing hanging on his saddle, or fastened to the horse's bridle in any way? You didn't see him drop or throw anything, except for his hat? He didn't have a powder horn hanging on a strap over his shoulder? We are puzzled, you see, because if Mr. Goss was killed with a musket, where is it? It hasn't turned up in the area, it is not hidden in the Goss house, so far as we have been able to discover, and the skin-divers have found nothing in the river for a hundred yards on either side of the bridge. It would seem that the murderer must have carried it off with him. Now, I don't want you to remember something that you didn't actually see, but we wonder if you might not have noticed a gun that was lying across the saddle, or attached to the horse's gear in some way?"

Arthur said, no, he didn't think so. "Unless it was attached to the other side of the horse, of course. I only saw one side of the horse. But if the gun was as big as me, I don't see how I could have missed it."

"All right, Arthur, thank you. Tomorrow we'll go back to the bridge and watch the horse jump the fence. You can go along now with your mother."

"Detestable child," said Chief Flower, watching Arthur waddle across the street with his large amiable mother. "Pompous little pain in the neck. I suppose we've got to be nice to him."

"We can be damn glad the boy was there," said Homer. "The horseman seems to have escaped observation by anybody else at all. Silverson was the one who followed his trail along the river? Can I see his report? Yes, here's where he went—right along the river and across lots until he got to the hard dirt road that runs down by the barns and sheds at the Hand place. And that's where they lost him, but they think he must have gone back to the Gosses' barn somewhere in there. I see they didn't turn up any gun, either. You think they were thorough?"

"They sure were. Got some state troopers to help 'em. Turned those barns and sheds upside down." Jimmy pulled at Homer's sleeve. "Look, what are we going to do with Charley? He's confessed, but his confession is as full of holes as a sponge. Ordinarily with a confession you'd keep him in custody until the next court session on Monday. I'm darned if I know what to do."

"Let him go," said Homer. "All we can have now is a medical examiner's inquest. I'm sure the D.A. would go along with that. It's just as you said—the boy only saw the man's back. About the only limits you can set are that it had to be somebody taller than a shrimp like you and shorter than me, and neither a fat man nor a walking skeleton, and probably somewhat less than ninety-five years old. There are at least two prime suspects without alibis, maybe more. How do we know there wasn't a third person present? He might have hidden under the bridge, then got away by water. Let them both go. They'll be around when we need them. And see to it that Charley gets himself a lawyer."

Homer put on his coat and his fur hat. It had occurred to him that somebody ought to go talk to the Hands again. It was mighty queer that nobody in that big family had seen that horseman. Besides, it was a good excuse to see that heavenly girl again.

"No, I didn't see anybody, did you, Tom?" said Gwen.

"No, I didn't either," said Tom. "Did you, Mother?"

"No, I didn't. Did you, Mary?"

"No. Did you, Annie?"

"No, did you, John?"

"No, did you, Freddy?"

"Horsie!" said Freddy, who was too young to count. So that had gotten him nowhere.

Chapter 24

≈§ *Such is the daily news...a parasitic growth....I
would not run around a corner to see the world blow
up....The morning and the evening were full of news
to you.*
HENRY THOREAU

The newspapers called it "The Minuteman Murder," and they
celebrated it swiftly. There were so many charming things about
it. For one thing it had happened on Patriot's Day at the Birth-
place of American Liberty, and for another it had apparently
been committed by a reincarnation of Paul Revere (this universal error brought joy to the heart of the Governor of the Commonwealth). How much juicier could a story get? the A.P. man
wanted to know.

"Well, the victim could have been a shapely blonde draped in
the American flag," said the reporter from the *Globe*.

For a week or so the story stayed on page one in the Boston
papers. The inquest in the District Court helped it along.

INQUEST FINDS MURDER
Widow Insane With Grief
"Ernest Goss met his death at the hands of a person or
persons unknown." This was the finding of Judge Harlow
Murphy this morning in Concord's District Court. His de-

cision was based on the report of District Medical Examiner Walter Allen and on an autopsy performed by Dr. Warren Betty of Harvard's School of Legal Medicine.

The nature of the wound, Dr. Betty said, was such that it could only have been inflicted from a distance of approximately six to ten feet. The angle of passage of the fatal ball through the body indicated that the weapon from which it was fired was held at a height. It could have been fired, said Dr. Betty, either from horseback or from the rise of ground below the obelisk in front of the bridge. Dr. Allen declared the time of death, one P.M., compatible with a shot fired about five minutes earlier, i.e. about the time Boy Scout Arthur Furry heard such a shot.

Mrs. Elizabeth Goss, widow of the murdered man and mother of Charles Goss, has been pronounced incapable of participation in the investigation, said Psychiatrist David Marks of the Massachusetts General Hospital. On the advice of Dr. Marks, Mrs. Goss, who is said to have lost her reason as a result of the tragedy, will be removed from her luxurious Concord home to McLean Hospital in Waverly.

That was the *Herald*. The *Every Morning* went in more for sex and sentiment. Chief Jimmy Flower looked at the picture on the front page with distaste. There was Arthur Furry, almost life size, upholstered in merit badges, looking prim and fat. SCOUT CONFRONTS SUSPECT. The account was highly colored. Jimmy read it aloud to Bernard Shrubsole, and got mad.

. . . and the brave lad paused. "Perhaps if he would just make his horse jump the fence," he said. The lip of Concord Police Chief James Flower tightened. "All right, lad, anything you say . . ."

("I—did—not! I've never called anybody 'lad' in my whole entire life!")

He gave the order for Charles Goss, dressed as Paul Revere, to jump his horse over the fence to the rear of the

Minuteman. "It's him!" cried the Honor Scout, as the great beast leaped the fence.

Questioned by Lieutenant-Detective Homer Kelly, Arthur admitted that he could not rule out the possibility that Philip Goss, brother of Charles, might have been the original horseman. "I'm sure as anything it was one of them," said the boy.

Philip Goss was not present during the re-enactment. Homer Kelly asserted that Philip was acting within his legal rights in refusing to take part.

Kelly also pointed out that Charles Goss had taken his horse over the fence with a fine display of horsemanship, whereas the escaping murderer had fallen off, demonstrating clumsiness.

On the editorial page of this newspaper a columnist gave the District Attorney of Middlesex County a hard time, remarking with thinly veiled candor that his pursuit of criminals had been lackadaisical to say the least.

"Oh, bah," said Jimmy Flower. He rolled up the newspaper and bounded around his office with it, swatting nonexistent flies.

Chapter 25

I like to deal with you, for I believe you do not lie or steal, and these are very rare virtues.
HENRY THOREAU, in a letter to Lidian Emerson

The telephone rang in Mary's library office. The thin hearty voice of Jimmy Flower was on the line. "That you, Mary? Look, sweetheart, one of these days I'll get around to proposing to you in style, but right now I've got another kind of proposition. You know Lieutenant-Detective Homer Kelly? Good. Well, he was up to my house last night, and he was saying he wished he had some kind of advisor on this case who knew Concord, and all its history and literature and so on, you know, and the people involved in the Goss case, and somebody who was smart, too, and my wife Isabelle suggested Mary Morgan, and I said, say, that's a good idea, but she's already got a job in the library there with Alice Herpitude, and she said to me (Isabelle) that maybe Alice would give you time off, like every Tuesday and Thursday and Saturday, and I said I'd ask Alice. Well, the upshot is, I just spoke to Alice and she says that's okay with her. How about it?"

Alice Herpitude was peeking around the door, nodding and smiling. Mary thought it over. She couldn't get Charley into worse trouble by being on the inside. Maybe she could help him. Then again, helping Charley might mean hurting his brother. Mary stared at the little bust of Louisa May Alcott on her desk. Louisa looked noncommittal. "What did Lieutenant Kelly say about it?" said Mary.

"Oh, he thought it was great."

Jump, Mary, jump. "Well, all right, I guess so."

Mary walked over to the station at lunchtime to see what was expected of her. Homer nodded at her, and snapped open a card table and squeezed it into the corner of Jimmy's office beside his desk.

"Grandiose appointments of your office completed just in time."

"Tell me," said Mary, "how a student of the Transcendentalists ever got to be a police lieutenant."

"Other way around. My father was a cop in Cambridge. Hence, Kelly. So I was more or less brought up on the force. And my mother was a classicist. Hence, Homer. Classicists live in libraries. So I did my teething on any old chewed-up volume that was lying around. Sucked out all the glue, gradually gummed my way through a five-foot shelf."

"Do you have a degree in anything?"

"You mean like a Ph.D. from Harvard? Look, my dear, the closest I ever got to Harvard was as a traffic cop like my father, shepherding Harvard students across Harvard Square. Picking up a law degree at Northeastern night school and reading Waldo and Henry on the side—those things were strictly extra-curricular."

He walked her to the corner, and the conversation galloped along in a sort of airy antagonism. A shot, a parting shot, and then Homer shouted a ricochet across the street. Mary found herself walking down the Milldam with a big grin on her face. She collided with Alice Herpitude, who was coming out of the First National grocery store.

"Oh, I'm so sorry, Alice. I wasn't looking where I was going." She leaned over and picked up Miss Herpitude's packages.

"We're such pygmies, Mary dear. I don't know why you Olympians take any notice of us at all."

Chapter 26

⮑ *My Aunt Maria ... was heard through the partition
shouting to my Aunt Jane, who is deaf, "Think of it! He
stood half an hour to-day to hear the frogs croak, and he
wouldn't read the life of Chalmers."*
HENRY THOREAU

It was Mary's first full day in the employ of the District Attorney of Middlesex County. Homer Kelly nodded at her curtly as she came in. He glared guiltily at his size 14 shoe. He hadn't told the D.A. about this yet. Hiring a secretary onto the payroll wasn't something to be done lightly, and it would probably be just as well not to tell the D.A. at all that Mary Morgan was the beloved of the chief suspect. One was supposed to stay strictly away from personal connections with possible criminals under investigation. But when it came to that, my God, there was Rowena Goss, Charley's sister. (Personal connections, Jesus.) Homer swung around in his chair and cleared his throat with a blast like the Last Trump.

"Now, the first thing I want you to do," said Homer, "is tell me about the members of the Alcott Association. Some of them felt pretty strongly about those crazy letters of Ernie's. And the letters have disappeared. Or at least we can't find them. Maybe he had them on his person there at the bridge, and somebody shot him and stole them after he refused to give them up. Now, do you have any idea which of these people might be fanatic enough to commit a crime just to protect the reputations of Emerson and Thoreau and all that gang they idolize so much?"

"Well, I idolize them myself, most of them," said Mary.

"I'm aware of that. And you wouldn't hurt a flea. And that reminds me. Where did you say *you* were when all this was going on?"

"Asleep in bed. And I would hurt a flea. I squash flies all the time."

"Tell me about Howard Swan."

"Howard? Well—I don't know any other way to describe him except to say that he's the best fellow in the world. One of those dependable people that everyone turns to and relies on. He's president of the Alcott Association, Secretary of the Thoreau Society, something or other in the Antiquarian Association, Moderator of Town Meeting, and probably other things, too. And not because he's aggressive and usurping but because everybody asks him to do the hard jobs nobody else really wants."

"Mmmmm," said Homer, scribbling it all down. Jimmy Flower came into the office, pulling on his coat. He picked up his Chief's hat and put it on. It was the smallest regulation size, but it still left a draft around the edges and rested on his ears, folding them over. "Jimmy," said Homer, looking up, "did you get a report yet on Howard Swan's story that he was in New York?"

"Yes, that's in. Those business buddies he said he was having lunch with all agreed he was with them on Patriot's Day, just the way he said they would. At one o'clock he was sitting right there in that restaurant off Wall Street. He was there all right."

"He's some kind of big wheel in banking, isn't he? What about the men he was lunching with? All solid citizens?"

"They sure were. Above reproach. Jeez, what a nice thing to be. I wisht I was above reproach."

Mary laughed and told him that he was, if anybody was. "Tell that to Isabelle," said Jimmy, going out again.

"Well, that's enough on Swan. We've been all over his house there on Main Street anyhow, and didn't turn up anything. He's not married?"

"No. There is some talk about an unhappy love affair, long ago. But then that's what people always say."

"All right, now what about Teddy Staples?"

"Teddy?" Mary smiled. "He certainly is a little nutty about Thoreau."

"Let's begin with Teddy."

Teddy's cottage on the Sudbury River was approached by a mile-long driveway off Fairhaven Road. Another driveway branched off his, leading to Alice Herpitude's house. Both houses looked out from pine woods on the wide bend of the river called Fairhaven Bay. Teddy's house had been built by the son of his illustrious ancestor as a summer camp, and basically it had once been a simple little house with a front porch toward the river, standing high and straight like an upright piano. But Teddy in a slack season for stonemasons had begun engulfing his front porch in a surging tide of cobblestones. Homer pulled up his car and stared at it, unbelieving. Mary explained that the Antiquarian Society was all upset about it, and was trying to make him stop. "But really," she said, "that would be too bad. Houses like the way it used to be are a dime a dozen. Now it's unique."

"Absolutely one-of-a-kind," breathed Homer.

Teddy was making a cobblestone birdbath in his front yard, which was really a beaten-down part of the woods, marshy at the bottom by the river, with ferns pushing up sticky fiddle-heads, and skunk cabbages, greener than anything else, putting out red snout-like flowers. It was chilly, and Teddy had on several layers of pants. The top one was split down the back seam where the staples had given way, showing a checkered pair underneath. Teddy waved his mortar trowel at them.

"You'll f-f-forgive me, if I go right on. I've got to work fast before the mortar dries."

"Oh, Teddy, isn't that a nice birdbath," said Mary.

Teddy looked up at her, his thin face shining. "Mary, I saw some red crossbills yesterday, in the very p-p-place *he* saw them, up the Assabet, by the hemlocks . . ."

"He . . . ?" asked Homer.

"Henry Thoreau," said Mary. "Teddy is bound and determined he's going to see every bird Thoreau saw in Concord. How is your list coming, Teddy? How many more to go?"

Teddy turned back to work. His eager look was gone, his face seemed to have closed in. "Oh," he said, "there's a few more . . ." He buttered a big round boulder with mortar and jammed it into place.

"I suppose it's harder now than it was in his day," said Homer. "Now that the area is so built up . . ."

"That's right," said Teddy, sounding grim. "And some of the birds were rare even for his time, even then."

Homer asked him what he thought about the death of Ernest Goss.

Teddy flushed and looked miserable. "I suppose you want me to say I think it's terrible. Well, I don't. The d-d-damn fool . . ."

"Were you at the parade on the 19th?"

"Me? At the parade? No, I was too busy."

It turned out after some pressing that Teddy had been out in his canoe on the river, watching a bluebird try to claim a nesting site in the hollow of a dead tree.

"Well, what did you do before and after that?"

"Before and after? Heck, I must have spent three, four hours watching the bluebird. It was having an argument with an English sparrow over its property rights, and they took possession one after the other. The sparrow finally won out, I'm sorry to say."

"Where was this hollow tree?"

"Where was it? Oh, I can show you the place. It wasn't far from the North Bridge, as a matter of fact. In fact every time those dern guns went off I was afraid the bluebird would give up and fly away. But she stuck to it. And unfortunately s-s-so did the sparrow. The black ducks didn't, though. There was a flock of them there, floating on the water, and one of the gunshots sent 'em all up—up and aw-w-w-ay."

"Which gunshot?" said Henry. "What time of day?"

"What time? Heck, I sort of l-l-lose track of time." Teddy was arranging small cobblestones artistically in a circle around the edge of his birdbath. "It was a long time after the others, though,

I'm pretty sure. Most of the people must have g-gone home."

"That was probably the shot that killed Ernest Goss. I don't know what good it does us, though. We have other witnesses to the sound of the shot, a little before one o'clock. Besides the Boy Scout there was Mrs. Parsons with her baby carriage. The baby woke up and started to cry. But anyway, maybe you'd better show us just where you were."

Teddy finished off his birdbath and cleaned his trowel. Mary made room for him beside her in the front seat of the car, and he sat down with his long bony hands hanging between his knees. She made small talk about birds, trying to ask sensible questions. Teddy answered in stammers, ill at ease. He showed them where to park on Monument Street, and then led them down to the river. "Here we are," said Teddy. "Right beside where the Mill Brook comes in. Here's the tree. See? The high water killed it, many years back. Those must be my footprints there, coming up from the shore. See there, where the g-g-ground is soft?"

"Did you see or hear anything else, Teddy, while you were here, any time during the course of the day? Anything that might have had a remote connection with the killing of Ernest Goss?"

"Me? Oh, no. No."

"Did you have those binoculars with you?"

"These? Oh, sure, I always carry my glasses and my f-f-field notebook." He patted his pocket. Then he stopped, his hand on his chest, and stared at the sky.

"What is it?" said Mary, turning to look where he was looking.

Teddy's voice trembled in a fusillade of stuttering. "I-I-I d-d-don't know. I-I-It's s-s-so h-h-h-high . . ."

He fumbled to free his binoculars and jerked them up to his eyes. Mary saw a dark speck wheeling and soaring very far up. It disappeared behind a clump of alders. Teddy, breathing rapidly, plunged along the shore and then into the water. He strode out, the water soaking up his trousers to his thighs, his eyes clamped to his glasses.

"What is it?" said Homer. "Looks like a gull."

Teddy stood silent, transfixed. Then his shoulders sagged. He lowered his glasses, and with his back to them, seemed to be trying to get hold of himself. "It's a d-d-duck hawk," he said. He started to cough.

"Come on out, Teddy," said Homer. "We'll take you home and you can put on some dry clothes." Mary wondered if he had another pair of trousers to put on. They drove him home, and she watched him stumble out of the car and start up the steep stony steps of his cobblestone porch. She felt extremely sorry for him. His trousers slapped against his legs, he was hunched over with uncontrollable spasms.

Homer backed the car around. "If you had to pick out one word to describe his mood, what would it be?"

Mary thought about it, then picked the right one. "Afraid."

"And there's another thing. Did you notice how he always repeated each question as though he were giving himself more time to think? That's an odd trick I associate with liars."

"Oh, no. Teddy isn't a liar. Not usually, anyway. I'm sure of it."

"Well, look. He could have paddled up to the North Bridge, bumped off Goss and paddled home again, and no one the wiser."

"Well, maybe."

The first thing Homer did when they got back to the station was to send Sergeant Shrubsole out to Monument Street to look in the hollow tree. "Do I have to have a search warrant?" said Bernard wittily. "I mean if someone lives there now..."

"Oh, hurry up. I can just see that fowling piece standing up inside. I suppose it would be too good to be true."

It was too good. There was nothing in the hollow tree but an extremely huffy English sparrow sitting on a nest of spotted eggs. She made a frightful fuss about the whole thing, lecturing Shrubsole roundly from a nearby bush, as he groped around inside her house. Gallantly, in spite of the superfluousness of any more English sparrows at all in the world, he put her nest back where it belonged, eggs and all. "Small thanks I got," he said.

Chapter 27

The Soul selects her own Society—
Then—shuts the Door—
On her divine Majority—
Obtrude no more—
EMILY DICKINSON

Miss Herpitude was no ordinary librarian. She did not regard it as her sacred task to protect her precious volumes from the clutches of the villainous defacing mob. Instead it was her faith that the proper destiny for any book in her car was to lie open upon the lap of a reader, whether he were taking notes soberly in school or simply holding his place with a buttery finger while he ate lunch at his own table.

Mary looked at Miss Herpitude with awe and wonder. That admirable woman was using a razor blade to cut a map out of a history book so that a boy doing his homework could hold it up to the window and trace it. When he was through with it Mary knew that Miss Herpitude would spend half an hour pasting the map back in. Her maxim was, and Mary subscribed to it with all her heart, that the books were there to be used and the librarians were there to be useful.

Be useful. Here came someone who was obviously in need of help. A stranger was goggling around at the pale watchers on the balcony, Ephraim Bull and Judge Hoar and Bronson Alcott

and Louisa May. Then he goggled at Mary and came right over.
When he opened his mouth his speech was one of the cruder
forms of British English, with an absurd affected accent thrown
in for good measure. Poor wretch. His posture was miserable,
his chest was caved in, his legs were bowed like a cockney
cowboy's. His eyes stared and stared at her, fixed and unblink-
ing.

"Can I help you?" said Mary.

"Oi hev something to show yew," he said. His eyebrows and
his hair, thick wiry stuff combed forward over his forehead,
were a dull black like lampblack. He wore glasses with round
celluloid frames. If he had stood up straight he might have been
about as tall as she was, but his posture was dreadful, and his
long neck thrust forward so that his Adam's apple hung down
over his collar. His collar was dirty, with a black line around the
edge. But all of these details were as nothing beside the awful
facts of his complexion. The poor fellow had a ghastly case of
acne, and its prominences were superimposed on the shallow
depressions and pits of old smallpox scars like the mountains
and craters of the Moon. Mary had to stare very hard at his
googly eyes in order not to be caught making a clinical examination of his pimples. As an unnecessary final flourish, his jaw
suffered from malocclusion and two yellow buck teeth rested on
his lower lip. Mary felt some anguish for him. But then her
sympathy vanished as it became more and more apparent that
he considered himself as sexually appealing as Tarzan the Ape-
man.

There was a sheaf of grubby typed pages in his hand. All his
own work. He laid it on the desk and ran his finger along the
lines, reading aloud. *Ralph Waldo Emerson's Philosophy of
Life, by Roland Granville-Galsworthy, Oxford University.*

What a charlatan. Mary nodded as though she believed it,
and then Roland Granville-Galsworthy asked for the complete
works of Emmanuel Kant. In German. "I'm afraid we have it
only in English," said Mary.

"Thet's quoite all roight. Thet will dew," said Granville-
Galsworthy. What a show-off. Mary bet he couldn't read Ger-

man anyway, the way he had pronounced Kant. She found him a watered-down version of the *Critique of Pure Reason,* and settled him down in the reference room. As she went out she could feel his eyes on her back like two dirty greyish-white balls. For the rest of the afternoon he kept coming to the doorway and staring at her, or going to the Men's Room, gaping at her over his shoulder. He went to the Men's Room twice, getting the key from her and returning it with his damp hand. Before he left he thrust his opus on Mary, writing on it graciously, "With the compliments of Arthur." Mary showed it to Alice Herpitude.

"But it's cribbed straight from that book by Claridge," said Miss Herpitude. "What an incredible man."

Mary started to laugh. "When I was in the sixth grade we had a health play, and I was supposed to be 'Malnutrition, First Cousin to Death.' I tried to make myself look just like that, with that same droopy posture and big lipstick pimples. I was a smash hit, too. I suppose I shouldn't be so hard on the poor fellow. He probably can't help being a wretch, a dolt and a fool."

"But surely," said Miss Herpitude, "he should have medical advice. I feel truly sorry for the poor man."

Chapter 28

Lectured in basement . . . of the orthodox church, and I trust helped to undermine it.
HENRY THOREAU

Poor Mary. The sham graduate of Oxford, having once set his googly eyes on her, would not take them off. He showed up everywhere. He came every day to the library, asked for some ponderous work and read picture magazines instead, like a boy with a comic book folded in his speller. When Mary didn't appear at the library on Thursday, he asked Miss Herpitude where she was and followed her to the Police Station, bobbing his Adam's apple up and down like a yo-yo. Mary couldn't understand him at all. His repellent skin was part of a hide so thick that he was sensitive to no hints and boggled at no excuses. Mary loathed the sight of him. When he began waiting for her at lunchtime, Jimmy Flower started to kid her about her boy friend. Mary took to ducking out the back door, but Granville-Galsworthy caught on to that trick, too, and she had no peace. Homer Kelly, shaking his head, would lift the corner of the shade and watch the two of them go off together, Mary marching firmly in advance, Roland Granville-Galsworthy skulking in the rear.

Even when one was trapped, one had to be polite. Mary, wedged into a corner behind a small restaurant table, would rack her brain for something to talk about. It was no good talking about Emerson. Roland knew nothing at all about Emerson. She had tried reminiscing about the colleges at Oxford, where she and Gwen had once spent a summer. Oh yes, he knew so-and-so, and he had met so-and-so. Mary made up a few preposterous people, and he was old friends with them, too. The ass. Why did he bother? What on earth was the man doing in Concord anyway? How was he supporting himself? He paid only for his own lunch, always, and ate an unvarying diet of Coke, potato chips and fried clams. Over the weeks his pimples roved from one part of his physiognomy to another, changing the lunar topography. The Apennines receded, Eratosthenes rose up in splendor.

And then one Sunday he showed up in church. He had seen Mary striding across the grass with her black choir robe billowing behind her, and he followed her in. She didn't see him, because she was looking up at the giant elm trees that stood on the lawn like old grandees, putting on new leaves like airs. Her transcendental jukebox was grinding . . .

Wasn't this church a copy of the one that had burned down? So it must have looked much the same to Waldo Emerson. He had retreated from Unitarianism, of course, or vaulted over it, one or the other, but he had been a gracious friend of the First Parish, as a good neighbor and fellow townsman. And, old hedonist of sight that he was, how he must have relished the domed spire and the heavy Doric columns, part of his daily horizon down the road. Mary climbed the steps to the balcony and sat down with the choir. The bell began to ring, and she cranked up Emily—

> How still the Bells in Steeples stand
> Till swollen with the Sky
> They leap upon their silver Feet
> In frantic Melody!

Then she apologized to the shade of Lidian Emerson, who had thought it wicked to go to church Sundays, and began to indulge in back-worship, her own private form of idolatry.

There came Alice Herpitude, a sufficiently splendid icon in her Easter outfit. In the library Alice wore garments that were modest and retiring, but in church she glorified God. Her hat was a fountain of rosy feathers, erupting to the sky, her coat was white with cabbage roses. She was a paean of joy and praise. Mary felt like cheering. But then she leaned forward and looked more carefully. What was wrong? Within her finery Miss Herpitude looked frail and old. She was clinging to the pew backs as she walked along the aisle. Now she was collapsing into an empty pew. Was she ill? Mary half rose to go and see. But then Miss Herpitude squared her shoulders and sat up straight. She picked up her hymn book and started leafing through it. Mary sat down again. She would try to speak to Alice afterwards. Here came the Hands, led down the aisle by the genial usher, Howard Swan. (He was a member of the Prudential Committee, too—everyone worked him hard.) Tom would be having his mind on spraying the orchard. His hose was clogged and giving him a terrible time. Gwen would be thinking about dinner, wishing she could peel potatoes in church.

Oh, damn. What was that NINcompoop Roland doing here? Couldn't she find sanctuary anywhere? Mary pretended not to see his dank salute, but he turned back when he saw her and climbed up into the balcony nearby, gaping at her. He was probably an Anglican or something. People should stay in the church they were born in, they had no right to go fishing around. She could see his pimples from here.

There was Charley Goss. Poor Charley. He was putting on a good front, coming to church. But he couldn't seem to face the whole congregation, so he headed for the balcony, too. Women and children in the balcony, please, and suspected murderers. Charley sat down in front of Roland Granville-Galsworthy. Roland gave him his adenoidal stare. Mary, feeling intensely sorry for Charley, attempted to catch his eye and smile at him. But

Charley had folded his arms and he was looking fixedly at the pew back in front of him. Granville-Galsworthy caught her look instead, and he wriggled all over with joy. Mary turned away angrily and looked down again at the congregation on the floor. She watched as Philip Goss came in with Rowena and Edith and Homer Kelly and sat down smack in the middle of the rows of pews. There was nothing on *his* conscience apparently. Edith rather stupidly waited to let Rowena go first, but Rowena frowned at her, and Edith, her heavy eyebrows lifting, scuttled in beside her brother. Rowena went in next, in her sensational black, and Homer sat solidly on the outside. Where had he got that outlandish haircut? His lank brown hair was shingled in layers. He probably did it himself, reaching around in back with the scissors. Mary had caught a glimpse of his tie as he sat down. It was one she had found in Woolworth's, with zebra stripes and horseshoes tipped in with glitter. Oh, go on, Homer Kelly, get along with you. Boston policemen are all Catholics anyway. Mary stared at Rowena instead. Rowena had a little itch behind her ear, and she scratched it daintily. She had one of those clean little necks.

The minister addressed God. Mary closed her eyes. Before long it was time for the anthem. Mary saw Homer look back curiously as the choirmistress pulled out the stops and the organ emitted small sounds of rushing air. The choir was not at its best that morning. Mrs. Jellicoe wobbled heavily all over the soprano part (everyone wished to God she would retire), and the choirmistress winced. The congregation sat through it upright and unflinching. After all, thought Mary, one didn't come to a New England church to enjoy oneself.

After the service the choir waited for the congregation to go out. Mary looked at Alice Herpitude and decided that she was all right. She was standing up, talking and smiling with Grandmaw Hand. Rowena Goss and Homer Kelly were stalled by a knot of talkers in the other aisle. Better have a pleasant expression ready in case they looked up. But they didn't. Mary's cordial smile became set and grim. She began to feel foolish, so she turned and stared with the utmost concentration at the last hymn, "Gird Your Loins, O My Soul," by the Reverend Maltby Trueblood, 1888. That's what she would do, all right. That was precisely what she would do. When Homer did at last look up at the choir loft he saw a tall black-robed back, bowed over, turned away. He wasn't aware that its soul was having its loins girt up, and that it was damning him straight to hell.

"Mary," Mrs. Jellicoe was prodding her and looking at her with her codfish eyes. "There's someone here to see you." Mary looked up. Oh no, not again. It was Roland Granville-Galsworthy. Couldn't the man leave her alone, even in church? He sat down beside her. He had written another opus. "Ralph Waldo Emerson, a Critical Bibliography." He wanted to know if Mary would look at it. Why didn't the man just forget the whole thing?

Everyone was gone. Mary got up to go. But Roland wouldn't let her. To her horror he tried to make a pass at her. "Oh, for heaven's sake," she said, "don't do that." But he persisted, and Mary backed away. "Stop it," she said. Good heavens. This was ridiculous. There was only one thing to do, and that was bolt. He was between her and the door. Mary found herself scrambling in undignified haste between pews. Roland seemed to think it part of a lover's game.

"Oi know how yew American girls are attracted to we Englishmen," he shouted, vaulting a pew back.

"You mean indiscriminately?" said Mary, trying to keep things, which had gotten out of hand, on a light level. She glanced back at him, and stopped for a second, appalled. What was that look on his face? The moon-calf expression had disappeared. There was a violent difference. The eyes were glazed —the lips were wet. Mary began scrabbling again at the backs of benches, pulling herself along, her heart in her mouth.

The balcony ran around three sides of the church. There was a door at the pulpit end. Mary grasped at the knob. It was locked. She turned and leaned against it. She was trapped. He was coming at her. Well, she could still scratch, bite and claw.

Then there was a laugh from down below. It was Rowena Goss. She was standing in the aisle with Homer Kelly, looking up. "Don't let us disturb you!" On Homer's face there was a look of pain. Rowena gave her enchanting giggle. "I'll just get my glove . . ." She nipped into her pew, picked up her glove and hurried out, with Homer following her, his face glowering.

Mary, pulsing red, ducked past Roland and ran for the stairs. She was down them before he had recovered himself. He let her go and stood where he had stopped, swallowing rapidly, his Adam's apple rising and falling, his chest heaving, a frustrated curtain falling on his vision of Sleeping Beauty. She was that smashing girl this time, but without the red, just white like wax, with her eyes shut. In his dream he came in to where she lay, just like that prince. But he didn't wake her up. No, curse her. That wasn't the way his dream went at all.

Chapter 29

He is not alert enough. He wants stirring up with a pole. He should practise turning a series of somersets rapidly, or jump up and see how many times he can strike his feet together before coming down. Let him make the earth turn round now the other way, and whet his wits on it, whichever way it goes, as on a grindstone; in short, see how many ideas he can entertain at once.

HENRY THOREAU

The District Attorney of Middlesex County was a devout man, passionately fond of his family, the Red Sox, freshly shelled peanuts and cold beer. Raised entirely in the city of Somerville, he had left it only once as a child for a single disastrous visit to the country where he had unexpectedly come face to face with a cow. Ever since that time he had been deathly afraid of cows; and even barns, hay, large dogs and the grass on Boston Common made him uneasy. He had been chosen to run for office for reasons other than his qualifications for the job, but on the whole he was an effective and conscientious public servant. His strong points were two. First of all, he was just intelligent enough to recognize his own deepseated befuddlement, and he made up for it by an elaborate system of self-prompting notes, charts and outlines written in his own painstaking rounded hand. Second, he was backed up by Miss Felicia O'Toole. Miss O'Toole was his secretary, a self-effacing homely woman with an I.Q. fifty points higher than the D.A.'s. She was incomparable.

Miss O'Toole had spread clean sheets of paper all over his big desk, and laid out four well-sharpened pencils and a big bowl of peanuts. The District Attorney pulled a sheet of paper toward him, and wrote carefully at the top, "Charles Goss." On another he wrote, "Philip Goss." Then he sucked his pencil and looked up at the vaulted ceiling. What other headings would he think of if he were smarter? Oh, well, they would come out in the discussion. Miss O'Toole sat a little to the rear, almost invisible in her grey dress, his shield and buckler and Excalibur invincible.

Homer Kelly reviewed the case swiftly. The D.A. scribbled things on his papers. Chief Flower was there, with Sergeants Shrubsole and Silverson and Patrolman Vine. Mary Morgan sat in one corner, listening and taking notes.

After two hours the men had all taken off their coats, a big fan was sucking in the tobacco smoke, and there were peanut shells and ashes all over the rug. Miss O'Toole went out for sandwiches. She had to march through a crowd of newsmen sprawled all over the wooden benches beyond the locked metal gate. "Plenty of time for you all to have lunch," she said kindly. "We'll be ages yet." When she got back the D.A. was mopping his thin sad face and ruffling the three long hairs he combed sideways over his bald head. His papers were covered with round scrawls. They were sifting over each other and getting lost. He doubted if he wasn't just getting more and more mixed up. Here is what he had.

CHARLES GOSS

Motive: strong. Revenge? Father a bast. Night before, was shot at by brother with musk. at command of Dad. Logical Ch use same gun bump off Dad.

Opportunity: last seen after parade-ride returning home horseback Barrett's Mill Rd. 11:15. Next seen by Flower coming from barn where suit found 1:45. No satisfact. explan. whereabouts meantime. (Murder 1:00).

Fax supporting Ch as X:

1. Confessed. Loopholes in confesh don't rule it out. Maybe diabol. clever ruse.

2. X wore Ch's outfit.

3. X's horse prob. Ch's horse.

4. Scout idents X as Ch or Ph.

5. Had motive.

6. Had opportunity.

7. Ch had access old gun, knew how fire it.

8. Scout sez X limped; Ch had hurt leg.

9. What he doing in barn, unless taking off suit?

10. Ch family black sheep, unstable.

Fax NOT supporting Ch as X:

1. Loopholes in confesh. Maybe Ch continues boy-
   hood custom, sez "I did it" when either brother
   accused. Ch assumes Ph did it, so protects him by
   confesh. Shocked when Ph doesn't confess, too,
   then clams up, assumes Ph trying pin murder on
   him. Big blow. (GOOD.) But maybe diabol. clever
   ruse (see above).

2. If Ch intended murder Dad, why do it in public place
   wearing own fancy suit? Unless crime of sudden
   passion. In which case, why? Why have loaded
   musk. with him? What reason for rondayvoo?

3. Not likely Ch would fall off horse, since expert
   horseman. But maybe unsteady becuz nervous?

4. Limp of X might be caused by fall off horse.

5. Boy Scout's identif. don't mean much, he only saw
   back of X.

PHILIP GOSS

Motive: weak. Suppose motive was revenge for Dad's making him fire at Ch night before—this mean Ph fond of
  Ch. Why, then, would Ph wear Ch's Paul Revere suit to
  murder Dad, thus pinning murder on Ch?

Opportunity: Ph was with Conc. Ind. Battery on arrival
  Rod and Gun Club noon. Shortly after (he say), he
  left, walked around fresh air, went to barn, came
  back. No witnesses. So no alibi. Gone full hour. Time
  enough.

Fax supporting Ph as X:

1. Alibi fishy.
2. Scout idents X as either Ch or Ph. But see above.
3. Gun handy, could fire it.
4. Logical he use same gun on Dad that Dad made him use on Ch. (But see under motive, above.)
5. VERY IMPORTANT: Ph nearly killed Dad with cannon same morning. Mistake, he say.
6. Ph's car found in parking lot at bridge after murder.

Fax NOT supporting Ph as X:

1. Motive looks weak.
2. Character good.
3. Why commit murder in public place? See above.
4. If Ph murdered Dad on horseback, didn't bring car. Car probly used by E. Goss to get to bridge from gun club.

QUERIES

1. Why E. Goss go to bridge?
2. Where gun?
3. Where hat?
4. Who E. Goss fight with before dinner? (Reported by Miss Morgan.)
5. DON'T FORGET BAWL OUT KELLY, HIRING GIRLS WITH-OUT PERMISH.

The District Attorney threw his head back and dropped peanuts down his throat. "Now for the Alco' Club. An' wha' abou' unknown persons, ou'siders?" he said.

Chief Flower made a sarcastic noise. "You mean beyond a couple thousand visitors to Concord to see the parade? They trampled up the place like a herd of elephants. But who were they all? Damned if I know. There isn't a prayer of tracking them all down. Say, there was one kind of interesting thing though. Loftus said he noticed a parked car in the parking lot there by the bridge the night before. Let's see, Bernie, that was a green Chrysler sedan, last year's, with a Massachusetts license, right? Bob saw it around midnight, and thought it was just a couple of neckers. Did that registration come in?"

Sergeant Shrubsole looked uncomfortable. "Well, yes," he said, "it did."

Homer Kelly, his face red, gave a snort. "Never mind, Sergeant, I'll confess. That was my car. It was me."

The District Attorney stared at Homer, his mouth open. Then he guffawed and made a lecherous remark. Mary Morgan, who had been doodling a face in the corner of her notebook, added a pair of horns and a set of villainous teeth.

Chapter 30

*I am tired of scraps. I do not wish to be a literary or
intellectual chiffonier ... let me spin some yards or miles
of helpful twine, a clew to lead to one kingly truth ...*
RALPH WALDO EMERSON

Miss O'Toole leaned forward and placed a scribbled note beneath her boss's nose. The D.A. took it in, cracked a peanut
between his fingers and cleared his throat. "Now then," he said,
"perhaps this would be as good a time as any to hear from
Ernest Goss's lawyer. Miss O'Toole, would you call him in?"
With his tongue sticking out between his lips the District Attorney printed WILL on the top of a clean sheet of paper. "All
right, Mr. Twells, here's a chair. You have a copy of Ernest
Goss's will?"

"I do," said Mr. Twells, sitting down stiffly. "Would you like
me to read it in its entirety? Or shall I just run down the list of
beneficiaries?"

"If you can spare us the whereases, Mr. Twells, we'd be
grateful," said the D.A., crushing another peanut. His own passage of the Massachusetts bar had been very shaky, and he
detested high-class lawyers.

Mr. Twells was a miracle of brevity. "Well, then. Ernest
Goss left nearly all of his estate in trust for his wife. She was to

receive the income during her lifetime, with the right to dispose of half of it in her own will, with the other half going in equal shares to her children. The trustees were myself and Mr. Philip Goss. And then there were a few other beneficiaries outside the immediate family. Mr. Goss left his collection of old guns and Indian relics to Mr. Theodore Staples. I understand that both of these collections were quite valuable. And there are a few others who will receive small sums."

"Could you run though the list of names for us, Mr. Twells?"

"Mrs. Annie Bewley, Miss Alice Herpitude and Miss Maria Fuller Alcott Emerson, of Springfield, Massachusetts. Each is to receive one thousand dollars."

"What?" said Homer Kelly. "Miss Maria *who?*"

Mr. Twells giggled nervously. "We don't know who this Maria Fuller Alcott Emerson is, and so far we haven't found anyone in Springfield who knows her. The bequest is not large, of course, but we will continue to look for her. No one in the Emerson family knows of her. Perhaps the similarity of her name is purely coincidental . . ."

Homer looked up at the ceiling and twiddled his thumbs. Mr. Twells put down his document and cleared his throat. "There is one thing more which I feel it my duty to say at this time. It concerns Mr. Charles Goss. About a week before his father's unfortunate demise, Charles came to me at my office. He needed money. He asked me to write a letter to a prospective lender stating what his expectations were."

Homer leaned forward and stared at Mr. Twells. "His 'expectations'? You mean like some young rake in a nineteenth century English novel? Fattening the usurers? Burdening the ancient family manor with debt?"

"Well, of course it would have been most improper to do so. I refused. I would not have done it without his father's permission, in any case. Charles insisted that he merely wished to be able to leave home and set up independently, and he promised that he would pay back the money as soon as he was employed. But there was no way I could help him. I offered him a small personal loan, but he turned that down."

The D.A. shuffled his papers around happily. "Say, that's first rate. Strawberry jam." He found the sheet headed CHARLES GOSS, and added a triumphant, "Needed CASH," under *motive*. "Thank you very much, Mr. Twells."

Miss O'Toole leaned forward and tapped the end of her pencil on a pair of photographs. "Oh, yes, the sisters," said the D.A. He picked up the photographs and looked at them. "Which one is the smasheroo?"

Jimmy Flower smiled. "That's Rowena. She came right home from the parade, she said, and went to bed with cotton in her ears. Didn't wake up until around quarter past one. As soon as she took the cotton out of her ears she heard her mother screaming, went downstairs, found her all alone having a conniption fit. Rowena said she'd had a late night the night before, and that's why she slept so soundly."

Mary drew a sharp-pointed tail on her devil and started surrounding him with the flames of hell. The District Attorney couldn't take his bulging eyes off the picture of Rowena. It was a studio portrait. Rowena had been wearing a low-cut gown apparently, and the photographer had snipped off the gown, so that it looked as if . . . boy. "Anybody see her coming home?"

"We can practically track her from point to point. When Rowena Goss goes by, people take notice. She must have driven up to the house at about 11:05. She was last seen on Barrett's Mill Road driving toward her house with the top down on her white convertible by a college boy on a bicycle and the fathers of three families driving home from the parade. The families didn't remember her, but the fathers all did."

Homer Kelly pointed out that Rowena had no particular motive for doing away with her father that anybody could think of, beyond of course his general hatefulness, and the company passed on to the contemplation of Rowena's sister Edith. The contemplation was less pleasant. Edith's introverted blank eyes looked furtively out at them from under her beetling brows. Her hair was gathered back unbecomingly at the base of her neck, and a piece of straggling ribbon showed.

"Edith drove her mother home from the festivities, and then

she says she went for a long nature-walk around Annursnac Hill. She came in around quarter of two just as we were driving out with Charley. Had her hands full of pussy willows."

"Any motive, in her case?"

"Well, old Goss picked on her, I understand, more or less the way he did on Charley. Less savagely, maybe."

The D.A. scribbled some more on his sheets of paper. "Aaalll right," he said, picking up a clean one. "Now, the Alcott Club. You say the members of this club had good reason to have it in for Ernest Goss because he was going to publish some scandalous letters from Louisa May Alcott and people like that. Right? And the letters haven't turned up? Say, let me stick that on my other sheet." He scrabbled among his papers, found the one marked QUERIES, and added, "Letters—where are they *at?*"

Homer got up and started walking around, one hand roughing up his cowlick. "Do you remember the argument Mary overheard, when Ernest Goss said something about a decision he had made? How he wasn't ashamed of it, he was damned happy about it, or some such phrase? Now suppose his 'decision' was the decision to publish the letters? The visitor might have been anyone in the Alcott Association. It might even have been a woman, threatening him with some sort of weapon. Suppose it was Teddy Staples. He failed, obviously, to persuade Ernie to abandon his scheme, so later on he boldly crashed the dinner party. He was getting desperate. Felt he had to hush those letters up, so people wouldn't laugh at his Henry Thoreau. But he failed again, and Ernie threw him out. So next day Teddy killed him. Now if this was the case, then the rider on Charley's horse might have been Teddy. Or more likely, Teddy came by the way of the river and the rider was more or less an innocent bystander. Well, this would mean that there were three of them there at the bridge—Teddy, Ernie Goss, and maybe Charley Goss. Charley could have brought the musket, Teddy could have fired it. Then Charley galloped away, without the musket, and was seen by the Boy Scout. In the meantime Teddy ran to the bridge and hid under it while Arthur Furry gamboled over the bridge and discovered the body. Then Arthur rushed off to alert the countryside and Teddy simply paddled off, with the musket lying in the bottom of his canoe, the letters in his pocket. By the time the mob arrived on the scene he could have been safely around the bend. What's the matter with that?"

Mary found herself just as unhappy with Teddy for a murderer as she had been with Charley. She couldn't picture him lurking under the bridge like the wicked troll while Arthur Furry frisked over it like the Little Billy Goat Gruff. She shook her head, scowling at her notes.

The D.A. was speaking. "You found no trace of the gun, though, at Teddy's house? Nor any letters?'

Jimmy Flower groaned. "We even got the skin-diver into the act again, in the river there at Fairhaven Bay by Teddy's house. No such luck. And that confounded hat wasn't there either."

The District Attorney yawned. His head was going around and around. What he wanted more than anything else was a can of cold beer. He usually had one about this time of day and then took a little shut-eye while Miss O'Toole held the fort. Wistfully he pictured the shining can, with the moisture condensed on the outside, and the *punkshing* sound of the can opener and the foam bubbling up through the opening. But it was out of the question. It would put him right to sleep. He shook his head and said drowsily, "Where's the ballistics man? He shown up yet?"

He had. His name was Lieutenant Morrissey, from the Department of Public Safety. He was ushered in by Miss O'Toole, with a long skinny case in his hand. Inside it was a musket very much like the one that had presumably killed Ernest Goss. In a small box in his pocket was the musket ball that had been found in Goss's body. Lieutenant Morrissey handed the musket around, pointing out its parts, explaining how the flintlock mechanism worked. He obviously enjoyed handling the old piece. He held the musket so that the District Attorney could peer sleepily into the muzzle.

"See?" said Lieutenant Morrissey. "No rifling. Smooth bore. Nothing to leave a trace on a projectile. So even if we had the musket we couldn't be dead certain that the ball was fired from it. It takes rifling to leave identifying marks. The round musket ball doesn't fit closely either, like a modern cylindrical projectile. This ball is about 60 caliber, and this particular musket I have here is 70 caliber. They always had room to spare. What you did was, you wrapped the ball in a patch, to make it airtight in the bore."

The D.A. made a heroic struggle to sound intelligent. "What happens to the patch? I mean when you fire it?"

"It flies out along with the ball. Here it is." Lieutenant Morrissey showed them a blackened piece of thin leather, cut roughly round. "This is apparently one of a bunch of them that Ernest Goss had in the drawer along with the black powder. Incidentally, all of the balls that Philip Goss made up the night of the 18th of April are missing."

"Humph," said the D.A., leaning his heavy head on his hand.

"What about the other guns in the collection?" said Homer. "Could this ball have been fired from one of them?"

"We looked into that, and of course that's possible. One or two of them had a big enough bore. The pocket pistol did, and the duelling pistol. But they were all clean as a whistle inside, and not one of them had lost its flint. And then what would the fowling piece be missing for?"

"And don't forget," said the D.A., making a supreme effort, "that the dying man said 'musket.'" That clinched it, as far as he was concerned.

Lieutenant Morrissey was all finished, so he packed up his gun and left, opening the door wide for someone else to come in.

"Hello, there, Mr. Campbell," said the D.A. "Come right in and make yourself at home. We're all ready for you. This is Lieutenant Morrissey's colleague from the Department of Public Safety, Mr. Robert Campbell. Anything he doesn't know about fingerprints you could write on your thumbnail. Ha ha, say, Mr. Campbell, how about that? Anything you don't know about fingerprints you could write on your thumbnail. Ha ha." Say, that was pretty sharp. (The District Attorney felt himself waking up again.)

"All right, Mr. Campbell," said Homer, "I know you haven't got any nice fat prints on a murder weapon, because we haven't got any murder weapon. Have you got anything else of interest? What about the other guns?"

"You mean in the collection? Well, they were all pretty well smudged from being handed around the night before. Except for a small one, like a pistol, with a flintlock. That one was nice and clean."

"That would be the other duelling pistol," said Homer. "We only passed one of them around."

"I suppose so," said Mr. Campbell. "I don't know one gun from another. One thing that most people don't realize is that you don't get good prints on a gun anyway. The rounded surfaces don't take a full print. But we got fragmentary prints on one gun or another from everybody who was there that night, including Staples. And we took prints off everything else we could think of, too, of course. The horse's gear didn't show anything. We took prints all around Charley's room, where Charley said he left his fancy-dress outfit after the parade. Turned up prints of Charley, his mother, his father, the maid, his brother Philip. Now, interestingly enough, there were no prints at all on the front of that dresser where the gun collection was kept nor on the front of the musket cupboard. They had been wiped clean, although the servant claims she hadn't done so in some time. (Say, do you think you can trust what that old woman says? She struck me as kind of . . .) Well, anyway, if someone had wiped them clean in order to erase his own fingerprints, he forgot something. There is a row of thumbprints as neat as you please up and down the *inside* of the musket cupboard door. You know how you hold onto a door that opens out to the left with your left hand while you're reaching in with your right? This door has a knob, but the door is hung in such a way that it swings around and bangs against the wall if you don't catch it, and when you catch it you leave a nice set of four fingerprints on the outside and a thumbprint on the inside."

"So whose thumbprint have you got?"

Mr. Campbell consulted his notes. "Oh, everybody's, just

about. Here's the list. Philip Goss, Charles Goss, Ernest Goss, Edith, Rowena and Elizabeth Goss, Thomas Hand, Mary Morgan, Teddy Staples, Howard Swan, and a few strangers."

That was the end of Mr. Campbell's information. He sat down. The District Attorney stood up and attempted to gather his wits. He then proceeded to make a very creditable summation, greatly assisted by the notes placed in front of him in large print by Miss O'Toole.

"It is my opinion," he said, "that the Commonwealth can make no arrest at this time. The case against Mr. Charles Goss is entirely too surrounded by doubt. Speaking personally let me say that I do not wish to add to my record in office a suit for false arrest. Let me point out that Charles Goss is not the only one who lacks a substantial alibi. Also there is the fact that the horseman was seen only from the rear. And it's difficult to see why Charley would commit a murder in such a highly public place dressed in an outfit uniquely associated with himself . . ." (The District Attorney stumbled over this phrase, and Miss O'Toole made a humble mental note, chastising herself for overreaching the District Attorney's vocabulary.) "May I suggest further investigation of that Teddy fellow, the nutty one that thinks he's Thoreau? He sounds like a good bet to me. And I assume that the search for the missing weapon will continue. And now, gentlemen," said the District Attorney, looking at his watch, which had stopped two days ago, "you must excuse me. I'm expecting a call from—ah—His Excellency, the Governor." With remarkable speed and efficiency the D.A. shooed everyone out of his office, while Miss O'Toole swiftly gathered up his disordered papers and took them out to her desk for her own superb recasting and thoroughgoing reorganization.

As the general exit began, the newsmen in the outer office came suddenly alive. The District Attorney showed his thin weary face only long enough to say, "No arrest at this time, fellas, that's all I can say now. Nope, no arrest. Excuse me, my phone is ringing. That must be my call from the Governor." The D.A. shrank back into his office, slammed the door of his sanctuary and collapsed with a contented sigh on his sway-backed cot.

Homer walked to his car with Mary Morgan. The Middlesex County Superior Court was surrounded by some of the scruffiest streets in Cambridge. On the clapboards of the dingy houses there were peeling election posters. It was too early in the year for the new ones to be in blossom, but before long the D.A. himself would be wooing the public once more—no easy task—his press was very bad. Homer looked back at the gold letters on the courthouse that said "District Attorney," and commented aloud on the shrewdness of Miss O'Toole. "What a jewel. It's a shame she's such a dog."

Mary made a face. "On behalf of all homely girls, I resent the word dog. It's not a nice word at all."

Homer looked at her curiously, and Mary bit her lip and (oh, damn) blushed. "Come to think of it," he said, "you sure do have an awful lot of mouth. It sort of goes on and on, like the big bad wolf's."

Mary opened her mouth up wide and gave a contralto roar. Homer clung to a telephone pole to keep from falling in. "Why can't you be sweet and nice like other girls?"

"Because I'm natural-born nasty and mean, that's why."

Chapter 31

I long ago lost a hound, a bay horse, and a turtledove, and am still on their trail . . . I have met one or two who had heard the hound, and the tramp of the horse, and even seen the dove disappear behind a cloud, and they seemed as anxious to recover them as if they had lost them themselves.

HENRY THOREAU

Then Teddy Staples disappeared. When the District Attorney was informed of this fact he thanked God that they had not been in a hurry to arrest Charley Goss. Teddy had last been seen by Tom Hand. It had been the last day of April, and raining. Tom was driving along Barrett's Mill Road in his pickup when he came upon Teddy at the foot of Annursnac Hill, leaning against the tattered bonnet of his old Chevrolet, coughing his heart out. "I stopped to see if he was all right," Tom said to Homer Kelly. "He looked terrible. His face was grey, and he could hardly stop coughing long enough to talk. But he insisted he didn't need any help, and he turned right away from me, and started walking up the dirt road there toward the hill. His knees seemed weak, and he had trouble walking. I got out of my car and started after him. But then he flung around at me, and told me in no uncertain terms to leave him alone. So I did. I went on home. After a while I came back, oh say an hour later. My conscience was hurting me for having left him when he was so obviously sick. But his car was gone by that time."

A couple of times during the day Tom had tried to call Teddy's house. No answer. When there was still no answer by eleven o'clock at night, Tom, a grim picture in his mind, drove across town and down the long dark lane to Teddy's house. It was pitch-dark, and groping his way up the path to the steps, he collided with Teddy's birdbath. Wincing, he shouted for Teddy, then felt his way up the steps, tried the door, went in and turned on the lights. Teddy wasn't there at all. His bed was rumpled, but Teddy wasn't in it. His trusty stapler lay on the chipped porcelain table in the grubby kitchen, his wooden flute beside it. When Tom poked around in the shed with his flashlight, he discovered only Teddy's canoe and his rowboat. His car was gone.

When Teddy still didn't answer the phone next day, Mary had called up Jimmy Flower and told him about it. Jimmy said, "Holy Horsecollar," and got on to it right away. He tracked down Teddy's only known relative, a sister living in Braintree. She hadn't heard from Teddy since Christmas, nor did she seem to care to. No, she hadn't the slightest idea where the fool had gone.

"He always was a bit cracked," she said.

Homer got out of his car with Mary and Jimmy Flower, and together they looked up at the bleak little house Teddy had called home. "Suppose," said Mary, "that Teddy had something to hide, like the letters." She stared at the birdbath. "Could he have stuck them in *that?*"

Jimmy and Homer looked at the birdbath. Then their two heads turned slowly as on a swivel and stared at the cyclopean breastworks Teddy had thrown up around his front porch. "Oh —my—God," said Jimmy Flower.

So Jimmy had his work cut out for him. Not only did he have to set in motion a statewide and at last a nationwide search for a slightly potty birdwatcher and possible murderer named Theodore Staples, but he also had to hire a crew of jackhammer operators to demolish the fruits of all of Teddy's labors with mortar trowel and cobblestones. For a week Teddy's quiet glade was hideous with noise.

But nothing turned up. Jimmy Flower looked at the shambles and smote his brow. "What do you bet Teddy comes driving up tomorrow, innocent as a newborn babe? Who's going to put all them rocks back?"

"You are, dearie," said Homer.

Chapter 32

Homer Kelly sat in Jimmy's office in the police station on Walden Street, waiting for Mary. It was Saturday, her day. What was she late for? He twiddled his ballpoint pen, then started chewing the end of it. The phone rang.

"Homer?" said Mary. In the background he could hear the children of the Hand household and a great clatter of dishes. "Gwen had to take Grandmaw into town for some new glasses, so I'm going to stay here with the children. I'm sorry."

"Oh, hell," said Homer testily. Damn the girl. She seemed to be public property. Any old body could call on her for any old thing any old time.

"Was there anything special? Could I do anything for you here?"

"Well, I wanted to go over Teddy's journal with you. There are some things in it I thought you might understand that I don't."

"Why don't you come by for lunch, and bring it with you?"

Be brusque. Step on the flowers. "Hmmm. Will all those kids be there?"

"I'm afraid so."

"Well, okay. But shut 'em up, will you?"

So he was that kind of man, thought Mary. Hated children. They would probably whine and fight all the time he was there. She hoped they did. Anybody that hated kids deserved what he got.

She was still slicing cucumbers when he came by a little early. "Goodness, where did you get that dreadful tie?" said Mary. It was a chaste green silk affair.

"Rowena Goss gave it to me," said Homer, looking down at it. "She doesn't like my taste in ties."

"Whatever can be the matter with her?" said Mary. She picked up three cucumber slices and arranged them on his tie like buttons.

Homer looked down at it admiringly. "What about some sliced olives scattered around in between?"

"Freddy's banana!" said Annie. "I'll cut it up for you!" She snatched it from Freddy. Freddy hollered. Annie squeezed the banana behind her and wouldn't give it back. Homer settled the argument with surprising tact, giving Freddy back all of his banana except a small piece, which Annie cut up and arranged carefully on his tie. "There now," he said, "what's for lunch? Or do we just eat our clothes?"

Lunch was canned ravioli. It was the children's favorite. (Mary had been darned if she was going to prepare something special for *him*.) Homer ate it gracefully and meekly asked for more.

John looked at him and pointed. "How do you like that plate?" he said.

Homer goggled at his plate. "Fine," he said. "It's fine."

"Isn't it clean?"

"Yes, sir, it's clean all right. Did you wash it?"

John nodded. "Annie did the breakfast dishes, and I helped her. She didn't even have to wash that one." He picked up his own plate, which was covered with ravioli juice and held it in front of his face so that it dripped, and licked it with his tongue. "See?" he said. Mary watched in dawning horror. John's tongue went around and around, thoroughly and efficiently. The plate was artistically, beautifully clean. Homer looked down at his own plate, his face lighting up with appalled understanding.

"John, you didn't!" Mary fell back against the wall and laughed. She couldn't stop. She went limp. Homer stared at her, then he snatched up her empty plate, licked it all over, spooned up a big helping of peas and dumped them on it. John and Annie got into the act and licked each other's knives and forks. Freddy understood the joke and licked his chair.

After lunch Mary put Freddy to bed for his nap and cleared the dishes off the table. Homer put Teddy's journal on it and started leafing through it. "I feel sticky all over," he said. "Now, where are we? Look, right here. Entry of April 6, this year. He starts out: 'Only one month more———' See those dashes? Then there's a quote, I guess from Henry Thoreau: 'For joy I could embrace the earth; I shall delight to be buried in it.' Then he goes on in his own words. (Look at his spelling.)

Why can't I delight in it? Alas, I cannot. If I could only find thatt which I seek I would give itt all upp gladly. (And if I could onnly be sure that Goss can be silenced. That is an addittional thorn in my side). That star that I worshipp from afar will shine on when I am gone, as though this speckk on a disttant planet had never been. Her light will be as raddiant as ever, when I am no more.

"I think I understand his spelling," said Mary. "You see? He doubles consonants. Maybe it's because when he's stammering through a word it seems to have more than one B or P."

Running down the sides of each page were marginal lists of the birds and wildlife seen each day. Mary read some of them. They were highly abbreviated and hard to decipher. She turned the pages slowly. The main part of the text was full of quotations. It occurred to her that Teddy had used Thoreau's journals as a kind of gloss on his own. Everything he did was seen in the light of something Henry had said or done. It was like her own movie music. She understood it very well.

"What do you suppose he means by that—'only one month more'?" said Homer. "What was he waiting for? His month isn't up yet, even now. Only one month till what? It sounds as though he felt doomed, as though he had some sort of incurable disease or something. But Dr. Cosgro hasn't seen him, nor any other doctor in town. He hasn't been to Emerson Hospital for a checkup or anything. Nor to any Boston hospital or clinic, at least not under his own name. We even tried using the name Henry Thoreau, feeling like idiots. No luck. Do you suppose he had TB? With that cough . . . But why would he say, 'Only one month more,' as if he knew for certain just how much longer he had to go? It's a queer thing. And who do you suppose his shining star was? Some Concord girl?"

Mary had a sinking feeling. She was afraid she knew. Then they found the answer. Homer put his big finger on a line, and looked at her peculiarly. The passage recorded their own visit to Teddy's house, when he had been working on his birdbath.

She likes my new birdbath. *She* understands everything I say or do.
    I satt next to her in the car, and she was sorry about my cough.

"It's funny," said Homer. "A girl that's as big and homely as you are and all. What do they see in you, anyway?"

"Oh, shut up." Mary shook her head in sorrow. Poor, poor Teddy.

"Look here," said Homer, "where he goes on about 'that which I seek.' This time he seems to be looking for a 'him.'"

I thought today, just for a minnute, that I had found him. No such luck. Am I doomed to die without him? Sommetimes I have believed that he might take me up to heaven with him, if he could . . .

"Homer, you don't suppose—I know this is silly, but you don't think Teddy was looking for Henry Thoreau himself? Up there on Annursnac Hill? It's crazy, I know, but then Teddy was . . ."

"I wonder. Crackpot notion. He doesn't sound as daft as all that in this journal. But maybe—after all, who else could Teddy's 'he' be?"

Chapter 33

A stony old road ran up Annursnac Hill. At the bottom was an old orchard of broken, bristling apple trees and a fallen wire fence like snarled bedsprings. The side of the hill was densely packed with blueberry and juniper bushes, and cedar trees standing like pikestaffs. At the top was a reservoir and a rocky pasture where the wind turned the white sides of the grass up in billows. Birch saplings with trembling new leaves grew along the barbed-wire pasture fence. Mary looked at them and found herself thinking of what Emerson had said about the mighty and transcendent Soul . . . *tenderly, tenderly does it woo and court us from every object in Nature* (from those trembling shiny leaves, opened only this morning, from those dried-up heads of sumac, from these wild strawberry flowers. Careful now, don't betray yourself).

"Wow," said Homer, "this is a swell place. Just look at that view."

It was the second day of May, and almost hot. Mary took off her jacket and sat down. Far below them they could see the hazy treetops bordering the Assabet, and Tom's cornfield, still dark brown, showing no sign of life. There was a green field next to it, with a blue puddle in the middle, and some white birds in the middle of the puddle. Next to the field they could barely see the complex rooftops of the Gosses' house, nearly hidden in its surrounding hemlocks, and far off to the right the tower of the Concord Reformatory. Homer lay down on his back and wondered what would happen if he were to put his arm around Mary. Or he might just tickle her a little in a friendly way...

"What do you suppose Teddy saw from here?" said Mary. "What could you see if you had binoculars?"

Oh, the hell with it. Homer sat up. "You'd see the souls of the Transcendentalists floating around over Concord. You could just sing out to Henry and he'd fly over and take you right up to Hebb'm."

"There are a lot of birds down there. You can see such a lot of sky. It's like a big blue soup tureen, not just that teacupful we see from under the elm trees down there." Mary glanced down at something shining beside her feet, then bent forward to pick it up. "Oh, Homer, look. I've found something."

"By God, it's a staple. Teddy must have sat right here and popped a gusset." Homer stood up, his brown hair rumpled upwards on the back of his head, and gestured at one of the state policemen who were searching the hilltop. Then he pulled Mary to her feet. "Say, I wonder how fine a fine-tooth comb Jimmy's men used when they went over the area where Goss was shot? Let's go see. If Teddy was there he may have come unstuck at the seams all over the place."

"If you had one of those back-and-forth hats you'd look just like Sherlock Holmes."

Homer was leaning over the path that led to the Minuteman, staring around through Mary's reading glasses, which he held halfway between his eyes and the ground. There was a group of tourists gawking at the grave of the British soldiers, telling themselves that they could still see where Ernest Goss's blood had left a stain. A small boy jabbed his father with his elbow. "Look at the detective," he said.

Homer played to the grandstand. "It's elementary, my dear Flotsam. Egad, sir, look at that lollipop stick. Lemon-lime. I think I can say positively, sir, that the flavor was lemon-lime."

"Query," said Mary, "which suspect has a passion for lemon-lime? In case you don't have a plan, Mr. Holmes, I have a plan."

The boy had a good idea, too, and volunteered, "What you could do is, you could have a whole lot of flavors in a dish, and then you pass it around and see which one . . . aw, you're just kidding me."

His father prodded him, and they moved away. Mary followed them across the bridge and looked up at the Minuteman. There he stood in his brazen calm with his bronze nose and ears and tricorn hat and his bronze buttons and the bronze wrinkles in his stockings and his bronze fowling piece and plow. Mary stared at the gun. What if the murder weapon was like the purloined letter, and the murderer had just stuck it in the Minuteman's hand where everybody could see it? The bronze gun was just like the one Ernest Goss had kept in his cabinet, even to the engraved pineapple on the bottom that showed it was British made. The flint mechanism was all there, with the frizen down over the powder pan. Mary called herself an idiot, but she reached up anyway and touched the stock. It was bronze, all right, not wood. And of course the murderer would have had to saw off the bronze one, and then get rid of *that*. Mary stood back and admired the monument, feeling a nudge again of that awareness of the reality of history, that awareness she found so hard to come by. It had all really happened. The Minutemen had looked very much like that, they had left their plows and taken up their guns and stood together in straight rows just over there, and the British had lined up across the river in columns for street firing, the first row kneeling and firing, then peeling off to the rear——

Homer spoke roughly behind her. "Look here." He had a

little pile of staples in his cupped hand, three or four of them, folded over on themselves.

"Where were they?"

"On the little hill where the obelisk is. You know what Thoreau said? 'Some circumstantial evidence is very strong, as when you find a trout in the milk.'"

Chapter 34

❧ *We are embarrassed with second thoughts . . . we are lined with eyes; we see with our feet.*
RALPH WALDO EMERSON

Jimmy was feeling testy. His expense account was worrying him, and the nationwide search for Teddy Staples was going badly. No picture of Teddy had turned up anywhere. The official description called for an itinerant stonemason about five feet eight inches tall, weight one hundred and forty pounds, brown hair, bad cough, peculiar-looking, poorly dressed. Across the broad face of the land the police had turned up plenty of five-foot-eight-inch, one-hundred-and-forty pound, brown-haired, peculiar-looking derelicts who had such atrocious health habits that they had coughs; but only a few of these were itinerant stonemasons. Jimmy had been called up three times in the middle of the night by excited members of far-flung police departments. "He denies it, of course," the voice would squeak, "but it's Staples, all right."

Twice Jimmy had turned them off with a suggestion given him by the Audubon Society. "Just one thing more," he would say sleepily. "Just mention sort of casually that you saw an evening grosbeak pulling up a worm in your back yard. If he disagrees with you, call me back. You heard me, an evening grosbeak. That's G, R, O . . ."

That had got rid of two of the suspects. But the third five-foot-eight-inch skinny itinerant stonemason with a bad cough had turned out to be a birdwatcher, too, and, glory be, he had boggled at the worm-eating grosbeak! "Hang on to him," shouted Jimmy over the long-distance line, "I'll be right there." *There* had been a thousand miles away in Cedar Rapids, Iowa, and to Jimmy's intense chagrin the man under suspicion had turned out to be a deacon in the Baptist church and the father of seven daughters.

This particular wild-goose chase had cost $172.53, and it looked terrible, really terrible on the tally sheet.

The next afternoon Homer Kelly snatched Mary out of her library early and marched her along the street to the little brick temple with the putty-colored columns that faced down Walden Street. It had once been a bank, but now it provided office space for insurance men and lawyers. Among the lawyers were Philip Goss and his partner George Jarvis.

"The heck with Teddy," said Homer. "I'm going to get back on the main track. Who was it the Boy Scout thought he saw a split second after the murder? One of the Goss boys. It's about time I started chivvying them around."

Philip's small office might have been on Beacon Street. There was a Turkish rug on the floor and the bookshelves were filled with old volumes in calf bindings. The roll-top desk was a piece of pleasant affectation. Philip was smoothly at their service. So was George Jarvis, who appeared out of nowhere and sat quietly in the background.

Homer wanted to know what it had been like to grow up in the Goss household. "Is it really true that your father dealt more harshly with Charley than he did with you?"

"My father's attitude toward Charley has always troubled me. My earliest memories are of shielding Charley from my father's displeasure."

"Why? Why was your father so hard on Charley?"

"I wish I knew. I think it was a tendency he had to see things only in black and white. Like in politics—everyone in the Democratic Party was assumed to be a knave or a cutthroat. If there were two sides to anything, one was dead wrong and one was right. He had two sons. One was good and one was bad. The same with his daughters. Of the two sons, I was the lucky one. I was the heir to the throne, the white hope, the serious student, the one who had his little nose pointed at Harvard from the beginning. Charley must therefore be the opposite of me. He was supposed to be unreliable, dreamy, wild. It's my personal belief that Charley isn't really so different from me at all, but he just hasn't been let alone, the way I have, to do what came naturally. He had to be made to fit this square hole they'd provided for him. So he was the one who always landed in the way-out progressive school, where you messed around with fingerpaint and got rid of your aggressions with drama therapy or some damn thing."

"But isn't it true that Charley has turned out to be a very different kind of person?"

Philip turned away to the window that looked down on the T-shaped crossing of Walden and Main. Patrolman Bob Loftus was standing in the middle of the crossing beckoning a pair of old ladies across the street. Who was that weird-looking character standing in front of Richardson's Drug Store, looking this way? Philip turned away from the window abruptly and glanced at Mary. He had seen that fellow with her. Was he waiting for Mary to come out? What right did he have to——? After all, some day Mary was going to be Philip's girl——

"You were saying . . . ?" said Homer.

Philip struggled to remember the question. "Well—as the twig is bent, so grows the tree, I suppose."

"So they say. Well. Let's go into this mutual-confession pact you boys had with each other. When did you start doing that?"

"I don't know. It wasn't a pact. It was just something we did, without ever thinking about it, as long ago as I can remember."

"Why didn't you carry through on it this time?"

Philip flushed. George Jarvis made a demurring noise.

"Well, forget it," said Homer. "Tell me this. What was Charley's attitude toward you throughout all the years you were growing up? Did he show any natural jealousy toward you because you were his father's favorite?"

"Yes, I guess he did. How could he have helped it?"

"And you had nothing against your father but his unfair treatment of your brother?"

Philip hesitated. George Jarvis answered for him. "You told me you had nothing beyond that."

"What about your mother? Did she show the same kind of partisanship?"

"Mother? Oh, she wasn't ever really 'there.' She lived in some sort of world of her own . . ."

She wasn't ever really there . . . That was it. Yes, that was just the way she had always seemed to Mary. Just a set of formal motions and gestures, with no one really inside. *When you knock,* said Henry, *no one is at home* . . .

Homer spoke softly. "Do you think Charley murdered your father?"

Philip looked wretched. His voice rose in pitch until it was almost a whine. "What else am I to think, for God's sake?" He collected himself then, and dropped his eyes. His question about Charley's prospects seemed mere formal politeness. Homer answered noncommittally, which was the way he felt.

Out on the Milldam again, Homer caught sight of Roland Granville-Galsworthy, and he took a firm grasp of Mary's arm. "It's almost five o'clock," he said. "I'll drive you home, and then you can repay me for my kindness by giving me a drink. Do the Hands have any gin? I'd better pick some up at my place. By rights I ought to bring some glasses, too. I don't trust the sanitary level you people put up with out there."

Half an hour later there was a cold pitcher on the round oak table under the Angelus, and Mary, Homer and Gwen were listening to old Mrs. Hand talk about her great-uncle George who had written "Rally 'Round the Flag, Boys." The pitcher was almost empty when Tom stuck his head in the door and hollered in, "Who left six bushels of apples right where I'd fall over them in the cider shed? Where in hell did they come from anyhow?" He glared at Mary, who shook her head and said, "Not me." Then he stalked across the room and yelled at his wife. "I darn near busted my head open. Did you put those apples out there?"

"No, dear," said Gwen. "Why don't you use them to run off some cider? We're all out."

"Cider!" Tom strode to the door and went out and slammed it. Then he opened it again and marched back in. "As if I didn't have enough to do, with all those trees to spray every time I turn around and fifty acres to plant and harrow and my machinery breaking down and those golblasted committee meetings and kids that don't do their chores and on top of everything I woke up in the night with the goldarnedest charleyhorse you ever saw. All we need this year is a real whooperdo of a hurricane. That's all we need. Besides, those apples are tired old winter-stored Macs. And nobody never made cider with them kind of apples."

"Nohow." Mary was sympathetic.

So was Homer. "The time for makin' cider is in cider-makin' time."

Tom was mollified. "Sorry if I shouted kind of loud," he mumbled and went outside again.

"Sorehead," said Gwen.

Grandmaw shook her head. "He always was an old fuss-budget, from a child."

Chapter 35

"Did it ever occur to you," said the District Attorney of Middlesex County on the telephone to Concord Police Chief Jimmy Flower, "that you're hanging an awful lot of your investigation on the word of that Boy Scout? How do you know he's telling the truth? I suppose you've ruled out the possibility that he bumped off the old boy himself, sort of as his Bad Deed for the day?"

"I wish you could see this kid," said Chief Flower, who had developed a really violent distaste for poor Arthur Furry. "He's so honest it's disgusting. We've talked to his scoutmaster, his teachers, his Sunday School teacher, his neighbors, everybody we could think of, and they all find him a bit lazy and not very bright, but about as far from being a juvenile delinquent as you can get."

"I hope you're being nice to him then. If his parents should take it into their heads not to let him testify. . ."

"What kind of nincompoops do you think we are? Chief Parker over there in Acton calls on them all the time, and takes

Arthur out in his Chief car with the siren going, and he gets rides on the fire engine, rings the bell and I don't know what all. Thank the good Lord he lives in Acton, and not in Concord."

"Let's see now," said the D.A. vaguely. "I had another question . . . Oh, thank you, Miss O'Toole. Yes. What about the mother, Mrs. Goss? Is she still unfit for giving evidence?"

"As a matter of fact Homer Kelly was over to see her this morning. She was still as crazy as a coot."

"Miss O'Toole suggested—that is, I wondered if even in her ravings she might say something that might be significant."

"Homer said she wouldn't even talk. When she saw him she dodged down the hall and peeked at him around the corner, wouldn't say a word. She's dyed her hair bright red and she goes around in this white nighty. She seems harmless enough, apparently, but there's no hope of getting anything sensible out of her. We thought we'd try the house again, though. Kelly wants to see for himself that there aren't any letters tucked away in some corner of the Goss place we haven't thought of yet."

Rowena Goss was playing her violin when Mrs. Bewley let them in. Mary suspected that Rowena had just whipped it out when she saw Homer's car turn up the drive, because her music was upside-down. She made a lovely picture, anyway. "Certainly, dear," she said. "Look around all you want. I wish we had some secret panels for you to discover, but I'm afraid we don't. I'll just go on with my practicing."

Jimmy and Homer wandered off to the cellar and started rooting around. Mary, with Rowena's "dear" sounding unhappily in her head, climbed the stairs and went back to Elizabeth Goss's bedroom. Downstairs Rowena was playing "Liebestraum." She played with plenty of vibrato and when she got to the end she started over again. She played it through six or eight times. Mary closed the door and began to look around.

The bookcase—the bed—the flower prints—the draperies —the dresser—the carpet. Everything seemed to fit the image of the woman Elizabeth Goss had been before she had gone out of her mind. Tasteful and uninteresting. Go around again. The bookcase—the bed—the flower prints—the draperies—the dresser—

The dresser. There was a chest on the dresser, a small black box. Mary moved closer and reached out to touch it. That wasn't black paint on the surface—the wood itself was very dark, nearly black. She lifted the lid and looked inside. There wasn't much in it. Jimmy's men must have examined the contents already. Sentimental keepsakes, most likely. Like that old dried-up daisy at the bottom—the memento of some girlish romance? (He loves me, he loves me not.) There was a small jewel case in the corner of the chest, half hidden by a fat envelope. Mary groped the case out of its corner and opened it. Inside it was an old ring with a purple stone, set in an antique fashion. Mary took the ring out of the case and held it to the light. Amethyst, probably. Now what about the envelope? Across the front of it someone had written, "great-grandmother's." She had to open it carefully because it was swollen from its contents and brittle at the edges. Why, it was hair, a braided mass of auburn hair—great-grandmother's? But it was as beautiful and shining as if it had been cut and braided only yesterday. She drew it out and held it in her two hands. It was wound in an intricate pattern, and Mary found her fingers picking at it, trying to find the beginning. She shouldn't be doing this, she shouldn't be doing this at all. But she went right on pulling at it. She just had to see. As she twisted it loose from its braiding, the hair sprang loose in deep ripples, like the silky fur of a spaniel's ears. Beautiful, it was beautiful. Awestruck, Mary lifted her right hand gently and let the hair fall over her left arm in a shining waterfall. She had forgotten that human hair could grow so long . . .

Then Mary shook herself and began to struggle with the problem of getting the hair back into the envelope. It was like trying to pour a river into a glass. She would have to braid it all up again. Furtively she glanced at the door. Rowena was still sawing away downstairs. Mary struggled to separate the cloudy mass into threes. What a job. It would take a good five minutes. Her fingers worked hastily. Left over right, right over left . . .

Red hair must run in the female line in Elizabeth's family—from great-grandmother to Elizabeth to Elizabeth's children. There was a picture downstairs in the dining room, painted in the style of John Singer Sargent, that showed Elizabeth as she had looked when she was married. She had been a redhead, all right, like her children, with a pretty, bushy bob. But not this color, surely? The hair in the portrait was a light red like Rowena's, not this deep, lustrous red-brown, the color of a sorrel horse . . .

Then Mary was struck by a thought, and her fingers shrank from the hair she was twisting. There was an old wives' tale (or was it true? perhaps it was true!) that the hair of a dead man goes on growing in the grave. A picture blossomed in her mind before she could stop it, a picture of a beautiful young corpse in a flowing white dress, with a pale pre-Raphaelite face, her white hands folded on the heliotropes of her breast, and her dark coffin filling and filling with the ever-lengthening coils of her glorious ghostly hair . . .

Chapter 36

How martial is this place!
Had I a mighty gun
I think I'd shoot the human race
And then to glory run!
EMILY DICKINSON

The D.A. had finally come out to Concord. He didn't do anything in particular while he was there except spend an hour in Jimmy's office, whining. Miss O'Toole was away on vacation, and the D.A. felt naked and defenseless. And it was a misty night. He hadn't liked the way the trees had hung over the road on the drive out. The country was spooky, with those *huge* barns, probably jam-packed with cows, and those *trees*, brrrr.

And the newspapers were at him again. A district attorney was supposed to come through with brilliant solutions to crimes and spectacular prosecutions. And here he was, getting nowhere as usual, the "Do-Nothing D.A." again. Well, they couldn't arrest the wrong man, could they? Then the papers would have at them for sure. And they couldn't arrest Teddy Staples, because they couldn't *find* Teddy Staples. Where in the hell was Teddy anyway? Brrrr, those trees!

After the D.A. left, Homer sat with his knees wedged into the kneehole of his desk, playing idly with his tie. He rolled it up from the bottom and then let go. As it unrolled, Mary and

Jimmy Flower could watch the girl who was diving off the diving board go through the various positions of a swan dive and end up with a big splash at the bottom. "Holy horsecollar," said Jimmy.

"It would look a whole lot better on a horse," said Mary.

Homer wasn't listening. He looked up from his tie and slapped the desk. "I know one place we didn't look for those letters, or that gun or the missing hat—the Gun House."

"The Gun House?"

"Where the Concord Independent Battery keeps its cannon. Come on. How can I manage to be so everlastingly dumb?"

Mary squeezed out of her chair and loomed up behind her card table. "Well I never," she said. "Homer Kelly being humble. What a nice change."

Homer laughed a huge basso laugh and lifted Jimmy right out of his chair. He dandled him up and down. "Well, if a person knows he's the cat's pajamas, why try to cover it up?"

"Ow," said Jimmy. "For Chris'sake, lemme down."

Jimmy didn't have a key to the Gun House, so they drove out by Harvey Finn's farm on Lowell Road and picked him up. The Gun House had been erected in the field next to Emerson's house by a patriotic town, the popular subscription taken up in a few days. Outside it a sign hung on a pole, displaying the crossed cannon insignia of the Battery. Harvey Finn opened the side door and turned on the light. The single room was like a big garage with a high beamed ceiling. Around the walls hung the harnesses for the horses. The two gleaming guns, copper-cent color, faced toward the big front doors, with the high-wheeled limbers behind them, their shafts resting on the floor. Homer stood between the guns and looked at them.

"What's today? May 6th. They won't be used again until Memorial Day, right? Suppose Ernest Goss was looking for a temporary place to stick his letters where he could get at them any time he wanted to. He had a key to the Gun House, didn't he? He might have planned to take them away again before Memorial Day. He didn't expect to die in the meantime."

Homer was stooping over, peering into the muzzle of the

right-hand gun. He took out his flashlight and pointed it inside. "Nothing here." Then he tried the other one. "Oh, hell." He sat back on his haunches and scratched his head.

Mary tried the ammunition boxes on the limbers. They were empty, too.

"It was a cute idea anyway," said Jimmy Flower.

"Harvey," said Homer. "Show me how they work. You use blanks to start them with?"

"That's right. See, here's the box that holds the charges, black powder in little red bags. The powder monkey puts it in the muzzle, the rammer rams it home, and the thumber, he stands in back and puts a blank cartridge here under this little screw (it used to be a thumb-hole) like this. Then the lanyard man pulls the rope on it when I yell 'fire.' Like this." There was a colossal BLAM. Mary shrieked, totally unprepared.

"Hey, hey," said Homer. "M-my God, man."

"That was just the blank. There wasn't any charge in it."

"Even so. Jesus. Say, what's in that bucket there, with the rag on top?"

Harvey Finn lifted up the rag and glanced underneath. "Oh, it's just . . ." He put the rag back hastily. "It's not anything."

"Well, what is it?" said Jimmy. He picked up the rag. The bucket was full of empty beer cans. Harvey Finn snickered. "Some of the boys must have had a party. Well, it's not like the good old days, though. We've really reformed since then. Don't forget, we're not a dry Battery . . ."

"I know, you're a wet cell."

No point in staying any longer. Harvey Finn walked around the big room, straightening a harness, patting a wheel-rim. He had the look of a housekeeper fussing about her parlor. Mary got a strong whiff of the feeling the members of the Battery had for their gear. It was an affectionate pride, a boyish pleasure in anything noisy and slightly dangerous. They were an easy-going unmilitaristic outfit that liked to have fun on the boys' night out.

Homer drove Harvey Finn home and then Jimmy Flower. Jimmy lived on Lexington Road in a tidy little house that had ice-cream-scoop hedges around the front porch. Isabelle Flower invited Mary and Homer in for coffee. She gushed over Homer and gave him a big squeeze around the stomach, which was all she could reach. "Boy, Homer," she said, "are you my type! I'll bet you make hay with all the girls. Say, wouldn't we make a cute couple?"

"And here it is, spring, and all," said Homer.

"How do the girls keep their hands off you?"

"They don't seem to find it difficult."

"For gosh sakes, Isabelle," said Jimmy. "Lay off of Homer."

Chapter 37

One need not be a chamber to be haunted,
One need not be a house;
The brain has corridors surpassing
Material place. . . .

Far safer through an Abbey gallop,
The stones achase,
Than, moonless, one's own self encounter
In lonesome place.
EMILY DICKINSON

"This isn't the way to my house," said Mary. Homer's car was turning up Bedford Street.

"Oh, come on. How would you like to go for a spooky walk in Sleepy Hollow cemetery? We'll just walk up to Authors' Ridge and pay our respects to the immortals. Come on."

The street lights were propagating rectilinearly, making straight paths through the mist. The elm trees had leafed out, and the shadows under them were black and huge. Homer waved his large hand overhead. "Thoreau called them chandeliers of darkness, when he walked under them of a summer night."

Mary looked at him sideways. He had almost sounded . . . Was he giving way at last to the spell of those old dead words, made alive again in Concord's elms and rivers and fields? But it couldn't be. Not the man who had condescended to Emerson and trampled on Margaret Fuller. No.

It took them fifteen minutes of fumbling along the misty paths with the help of a flashlight before they stumbled on the steep rise of Authors' Ridge. They climbed to the top and looked around.

"Look," said Mary. "That's Bronson Alcott's stone, the fancy one. And this little marker is Louisa's." They stood a minute looking down at it. Then Homer moved away, groping for the iron chain around Emerson's big piece of quartz. Mary knelt down and touched the simple marker that said L.M.A. She thought of Louisa's bust in the library, with the gentle plaster face and the heavy chin and the enormous coil of plaster hair hanging over the collar in back. Then she thought of the rows of dead, lying side by side beneath her feet—Louisa and her sisters, her mother. *Was their hair still growing and growing in the grave—their long, long hair?*

Mary struggled to her feet, and looked around in the dark. She began to feel panic-stricken. Oh, now look here. Don't be idiotic. But—where was Homer? If he didn't come back soon, she would be compelled to call out for him, and she was determined not to do that. Mary stood still, trying not to tremble, trembling all the same. She could hear his steps crunching on the gravel, off to the right. But he had gone to the left, to see Emerson's grave. Suddenly Homer took her hand, and she jumped spasmodically, jerking her hand away.

"Mary," he said huskily.

Mary began to babble. She had just had an extraordinary idea. "What day did you say it was?"

"What? I don't know, for heaven's sake. It's May sixth."

"That's what I thought you said, that's what I thought. Homer, do you know what today is?"

"Darned if I know. Your birthday? Happy birthday."

"No, no, not mine, it's Henry Thoreau's birthday. I mean it's the anniversary of his death. He died a hundred years ago today, in that house on Main Street. I knew that, and then I forgot. They're having a big celebration in New York at the Morgan Library."

"Well then, all the more reason for paying Henry a call. So it is—so it is—well, well. A hundred years since he lay there in the front room, dying of TB and failure of the legs, with spring breaking forth outside his window . . . And somebody (who was it?) asked him if he had made his peace with God. 'We have never quarreled,' says Henry. I like that."

"Wait, wait," said Mary. "Listen!" There was that crunching sound on the gravel again. "It's over there where Henry is buried. *Homer, he's walking.*"

"Good God, girl, what's the matter with you? I'll know better than to take you into a cemetery at midnight any more." He stopped, then, and listened. "Hey, you're right. There is somebody over there."

The crunching sound grew more audible. Grate, grate, grate. Then it stopped. There was a swollen piece of fog hanging over Thoreau's grave. (Like a winding sheet—or a cocoon about to loose some great shadowy moth—and the moth would flutter its huge grey wings and then blunder against Mary's cheek and grapple in her long hair.) She shuddered violently, and struggled to master herself. But then out of the fog there came a voice, and Mary was suddenly calm and still, listening. The voice had a low sepulchral hollowness, as though it came from some body that had gently laid aside its coffin lid like the newly risen dead.

"Know all men by these presents, that I, Henry Thoreau . . ."

It broke off. Homer gripped Mary's arm. But her fear had turned to a weird longing. She felt an intense desire to walk forward, rend the mist and find Thoreau inside it, reborn, alive, clothed in flesh, his eyes upon her—those great, burning eyes! The voice began again, more loudly this time, more firmly.

"Those who call themselves Abolitionists should not wait till they constitute a majority of one. It is enough if they have God on their side. Any man more right than his neighbors constitutes a majority of one already."

The voice stopped again. Homer recognized the statement: it was a fragment of Homer's essay *Civil Disobedience*. He remembered some of it himself, and he spoke up cheerfully. "Under a government which imprisons any unjustly, the true place for a just man is also a prison." He lifted up his flashlight and switched it on, pointing it at the chrysalis of fog. The fog expelled its contents, and a man stepped forth. It was Howard Swan.

"Is that you, eh, Teddy?" said Howard.

"No," said Homer. He turned the flashlight up under his face and then turned it momentarily on Mary. "It's Kelly and Mary

Morgan. Well, well, Howard. Happy anniversary."

Howard Swan scraped the gravel with his foot. "I had to come," he said. "I was sitting at home there, reading Henry's journal, and I got to thinking about him you know, lying up here alone for a hundred years, and I just had to come over." He gestured sheepishly with his hand, which had a bunch of flowers in it. "I brought him some wild flowers."

Homer spoke softly. "Did you expect to find Teddy Staples here?" He directed his flashlight at Howard's face. Howard looked distressed.

"No, of course not. He's still missing, isn't he? I just thought when you spoke up, it might be Teddy. I mean, who else cared enough about Henry's memory to come up here like this, and could quote him, and so on? As a matter of fact, for a minute there, I almost thought you were . . ." His voice drifted off, and he turned and bent over and laid his flowers in front of the Thoreau family marker.

"Thanks for the compliment," said Homer. "We thought the same about you." He turned off his flashlight, and the three of them stood in the swirling mist looking at the blocky shadow that marked the resting place of Henry Thoreau, his father and mother, his beloved brother John and his two sisters. (The sisters had probably worn their hair long, like the others. They had parted it in the middle, and combed it flat and smooth each morning, and twisted it and braided it and lifted it up and interwoven it and pinned it together at the back of the head with long, long hairpins. Strong sharp hairpins firm enough to hold their heavy masses of hair . . .)

"Well, so long," said Howard Swan. "I'll go on home, I guess." His footsteps went off, crunching along the path.

Mary and Homer followed slowly. Homer whistled quietly, the only tune he could think of to honor the man a hundred years dead. It was *John Brown's Body*. Henry had been a passionate defender of Brown.

Then Mary had another rush of insight, and she felt tears springing up in her eyes. How could she have been so blind? "Homer, I know now what Teddy meant, when he said he had only one month more—he was born on the same day as Thoreau, remember? July 12, 1817. Only in 1917, of course, exactly one hundred years later. I told you about that, didn't I? And Thoreau *died* exactly one hundred years ago today. Teddy must have thought that he, too, was going to die on the same day! Don't you see?"

"My God, I think you're right. And Teddy had the same symptoms, too—the pulmonary consumption, the coughing, the legs going out from under him. And all completely induced by hysterical identification. You're a genius," Homer clapped her on the back.

"Homer, Teddy's gone off somewhere to die, like a poor sick dog. Can you die of hysterical identification? I'll bet you can."

"The question is, did he do in Goss first? If Teddy thought he was going to die anyway, what was there to stop him? And then where the heck did he go?"

But if he was dead anyway, what did it matter? Mary found herself remembering the words in Teddy's journal: *Her light will be as raddiant as ever, when I am no more*. She said nothing, and stared up at the mist. It had risen and it hung now in the treetops, like layers of spun glass shredded out into stringy banners, or long hair tangled in the treetops. Long, tangled, witch-white hair . . .

Homer could feel her shaking. "What's the matter with you? Here, dearie, let's talk about something else. We'll be out of these meeting places for spirits pretty soon. Just hang on." He put his arm around Mary's waist (it was easy) and began to talk amiably about Paul Revere, squeezing her tightly against his side. "I was reading those three accounts of his today, that he wrote about his famous ride. That Prescott fellow of yours must have been a bold fellow. The British said, 'G-blank-D D-blank-N you, stop, or you're a dead man!' Or so goes Paul's story. Imagine his politeness, writing in those blanks. And then they herded Revere and Dawes and Prescott into a field, and then Prescott jumped his horse over a stone wall and got away to Concord. So he was a jumper, too . . ."

"But, you see, that doesn't matter," said Mary. She shook her head and pulled away from Homer, rubbing her arm over her forehead. "I keep getting the past and the present all mixed up. As though Henry Thoreau really took Teddy away with him, or as if the murderer was really Dr. Sam Prescott, and as if he shot Mr. Goss with a ghostly old flintlock and then vanished into thin air. And of course it's ridiculous to think that way."

Homer chuckled. (Cheer the girl up.) "I bet you don't know what Paul Revere said at the end of his famous ride?"

"No, I don't."

" 'Whoa.' "

And then suddenly there *was* a horseman, and the sound of a horse's hooves cantering along the gravel path behind them.

"G-blank-D," said Homer, "if it ain't old Dr. Sam himself, come back as a ha'nt!"

Mary, too frightened to speak, stood rigid in the middle of the path, her head wrenched back over her shoulder, listening. The cantering sound changed to a gallop, and Homer at last had to snatch her roughly out of the way, as a great shape plunged heavily by, going like the wind down the hill. The horseman was leaning forward, his jacket flying behind him. They could see his hair in silhouette, caught by a ribbon in back, bobbing up and down. He called something to his horse, and leaned over farther. "Hey," shouted Homer, "whoa up there!"

They could see the rider pull at the reins with a sort of convulsion, and half turn his horse to glance back at them. Then he wheeled his mount around and, kicking with his heels, started downhill again at top speed.

Mary could feel hysterical laughter welling up inside her. She found a grave that was a lichen-covered marble bench and sat down on it, covering her mouth with her hands. It had been Prescott, the real Dr. Samuel Prescott.

"Now, don't get excited, you idiot," said Homer. "You know who that was? I heard the voice. There was no mistaking that flat monotone. That was Edith Goss."

Chapter 38

The melting snow and the rains of March and April had swollen the river that flowed at the foot of the sprouting fields. But the weather of May and June, normally an occasion for irritation, abuse, misery, tears, pain, distress and withered hopes, had turned out so long and golden a succession of days that one almost forgot to take note any more or thank God or rejoice. It was like a king's grant, signed and sealed, or a special dispensation of Providence. The greenish-white blossoming of Tom's trees was over now. It had been a spring when one walked carefully, afraid to tear or crush something incredible. But the most fragile time was past, and now there was strong ugly plantain in the grass.

Mary woke up on a Tuesday morning that was like the rest, clear and bright. Outside her bedroom window the fully-globed maple trees stood glittering like jeweler's work. In the elm tree a hoarse-throated bird had sprung a leak in his kettle and was dripping rusty splashes of song on the lawn. Mary got out of bed and pulled on her clothes, reflecting. It was the combination of things, perhaps, that had made it inevitable. Given a crop of young men with classical educations and given a succession of nurturing springtimes, how could New England *not* have produced a rash of transcendentalists? Or even so rare a flower as a Thoreau? Perhaps you shouldn't wonder at genius. Sometimes, maybe, it grew as naturally as weeds.

Gwen put her head in the door. "Mary, I don't suppose you have any white elephants for the church bazaar?"

"Oh, I don't know. Let me think."

"Anything will do, you know, absolutely anything. Old worn-out pieces of electrical equipment, toasters and irons. Remember the hair-dryer that John bought once? The heating unit didn't work, but he used it for a fan and gave himself chilblains all summer."

"I'll look around. Isn't that Mrs. Bewley vacuuming? Why don't you ask her? You know, she's got a whole houseful of white elephants."

"Oh, you bet I'm going to. She's our old reliable."

Gwen had graduated to little maternity jackets. She was keeping her weight down with difficulty, and already found the stairs hard going. Mrs. Bewley, who loved babies and motherhood, had offered to come in on her day off and help out. Now she stood in John's room, pushing the vacuum cleaner back and forth. Gwen came up behind her and turned off the switch. Mrs. Bewley didn't realize it was turned off, and she continued to push it back and forth dreamily. Gwen had to pull on the paw of her squirrel neckpiece. "MRS. BEWLEY," shouted Gwen, "I HOPE YOU'LL HAVE SOMETHING FOR ME AGAIN THIS YEAR FOR THE WHITE ELEPHANT TABLE?"

"SABLE?" bawled Mrs. Bewley. She patted her neckpiece. "NO, DEAR, IT'S SQUIRREL."

"TABLE, TABLE," bellowed Gwen. "DO YOU HAVE ANYTHING FOR THE WHITE ELEPHANT TABLE?"

"WHAT SAY?"

Gwen took a deep breath and tried again. "WHITE ELEPHANT," she shrieked. "WHITE ELEPHANT."

At last Mrs. Bewley understood. She vaulted with her

scrawny old legs over a small chair and stuck her head out the window. "WHERE? WHERE?"

Gwen thought it over. If she screamed any louder she would have a miscarriage on the spot. She picked up a piece of John's drawing paper and a crayon and beckoned to Mrs. Bewley. It was no good writing, because Mrs. Bewley couldn't read. So Gwen drew a rough picture of the First Parish church. Then she outlined a table with some chipped dishes on it and a sign on a stick. Carefully she made the sign in the shape of an elephant, with a long trunk in front. Mrs. Bewley began to smile all over her gaunt old face. "OH. YOU MEAN WHITE ELEPHANT TABLE. YES, YES. I'M SURE I CAN SPARE A FEW THINGS FROM MY COLLECTION."

"THAT'S NICE. YOU'RE ALWAYS SO GENEROUS, MRS. BEWLEY."

Mrs. Bewley nodded and smiled. It was true, she was.

Downstairs Mary was ready to go. But at the front door she blanched. That Granville-Galsworthy fellow had taken to hanging around in the morning. He had a room on Belknap Street but some mornings Mary had suspected that he had been lurking outside all night. Grandmaw had complained of prowlers, and the other night Tom had nearly caught someone in the barn. It gave Mary the shivers. She opened the door a crack, thinking to dodge out the back way if he was there, and try driving off as if she hadn't seen him. But his sallow face swam up to the crack in the door. She jumped. He had been standing on the great granite step before the door.

"Oh, hello. Good morning."

"Good morning tew yew."

Mary walked quickly toward her car. Roland came, too. There was nothing for it but to ask if he'd like a lift. Where did he want to go?

"I'm going tew dew some research," he said. "Just let me out wherever you're going."

Research, my eye. "Well, I'm going to the police station. Is that all right?"

That was all right. Mary parked her car beside the station, and he got out and followed her to the door. She despaired. Was there no way she could rid herself of this limpet? Then he collided with someone who was hurrying around the corner of the building. It was Homer Kelly.

"G'morning," said Homer, scowling. Roland lifted his hat and faded away.

Mary silently thanked God. "Nice day," she said meekly. Homer glared at her, opened his mouth to say something, and then thought better of it. Instead he opened the door for her, went in and leaned on the counter.

"Shrubsole," he said, "it's June."

"That's right, sir; lovely day."

"Miss Morgan and I will be out all day. Mind the store."

"Working on the case, are you, Mr. Kelly?"

"Naturally. You didn't think we would take a day off, and go boating on the river, or some frivolous thing like that, did you? We're just going to be doing some miscellaneous—ah—"

"Research," suggested Mary.

"That's it."

Sergeant Shrubsole was looking curiously at Homer. He lifted up his forefinger, rubbed it on his superior's cheek and looked at it. It came away pink with lipstick. Shrubsole shook his head, winked at Mary and drew an obvious conclusion. Homer hastily pulled out a handkerchief and rubbed his face. Mary blushed, and, trying hard not to look unhappy, succeeded in looking guilty. But it wasn't *her* lipstick.

"Come on," he said testily to Mary, pushing her out the door ahead of him. He slammed the door. "Impertinent young fool."

"You've got some on your collar, too," said Mary. She licked her handkerchief and wiped at the smudge. Homer looked down at her and growled, "Where can we hire a canoe?"

"A canoe? Oh, I see. Our research is going to be . . ."

"Naturally. Boating on the river."

Chapter 39

⤙ *I left the village and paddled up the river to Fair Haven Pond . . . I was soothed with an infinite stillness. I got the world, as it were, by the nape of the neck, and held it under in the tide of its own events, till it was drowned, and then I let it go down stream like a dead dog.*
HENRY THOREAU

"Wish I could go with you," said Tom. "I sure love this river. But what with crating asparagus and one thing and another a man hasn't a moment's peace this season. Here, why don't you use the outboard? See, it has its own battery. Doesn't make any noise at all."

Homer looked at the motor doubtfully. "Maybe we'd better just paddle," he said. "I don't know a thing about making motors work."

"Nonsense. You don't have to. This one's good for ten, eleven hours. Here, I'll start her up."

Gwen had made them a lunch in Annie's old plastic lunch-box. She came down to the edge of the river with Freddy to see them off. Freddy wanted to go, too. He wept as they shoved off from the shore into the middle of the dark stream. "Goodby, Freddy," shouted Homer. "Don't cry, and we'll bring you a turtle."

Freddy stopped crying right away. "Big," he said. *"Big."*

Out in the middle of the Assabet Mary could feel the sun drawing all the slivers from her mind. She knelt facing forward in the bow of the canoe and stared straight ahead so that Homer wouldn't see her smile. Grind away, hurdy-gurdy. (Henry Thoreau had spent half his life on the rivers.) Homer sat still in the stern, his hand on the tiller of the motor, his eyes on Mary's back. She was wearing a white dress. Unbidden, a quotation from Emerson floated into his head. *Beauty is the mark God sets upon virtue*. There was an asinine remark if ever there was one.

Mary pointed silently to a half-submerged log on which five turtles lay basking, leaning upon one another. They looked like overgrown shiny black beetles. Homer aimed the canoe that way, but when they came near, the turtles all slid into the water. "Better on the way back, anyhow," he said.

They passed a heron, standing motionless, and later a fisherman, motionless as the heron. Cloudy heads of water willows filled the edges of the river. "We could be Indians," said Mary. "Everything must have looked just the same when they lived along this shore."

"You awful heap big squaw," murmured Homer. "Squaw Head-in-Clouds."

"Look," said Mary, "here's the junction of the three rivers. See? This is where the Sudbury comes in and joins the Assabet to flow on downstream as the Concord. We'll be at the North Bridge in a minute. It's just around the bend."

The Concord River was slower-moving, but the surface rippled slightly in the warm breeze and slipped over the still body of the rest. The reflections in the water were upside-down impressionist pictures of the shore. Then a pair of redwing blackbirds fluttered out of the buttonbushes and Homer lost his self-control. That did it. It was all so damn pretty. Almost as if it were trying to persuade him of something he didn't want to be talked into. Homer looked around nervously and started tearing into Concord. In his opinion it was a polite little suburban pesthole, living on its picayune history, full of proper little anglophilic old biddies in sneakers. It made him sick. It was like Brattle Street in Cambridge, where you could feel the ghostly whiskers of old dead professors tickling your cheek. Creepy, that's what it was.

Mary promised herself she wouldn't get angry. She looked up at the watery light under the arch of the Red Bridge and remembered that Henry Thoreau had cooled himself in the same spot on hot days. That was it. Cool down. Just cool down.

"And the Battle. Some battle. Absurd little hesitation waltz of a skirmish. Cradle of American liberty, my foot."

Well, all right then. Jump in when the rope swings. Jump, jump. Mary swung around to talk back. "You know what Emerson said about the battle? 'The thunderbolt falls on an inch of ground but the light of it fills the horizon!'"

"Very pretty." Damn it, those things in the water were water lilies. Wouldn't you just know. Blasted river. Blasted town. Double blasted girl. Then a mallard took off in its stooping flight from a stand of weeds in front of them, and Homer jumped. The canoe swerved and almost caught a snag. "You've always got a quote, haven't you? Typical intellectual female. Talk talk talk."

"All right then. You don't have to speak to me. Just shut up."

"Okay. Who wants to talk to an intellectual female anyhow? Not me. There are two things that don't go together, and that's females and brains. Women weren't meant by God to talk in words of more than one syllable."

"Well, I'm not, am I? All I said was, shut up." Mary stared grimly ahead at the North Bridge. What an irascible boor.

The railing of the bridge was lined with tourists. The tourists were all staring back at them. For some reason people beside a body of water always assume that anybody in a boat must be deaf and dumb. A woman from Belmont dug her elbow into her husband's side. "Look," she said loudly, "lovers." Her husband lifted his camera and leaned way out over the railing to take a snapshot. Another fellow laden down with equipment was making an artistic home movie. He hung over the side, too, found the canoe in his finder and adjusted his new zoom lens. Idyllic picture—lovely girl in white, tall fellow with sleeves rolled up, lock of brown hair on forehead. Charming. Now. Come in close on the girl. *Zooooooom.* Boy, she's a dilly. Looks a bit stiff though. Now for her beau. (Homer adjusted his features into a grimace, rolled up his eyes, crossed them, and lolled his tongue on his chin.) The movie expert shifted his focus, zoomed in on Homer, and nearly fell off the bridge. He just managed to save himself, but his Bell and Howell Director Optronic Eye Reflex Camera ($249.95) fell into the middle of the Concord River, along with his Pistol Grip ($16.95) and his Luxury Contour Camera Carrying Case with smart Chrome Trim ($24.95). As Mary and Homer passed under the bridge, the movie expert was jumping up and down and waving his arms around.

Homer could feel his good humor coming back. Come on, rile her up some more. "Of course what I really don't understand is why Concord has any claim to fame at all. It was Lexington where the first blood was shed. And there wasn't any indecision and running around behind hills there. What did they do? They stood there on the Common and met the enemy face to face. Besides, Lexington was where the brains were, with Hancock and Adams holed up in Jonas Clarke's house."

"I sometimes wonder," said Mary acidly, "what would have happened to the history of this country if it hadn't been for Jonas Clarke's wife. Do you know how many children she had? Twelve. And on top of them she had all those important people and their aunts and cousins sleeping and eating in her house for weeks at a time. What if Mrs. Jonas Clarke had thrown in the towel? The whole thing might never have come off at all."

Homer snickered. "You're probably right, at that. What is there behind every great man? A great woman." Homer pulled back on the tiller, and the canoe made a wide turn and started back toward the bridge. The man who had lost his camera was kneeling on the bridge, poking around in the water with a golf club. Homer agreeably turned off the motor and fished around in the water with the handle end of a paddle. He got the handle neatly under the strap of the camera case and brought up the whole thing, streaming water and trailing weeds, but still grinding away, five dollars' worth of color film wasted on a lot of curious out-of-focus bass who had nosed up in a school to see what the funny noise was. The owner of the camera took it back with bad grace, and then Homer pulled the switch of the inboard and they headed upstream again. At the joining of the rivers they took the left-hand branch and nosed their canoe up the Sudbury River. Suddenly they discovered that they were ravenous, and Mary opened up Annie's lunchbox.

"I like to fight with you," said Homer, with lordly condescension.

"Thank you," said Mary, nodding graciously. "How nice of you to say so."

The river was becoming domesticated, flowing past the green lawns behind the houses on Main Street with their small docks and their canoes leaning up against trees. A noisy powerboat piloted by a man in a duck-billed hat beat them to the railroad bridge. They joggled pleasantly in his wake, and presently the river became wild again. Tom's little motor pushed them silently past Thoreau's Conantum, with its tall pines and its discreet development of new houses, half hidden in the trees.

"What happens here?" said Homer. The river was opening out into a lake. "Oh, I know." There was a shade of reverence in his voice. "It's Fairhaven Bay."

"Yes. And there's Teddy Staples' house. And that white one next to it is Alice Herpitude's."

"Look over there," said Homer. "There's an island. Funny, I don't remember any island on the map. Holy smoke, look at the size of that pine."

"Well, most of the year the island is connected to the mainland by a marsh, but it's all high water around it at this time of year. Would you like to land over there and look around?"

The island was about as big as a baseball diamond. There was a clearing near the place where they drew up their canoe, and at one edge of it the tall pine tree grew. It was a magnificent specimen with irregular outflung branches at the top, a long bare trunk and a bristling set of broken snags below its evergreen arms. They walked to the other end of the island, knee-deep in blueberry bushes and the pale stars of Quaker Ladies. Then they walked back again, pushed the canoe off and climbed in. Misfortune struck. Tom's little motor wouldn't catch. Homer fiddled with it clumsily. "I think the blasted thing's out of juice."

"That's what's so exciting about Tom's gadgets. You never know what will happen next. I'm afraid we're in for a lot of paddling. Horrors, there's only the one paddle."

"Oh, well, give it to me. Me heap awful big chief. Bendum mighty arm." Homer's paddling was inexpert and splashy. He caught a crab and doused Mary with water.

"You heap big lousy paddler," chortled Mary. "Here. Me paddlum with lunchbox. Don't dip down so deep."

The lunchbox provided just enough extra movement of water to allow them to creep forward. The sluggish current was with them, but the wind wasn't, and they made slow progress. They inched past Conantum. An hour later they we struggling past the Main Street lawns. Homer had taken over the lunchbox and he was plying it in rhythmic sweeps and bellowing in basso profundissimo a hymn he had made up called "Arise, O Man, and Curse!" He called it a typical Protestant hymn. Mary sang a dreary alto part—fa, fa, fa, fa, mi, fa. The whole effect was altogether too plausible. She asked a question that had puzzled her. How could anybody who called himself a Catholic have anything in common with the Transcendentalists?

"That's easy," said Homer. "Awe and majesty and glorification of the spirit, that's all. The mystic sense of God the Creator, what Emerson called the geometry of the City of God. You Protestants had a good thing in Martin Luther, and then you let it all go down the drain and replaced it with ethical culture and rationalism and humanism and Japanese flower arrangements. Corpsecold Unitarianism, that's what Emerson called it. A society of the diffusion of useful knowledge."

An hour later they were still bickering. "Oh, for God's sake, let's go ashore," said Homer. They had reached the joining of the rivers.

"But we've still got to go upstream on the Assabet," said Mary. "That'll take ages."

"Go ahead. You go upstream. Be a hero. I'm getting out right here." Grumpily Homer took off his shoes and socks and jumped out of the canoe. It rocked wildly from side to side. Homer's feet found a mushy footing and he pulled the canoe after him toward the left-hand shore. Mary found this action highhanded and she began to protest.

"Squaw talkum too much," growled Homer. "Squaw shut-tum-up and come ashore." Then suddenly he began to howl and hop around on one foot. He lifted the other foot out of the water. There was a small snapping turtle attached to his toe. *"Ow, ow!"* roared Homer, trying to kick it off. The turtle hung on like grim death.

Mary was overjoyed. She clapped her hands. "Freddy's turtle! Oh, good for you. Here, don't lose it. Just hold still." She reached over the side with the lunchbox, held it open like a clamshell, and then clamped it hard around the turtle and Homer's toe, *slam*. Homer hollered and jumped around, and Mary, hanging on, fell clean out of the canoe. She went under, and stayed there, and Homer found himself groaning and fishing around for her desperately. But in a minute she was up, smiling radiantly, her hair streaming, her wet dress clinging, clasping a lunchbox that was shut and locked on the bloody mingled waters of the Assabet, the Sudbury and the Concord rivers and on a snapping turtle that was digesting a piece of Homer Kelly's toe. "It's all right," said Mary brightly, "I've got him!"

"Who's worried?" snarled Homer. He turned to wade toward the shore, hobbling, hanging onto his toe. Then he stopped, and hopped up and down in one place, and pointed. "What's that?" he said.

Facing them was a great grey rock. There was an inscription carved into its face. "That's Egg Rock," said Mary. "We went right by it twice before."

Homer waded clumsily to the edge of the water, and read the inscription.

ON THE HILL NASHAWTUCK
AT THE MEETING OF THE RIVERS
AND ALONG THE BANKS
LIVED THE INDIAN OWNERS OF
MUSKETAQUID
BEFORE THE WHITE MEN CAME.

"Musketaquid," said Homer. "That's the old Indian name for
the river."

"Yes, and of the tribe. It means Grass-ground River, or river
surrounded with grassy meadows. Thoreau liked to call it that,
too. He called his little boat *The Musketaquid.*"

Homer was bleeding into the water, but he let go of his toe
and ran his finger over the word *Musketaquid.* "Musketaquid.
Musket-a-quid. Musket..." He looked at Mary. "Say, you
don't suppose that was what Ernest Goss was trying to say
when he died?" Mary stared back at him. Could it have been?
Then Homer tugged at the canoe and dragged it up on the sloping shore. Mary wrung out a streaming handkerchief and tied it
on his wounded toe. It was hard to do because he kept hopping
around.

"What do you think you're doing?"

"I don't know. Looking for something. Doing research."

"Oh, I see. Well, hold still. Golly, I'm afraid you're going to
bleed right through this bandage. He really took a piece out of
you."

Homer got away and hobbled all over the small point of land
that marked the joining place of the rivers, leaving wet red
drops on the ferns that grew in clefts in the granite outcropping.
Then he found something. It was a small tin bait box, wedged
deep down in one of the clefts. It was fastened shut by a heavy
padlock.

"Zowie!" shouted Homer. "My letters! What do you want to
bet?" He rattled the box around. "Something in there all right."

"You're sure it's not just a lot of smelly worms?"

"Doesn't sound like worms. Sounds like papers."

"Well, it could be a club that some boys have, and this is

their secret hiding place, and the papers tell who's president and what the password is. Oh, Homer, look, you've got to sit down and put your foot up. You'll bleed half to death. You stay here. I'll find a house and call Tom and get some bandages and he'll bring the car as close as he can."

"You go wigwams? You one heap awful big wet squaw."

"You one heap awful big bloody mess, go Happy Hunting Ground." Mary climbed over a great fallen log, rotten and soft, and started up a barely visible path. Old Squaw Sachem had had a trail somewhere here, and up on Nashawtuc Hill there were some houses.

Homer stretched out on the ground and put his foot up on the canoe. He held the bait box on his stomach and patted it. "Me findum plenty wampum. Me plenty heap awful smart."

Chapter 40

Homer was for opening the bait box with a can opener, but Jimmy Flower would have none of that. He brought out a manila envelope that held the contents of Ernest Goss's pockets, and poured them out on his desk. Small change, wallet, penknife, key chain. And on the key chain there was a small key for which they had as yet found no matching lock. "Will wonders never cease," said Jimmy. The rusted padlock was reluctant, but it gave way. Inside the bait box was a plastic folder, and in the folder was the batch of letters. Mary recognized them at once. These were *the* letters, the letters Ernest Goss had read to the Alcott Association, Transcendental dynamite.

"Now don't you go handling them," said Jimmy. "We'll let Campbell at Public Safety work them over. I'll get them off to him right now."

"So if I'm right," said Homer, "Goss wasn't saying *musket* at all as he lay dying. He was trying to say something else entirely. And that's why Arthur Furry didn't really need to strain himself to remember a big gun. There was no big gun. No musket at all."

"Hold on there, not so fast. Don't forget, he was killed with a musket ball and there's a musket missing."

"But why should a dying man waste his last words on the weapon that killed him? That's what's bothered me all along. He didn't even bother to tell the name of his murderer. Something else was more important to communicate—the whereabouts of the letters on which he planned to raise a big reputation. He wanted them found and saved and published and credited to his own glory."

"Well, could be. I don't know. I'm not going to make up my mind yet. Say, how do you suppose Goss got the letters to Egg Rock? By boat?"

"He probably just drove down Nashawtuc Road and walked over. And he could have left them there any time after he read them aloud to the Alcott Association, afraid they might be stolen if he left them around the house."

"But what did he pick that particular place for?"

"I know," said Mary. "It must have been an old haunt of his. He was a great arrowhead collector, don't forget, and he must have scratched around there a good deal on the site of the old village, looking for Indian artifacts."

Mr. Campbell, the fingerprint man, made an informal report by telephone to Jimmy Flower. "Of course," he said, "paper isn't the best stuff in the world to get good prints from, but fortunately these didn't dry out too badly, being out-of-doors the way they were. So the sweat prints didn't fade too much for us to make some indentifications. Well, there's two sets of prints on them, on all of them. Right thumb prints on the upper righthand corner of each sheet. That's where you hold it to read it over after you write, or to read it for the first time if you've just received it. One set of prints is Ernest Goss's, the other is his son Charley's."

"Whose? *Charley's?*"

"That's what I said. And Ernie's appear to be on top of Charley's in some cases, which makes it look as if Charley wrote them and Ernie received them."

(Charley's? Mary, sitting at her card table in the corner, felt her heart sink. Another bad mark for Charley.)

"What about real old prints? Like a hundred years old? You didn't find any of those?" said Jimmy.

"That's a different kettle of fish. You have to use a different way of bringing them out. You see, the sweat prints evaporate after while, so you have to use a system that looks for acids that don't evaporate. Well, we used it on these letters. It's called the ninhydrin method. Of course we can't be positive, since we never tried it on anything as old as these letters were supposed to be, but we didn't turn up a single print."

"There was nothing on them, then, but prints by Ernest and Charley Goss?"

"That's right. Now, do you want me to send these down to the lab, so they can look into the paper and ink? They look to me like they're all done with the same brown ink."

"Okay. But I bet we can get Charley Goss to talk. Say, what about the bait box? Where Charley's prints on that?"

"No, just his daddy's. And of course about a million big huge blobs belonging to one Homer Kelly. Tell him from me he's a great big overgrown blundering oaf."

Jimmy passed along the message, and Homer grinned. "Tell him from me he's a dear boy and thank him very much."

Charley Goss had given up trying to find a job. He had planted a colossal vegetable garden behind the house and he was spending his time caring for it. He threw himself into it, hoeing and weeding and setting out branching sticks for the peas to climb on and tented stakes for the tomato plants. Only Rowena and Edith and Charley himself were left to eat the results, because Philip had moved into George Jarvis's bachelor apartment on Thoreau Street. But the garden gave Charley something to do, and he gave most of his produce away.

Mary looked at him guiltily, as he came into Jimmy's office with Sergeant Shrubsole. Charley's face was red and healthy-looking from the sun, but his eyes looked miserable. He glanced at her, and then looked away without speaking. She had tried to tell him privately that her time spent with the lieutenant-detective from the District Attorney's office was an effort to help him. But

Charley had merely looked at her with red eyes, and said, "Oh, sure." Mary had bitten her lip and said nothing. Perhaps he was right. Perhaps after all her motives were not as clear as all that.

Jimmy Flower brought out a chair for Charley and started talking. Charley listened to the facts about his fingerprints on the letters, and then confessed right away. "Sure," he said, "I wrote them. But let me tell you how it happened." He turned to Homer. "You know what a great practical joker my father was? A real joker. You saw him that night going after poor old Edith with that paper napkin. Well, it occurred to me (back in February I guess it was), after a particularly nasty trick he had played on me, that one way of getting back at him was to try it myself. Let him slip on his own banana peel. I thought it over for some time before I finally came up with this. The thing that made me think of it was an exam I had in one of those crazy schools I went to. They didn't really have exams, just something they called CTPs, Creative Thinking Projects. The course was a sort of Renaissance History Seminar, or something. You were supposed to write an imaginary letter from Savonarola to Pope Alexander VI. Well, I had a wonderful time. I had Savonarola threatening to hire Leonardo da Vinci's flying machine and drop burning coals on the Vatican. Got a very good paragraph on my PCP. That is, my Personal Critical Profile. In other words, my report card.

"But anyway, the point is, it gave me this idea of writing letters from one Transcendentalist to another, making them ridiculous but sort of superficially convincing. I did a whole lot of reading, and I even copied the handwriting, when I could find the originals. There's a glass case there in the library with samples of writing by Emerson and Thoreau and Louisa May Alcott."

Homer shook his head. "I've got to hand it to you, Charley. You did a magnificent job. Works of art, all of them. What did you do for paper and ink?"

"It was just good bond paper in various weights and sizes. And brown India ink. I left the paper in the barn a while to get weathered. Any even slightly scientific examination would show that it wasn't old paper."

"What did you do with them when they were finished?"

"Well, that took a bit of thought. I finally wrote another letter. This one was supposed to have been written by a sweet little old lady in western Massachusetts by the name of Miss Maria Fuller Alcott Emerson . . ."

"Maria Fuller Alcott Em——Say, that's the mysterious lady in your father's will! Okay, go ahead, what was she for?"

"She was supposed to be a genteel old lady in reduced circumstances, descended on both sides from Concord greats. She flattered my father up and down, going on about how much she had heard about his integrity and honor and all that bilgewater, and how her grandfather had known his grandfather, and how ashamed she was to be selling the souls of her great ancestors, so she didn't want her name mentioned, but her poverty had reduced her to this extremity. So would my father publish these letters under his own name and divide the royalties with her, that was all she asked, some fraction of the royalties, and would he please memorize her address and burn this? Well, of course, Dad fell for it. He wrote her this big pompous magnanimous letter, agreeing to the whole thing, and then she sent him the letters."

"He really wrote a letter to some fictitious lady?

"Oh, I have an old buddy out there in Springfield. He's a postman. He agreed to send and receive letters for her. I guess he's kept his mouth shut."

"Well," said Homer. "It all worked just the way you hoped."

Charley flushed. "Not quite," he said. "Of course I was delighted when I heard he had read them to the Alcott Association and that they had laughed at them. I thought that would be the end of it. I'd had my revenge. But I didn't dream he'd go on taking them seriously after that."

"Didn't that put you on the spot then?"

"What do you mean?"

"Your father *did* go on believing in them. That meant that there would eventually be a good deal of notoriety and investigation and damage to literary reputations, and it probably meant that the letters might be traced back to you. How would you have explained to the press, for example, your responsibility for such spectacular forgeries?"

Charley was silent.

"And your father. What would have been his reaction to the discovery that his own son had made a fool of him before the world? Had you thought that through?"

Charley still said nothing. He looked down at the red backs of his hands, which were clutching his knees.

"Isn't is possible," said Homer, "that you feared your father's anger because you thought he might cut you out of his will? You hated him anyway. Isn't it possible that you decided there was only one thing to do, to kill him? You arranged a rendez-vous with him, again by letter, posing as a literary agent or a collector, or something. You also made arrangements to be sure that your brother would have no alibi for the time of the rendez-vous. Then you killed your father..."

"What arrangements?" said Charley. "How could I know Philip was going to leave the Rod and Gun Club and go out for a walk?"

"We don't have the whole story on that yet," said Homer. "But his slip with the cannon firing that morning was just the break you needed, wasn't it? You counted on the double confession you assumed he would make, on his opportunity to commit the crime and on his unlucky mistake of the morning to so confuse the police that they wouldn't dare to arrest either of you, afraid of condemn-ing an innocent party—the very same ruse you had practiced throughout your life to escape punishment at the hands of your parents. Your Sam Prescott outfit and your false 'confession' were all part of the trick. Isn't that so, Charley?"

"No, no," said Charley, "that's not so. That just isn't true. It is true that I was unhappy about the letters when my father insisted on going ahead with them. But I didn't think any repu-table publisher would take them seriously. Then, I thought, he would drop the whole thing."

Homer made a church of his fingers, and opened and closed the front door that was his large thumbs. He shifted his ground. "I didn't know your sister Edith was a horsewoman, Charley," he said. "She denied it when we asked her, way back in April."

Charley was startled. "Why, yes. Yes, she is. It's one of the few things she's any good at."

"She rides your horse, Dolly?"

"Sure. It's the only one we've got. She likes to go out mostly at night. It's kind of hard on Dolly, but, heck, it's one of the few pleasures the poor girl has. Say, look, you don't think that Edith . . ."

"No, as a matter of fact, we don't," said Homer. He clapped shut his church doors like the snapping of a trap.

"I mean, she's just not strong-minded enough . . ." Charley stopped abruptly, and looked at Jimmy Flower. "Are you going to arrest me now?"

Jimmy looked at Homer. Homer's little eyes blinked. He rubbed his hair up the wrong way on the back of his head and leaned back in his chair. "No, Charley, you can go on home."

The door closed behind Charley. "What do you think?" said Jimmy Flower.

"Well, with Teddy still missing, what can we do? Besides, it doesn't really hold water yet." Homer looked gloomy. "Do you suppose Charley and Teddy were really in it together, and afterwards Charley murdered Teddy to shut him up?"

"In that case," said Jimmy, "where's the corpus delicti?"

"That's just it. Where *is* Teddy?"

"Well, I'll tell you what I think, Teddy or no Teddy," said Chief Flower. "I'm sick and tired of us being so clever. Here was somebody wearing Charley's own bunny-suit, seen practically at the moment of firing the fatal shot. Charley had the opportunity, he had the motive, stronger than ever now, with these letters to hush up, and he was witnessed by a real live witness. Why do we have to think up all these ifs, ands and buts? I'll tell you something else—all it would take to convince me is one more scrap of evidence against Charley—just one more little scrap."

Chapter 41

What you seek in vain for, half your life, one day you come full upon, all the family at dinner.
HENRY THOREAU

Tom and John were helping Gwen load her white elephants into the pickup. John had worried circles under his eyes. One of the white elephants was a huge mahogany-veneer loudspeaker cabinet, and John wanted it desperately. He sat beside it in the truck and followed it possessively into the vestry of the church, where Gwen was setting up her table. She had to shoo him out. "No customers till the bazaar opens at ten o'clock," she said.

"It seems awfully stupid to me," said Tom, "to haul this thing all the way to church and then all the way back again." But Gwen, who had a stern New England conscience, didn't think it was moral to sell her elephants ahead of time.

"Please, Mom, you won't sell it to anyone else, will you?"

"Whoever gets here first," said Gwen piously. "It wouldn't be right to hold anything for my own family."

So John hung on to the doorhandle outside the entry, scorning the pony rides that had started early. Mary stood beside him, and when the chairwoman of the bazaar opened the door, Mary managed to block a large crowd of greedy-looking children and let John squeeze in first. He streaked for his mother's table.

"Well, hello there, John. Anything I can do for you today?"

"H-has anybody——?"

"No, dear, of course not. It's all yours."

Later in the day Mary walked back from the library to check on her sister. "Aren't you tired?" she said. "Isn't someone going to take over and let you get some lunch?"

"I'm fine," said Gwen. "Grandmaw's going to come over after while and take my place. Do you know, someone actually bought that defunct ant-farm and the inside-out umbrella? They went the first ten minutes. Maybe I underpriced them. I've still got lots of lovely things, though. Don't you want to buy something? We can always take it to the dump on the way home."

Mary looked the collection over, to see if there was anything less useless than the rest. She passed over the salt-and-pepper shakers shaped like drunks leaning on lampposts, the cut-glass pickle dish, the old phonograph records, the cracked dishes, the yellowed dresser scarves, the Donald Duck doorstop, the dented-in ping-pong ball . . . and her eyes came to rest on the tricorn hat.

"Where did that come from?" she said. "It wasn't here this morning."

"Mrs. Bewley brought it over. She brought the glove, too, and the half-harmonica and the rusty letter-opener and three pairs of broken sunglasses and this nice trylon-and-perisphere paperweight. She wanted to give me her neckpiece, too, but I made her keep it. I don't think the First Parish should ask for that much of a sacrifice. She helped herself to a few things while she was here, of course, but I was glad to get rid of them anyway."

Mary bought the tricorn hat for a quarter, and looked around for Mrs. Bewley. She found her at the food table, swiping a cooky and being glared at by Mrs. Jellicoe. Mary clung to Mrs. Bewley's bony arm, bought her a dozen brownies and then drew her out into the corridor. But the uproar from the Children's Midway downstairs was so great that she had to lead her out of doors. Freddy was going by on a pony, with Grandmaw walking beside him, holding him on.

"MRS. BEWLEY," shouted Mary, "WHERE DID YOU GET THIS HAT?" She waved it at Mrs. Bewley and pointed at it.

Mrs. Bewley clasped her hands. "THAT'S GOING TO LOOK REAL NICE."

"No, no, Mrs. Bewley. WHERE DID YOU GET IT?"

"WHAT?"

"THE HAT. WHERE—DID—YOU—GET—IT?"

"OH, OH, I SEE. LET ME SEE NOW, I WAS JUST COMING BACK FROM THAT PARADE, YOU KNOW, THAT THEY HAVE? AND I FOUND SOME REAL NICE THINGS. THERE WAS A NICE BEER BOTTLE, THE GREEN KIND, NOT THE BROWN KIND, I DON'T COLLECT THE BROWN KIND, AND A WALLET WITH TEN DOLLARS IN IT THAT BELONGED TO MR. RICHLEY, I COULD TELL BY THE PICTURES OF HIS FAMILY. WANT TO SEE? THE BABY'S ADORABLE."

"YOU MEAN THE APRIL 19TH PARADE? WAS THE HAT THERE AT THE BRIDGE?"

"NO, NO, IT WAS IN THE FIELD THERE, OVER THERE ON THE OTHER SIDE."

"DID YOU SEE ANYONE THERE AT THE TIME? A BOY SCOUT? A MAN ON A HORSE?"

"OH, IT DIDN'T BELONG TO A SOUL, IT WAS JUST LYING THERE ALL ALONE."

"THANK YOU VERY MUCH, MRS. BEWLEY."

"OH, DON'T MENTION IT."

Chapter 42

'Miracles have ceased.' Have they indeed? When?
RALPH WALDO EMERSON

"It's the Prescott hat, all right," said Chief Flower. "This strand of fiber that was stuck inside the band matches that cheap orange wig. But that doesn't tell us whether it was worn by anybody else after Charley wore it the first time."

"You know," said Mary, "this is probably a waste of time, but do you think there might be any point in our looking around Mrs. Bewley's house? Maybe she picked up something else. You don't suppose she carried home that great long gun, too?"

Homer threw back his head, convulsed by the picture of Mrs. Bewley as a Minuteman. But then they went and paid her a call. She lived in a small house on Lowell Road, with an infinitesimal parlor, a miniature bedroom and a dollsize kitchen. Mrs. Bewley herself was quite large and angular, and she had to bend herself around her furniture. She was overjoyed to see Mary and Homer, and she shouted them in for tea. It was pouring rain outside and Homer and Mary were glad to duck indoors and take off their wet coats. There was no difficulty in getting Mrs.

Bewley's permission to look around. She adored exhibiting her Collection of Things.

Homer was particularly impressed by her collection of beer bottles (the high-class green ones only). She had a whole lot of matchbooks with pictures of pussycats on them, and a drawerful of miscellaneous mittens. Mary recognized one that had belonged to Annie. She had NEVER SEEN SUCH A DARLING MITTEN.

"OH, TAKE IT, TAKE IT," hollered Mrs. Bewley.

The little room was overwhelming. It seemed bursting at the seams with overstuffed plush decked with antimacassars. Antimacassars were Mrs. Bewley's favorite swiping material. It was so easy. Just *swish, pop,* and there you were. Stalking around the room were her little pets, four or five bantam hens and a tiny rooster. They kept getting their claws tangled in the antimacassars. Homer made the mistake of sitting down without looking in one of the chairs. There was a small *punksh,* and he got up with an infinitesimal egg dripping from his backside.

"OH, TOO BAD," cried Mrs. Bewley, dabbing at him with an antimacassar. "BRIDGIE'S SUCH A GOOD LAYER, SHE DOES LIKE THAT CHAIR, SEE?" Mrs. Bewley felt around in the voluptuous bulges and crevices of the chair and triumphantly brought up two more small eggs, like a child finding jelly beans at Easter.

Mary decided to remain standing. "WHAT'S IN THOSE PAPER BAGS, MRS BEWLEY?" she shouted.

Mrs. Bewley looked ecstatic. "MESSAGES, ALL MESSAGES."

"MESSAGES?"

"FROM JESUS. HE SENDS ME MESSAGES ALL THE TIME."

For a wild moment Mary wondered if Mrs. Bewley was a sort of super-Transcendentalist, seeing sermons in stones and lessons in the running brooks. Or was she a sort of innocent natural saint, and were the paper bags filled with long curling ribbons inscribed with Gothic messages in Latin, like the ones you saw in old Flemish pictures with the Virgin and the angel Gabriel?

But the first thing that came out of a paper bag was a startled hen named Priscilla. ("WHY, PRISCILLA, YOU NAUGHTY GIRL, SO THAT'S WHERE YOU'VE BEEN.") Next Mrs. Bewley had to scrabble around until she brought out Priscilla's six teeny-weeny eggs and established them under Priscilla again on top of the sofa. Then she plunged back into the bag again, peering into the top like a skinny Mrs. Santa Claus and then rolling her eyes up at the ceiling while she felt around. "THERE!" She came up with her hand closed around something and held it behind her back coyly. "WHICH HAND?"

Homer groaned under his breath, but Mary heroically chose the left. That was wrong. She chose the right. Mrs. Bewley brought forth her treasure. It was a message, all right, from the Jubble Bubble Chewing Gum Company. It had once encased a large pink piece of bubble gum, long since chewed and gone to glory. Mrs. Bewley reached for another grab. This time it was a torn campaign poster advertising Harry J. Croney for County Clerk. Mrs. Bewley leaned Harry up against the wall like an icon and beamed at Mary and Homer, expecting homage.

They were stunned. Mrs. Bewley, taking their gaping for awe, decided to do the thing up brown. She turned the paper bag upside down and dropped a fluttering shower of trash on the floor. And there among the candy wrappers and cigarette containers and throwaway mail advertising specials on pork chops, Mary saw a message from Jesus that was worth the salvaging. She reached for it and picked it up. It was another one of Ernie's letters, the one that had fallen under her chair at Orchard House. It was the tenderly beautiful letter that Henry Thoreau was supposed to have written to Emily Dickinson. What on earth was it doing here? Mary showed it to Homer.

"What a stroke of luck," said Homer. "It never occurred to me that one letter might be missing from that bunch in the bait box." He read it over. "What a genius that Charley is. This is a masterpiece. Mrs. Bewley must have lifted it off Ernie's desk before he decided to hide them away. Say, maybe that's why he had to hide them in the first place. Someone was swiping them."

"Ssshh." Mary looked apprehensively at Mrs. Bewley. But Mrs. Bewley was delighted by their interest in the central feature and mystic heart of her collection. Struggling behind her sofa, which was kitty-cornered artistically across the angle of the room, she moved aside a wickerwork plant table sprouting a hardbitten rubber plant and yanked at a closet door. It opened just wide enough to show what was inside. It was jampacked and bulging with brown grocery bags chock-full of messages straight from Jesus.

Homer clapped his hand to his brow. The worth of Mrs. Bewley as a collector on a par with Bernard Berenson and Andrew Mellon was just beginning to dawn on him. He fell down on one knee and shouted humbly, WOULD MRS. BEWLEY, COULD MRS. BEWLEY SEE HER WAY CLEAR TO LETTING THEM BORROW HER COLLECTION OF MESSAGES? THEY WOULD BE SO CAREFUL, SO VERY CAREFUL . . .

Mrs. Bewley climbed eagerly over the back of the sofa, stepping gingerly on either side of Priscilla, and gave them her blessing.

Chapter 43

*Let such pure hate still underprop
Our love . . .*
HENRY THOREAU

Mary was still hoarse from shouting at Mrs. Bewley. She cleared her throat. "Why don't we sort them for her?" she said. She was watching Patrolman Vine and Sergeant Ordway turn over mountains of trash, spreading them out neatly on the floor of the firing range on six of Isabelle Flower's clean white sheets. "Maybe she'd like all the Choko-wrappers in one bag and all the popsicle sticks in another."

"No," said Homer. "She may have some profound system of classification all her own. Let them alone. Mrs. Bewley knows best."

It took them two hours to go through the entire collection. Some of the pieces were sticky and had to be soaked apart. Luther Ordway picked up the last of these from a towel in the darkroom and brought it out into the light to look at it. He was whistling, but then he stopped whistling, and read it through again. Then he brought it to Chief Flower. Jimmy read it a couple of times, looking sober and brought it over to Homer's desk.

"Oh, good," said Mary. "Did you find something else?"

Jimmy glanced at her, looking troubled, then shifted his glance away. Homer read the scrap of paper through twice, then slowly lifted his small sharp eyes to look at her.

"Well, what is it?" said Mary. She walked around behind him and he held the piece of wrinkled paper so that she could see. It was a short typewritten note.

Dearest Philip,
I have something to tell you that I hope will make you happy. Can you meet me at Nicholson's Barn between 12:30 and 1:30? Please don't say anything to anyone—and destroy this.

It was signed in ink. The signature had run, but it had a homely look, and it jumped out at Mary from the page. It was her own.

Homer looked up at her. His face was still with an arctic calm, his eyes buckets of nails. Mary couldn't speak. She didn't say anything at all. She stared at the signature. That was her M, her closed A and careless R, and her Y that was just a bump and a straight line without any loop.

Then Jimmy snatched the paper suddenly. "I'm going to tear it up," he said.

"What do you want to do," said Homer, "lose your badge? That's evidence."

Jimmy glared at him. "It don't mean anything and you know it."

"Oh, but it does," said Homer. He stood up and reached out, gripping Jimmy's wrist. He squeezed the wrist in his large hand until Jimmy's fingers went limp and dropped the paper. "Thank you," said Homer. He picked it up. "This note calls Philip away from the place where he was surrounded by witnesses who could furnish him with an alibi for the time of the murder, to a lonely spot where no one would see him coming or going. He could walk to the barn from the Gun Club right across a dry field." Homer looked at Mary coldly. "Did you meet him there?"

Mary dumbly shook her head.

Homer started walking around the room. "Philip Goss received this note some time during the morning of the murder. Expecting a declaration of love he walked eagerly across the field to the barn, arriving around 12:30. Impatiently he waited there for Mary for a full hour, maybe longer, before giving up. Then he tossed the note aside in disgust, returned to the Rod and Gun Club and started to drink himself under the table. Afterwards, when asked about his whereabouts, Philip was gallant. He refused to name the reason he was missing, for fear of getting into trouble the girl he loved. A gentleman of the old school."

"That's more than you are, I see," said Jimmy, his voice rising. "Listen here, Homer Kelly, if you say a word, just one word, that harms a hair on the head of my Mary, I'll . . ."

Homer interrupted roughly. "Oh, so she's *your* Mary now, is she?" Jimmy made an angry lunge for the piece of paper, but Homer snatched it away and held it behind his back. He looked at Mary and spoke softly. "Split the lark, and you'll find the music. Mary, did you write this?"

Mary hugged her arms and shivered. She found herself noticing the way Homer's head was arranged on his neck, the way his neck grew out of his collar. His head was different from the bald knob that rested on Jimmy's shoulders like a friendly turnip. It was erect like a dog's, furry and cocked and alert. Cocked. Cocked like a gun. "No," she said. "I don't think I did. I mean, of course I didn't. I know I didn't."

Homer blinked. He lowered his eyes to her desk and touched her typewriter. "We can find out what machine it was typed on, probably. I'll bet it was Charley's. And anybody could have traced your signature. Charley had letters from you?"

Then he wasn't—it was all right. Mary nodded without speaking.

Homer glanced at the note again. "Elite type. Small portable, most likely. Is that what yours is? I mean the one you use at home?" Mary nodded again, and looked at the piece of paper. Even with its soaking it looked grubby, and she was reminded of the dirty typed sheets of plagiarized scholarship turned out by Roland Granville-Galsworthy.

"Jimmy," said Homer, "have you got some typewriter experts up your sleeve?"

Jimmy was still glowering. He shook himself and spoke grudgingly. "We'll look into it."

Mary took Jimmy's phone call in her library office. "Well," said Jimmy, "his lordship had to admit that it couldn't have been your typewriter that wrote that note. The expert identified it as Charley's, all right. The A tended to skip, the type needed cleaning, the E was tipped off-axis to the right, and so on and so on. But of course the Great Kelly hastened to add that you or anybody else could have used Charley's typewriter. But what this really amounts to is one more little piece of evidence that doesn't do Charley Goss any good."

"But why would Charley forge a note from me to Philip?"

"It's like Homer said. To get Philip away from witnesses, to take away from him the alibi he would have had for the time of the murder."

"But if Charley was planning to kill his father and pin the murder on Philip, why did he wear the Sam Prescott outfit and do it in a public place?"

"Just so that you would ask that very question."

"Oh. Well, did you ask Charley about it?"

"Oh, he denied it. Categorically. Then we talked to Philip, and he admitted receiving the note. He said he found it on his pillow before the parade. Said it got him all excited. (You sure have a powerful effect on us men.) But then he got very angry when you didn't show up. He didn't remember dropping the note, but he supposes he probably did. And it could have blown into the road where Mrs. B. could have found it. And, say, we found the letter that your signature was traced from. It was one of the letters you wrote to Charley from Amherst, that summer when you were working on that female poet. What's her name?"

"Emily Dickinson. What did my letter say?"

"Oh, you needn't worry. It sure wasn't any smoldering billy doo, it didn't even smell pretty. Say, Mary, listen here, were those boys jealous of each other over you?"

"I told you," said Mary. "I turned them down, both of them, a year ago. They weren't really serious about me any more. I just came in handy to take out."

"Is that so? Did they have any other girl friends?"

"Well, no, not that I know of."

"Do you think they still hoped to win you over, either of them?"

"Oh, maybe, but I did everything I could to discourage it."

"Well, I just wonder if one of them could have been all worked up with jealousy on your account, and tried to eliminate the opposition by getting it accused of murder."

"Oh, no, no, I'm sure not." That was absurd. Mary hung up and turned away from the telephone, looking troubled. She folded her arms on the sash of the window and stared out at the rain that had been coming down obstinately for a week now. But she didn't see the lowering sky and the sodden leaves. She was aware only of a heavy feeling of increasing guilt—the more she took part in the investigation of Ernest Goss's murder, the more deeply entangled in suspicion Charley became. Whether you loved someone or not, if they loved you, you had a certain responsibility not to hurt . . .

Alice Herpitude was looking at her, questioning her, picking at her sleeve. Mary had to say it out loud, and admit it to herself as well as to Alice. "Things look pretty bad for Charley Goss."

Then Miss Herpitude did an odd thing. She started trembling all over. Her pale old lips looked thin and tight. "Are you sure?" she said. "Do you think they'll accuse him of—of—?"

"I just don't know," said Mary.

Chapter 44

There is one field beside this stream,
Wherein no foot does fall,
But yet it beareth in my dream
A richer crop than all.
HENRY THOREAU

The rain had stopped at last, and the sun was out, hot and bright. Tom came back from a trip to the Fulton Box Company in Boston with a load of crates for packing corn, five dozen to a crate. He was stacking them in the loft in the barn. John was helping him. "Boy," said John, "I sure wish we still had some cider froze from last year. It sure is hot. Boy, I sure am thirsty."

"We'll try to make more this year than we did last," promised Tom. "And we won't wait for our apples, we'll get some early drops down from Harvard."

"Boy, if we just had a good hurricane, then we'd have plenty of drops."

Tom stopped tossing crates and scowled at John. "Don't you go tempting fate to destroy our apple crop again. Plenty of drops, plenty of cider, sure, but plenty of money down the drain, plenty of kids that don't go to college."

"Well, I love hurricanes anyway."

"You just go in and wash your mouth out with soap. I'm going to get out the John Deere and harrow that corn stubble in

across the way. You go tell Annie. She's been wanting a ride."
Tom mopped his forehead and unbuttoned his shirt. A little later
he was heading the tractor down the dirt road that led past the
cider shed and into the cornfield. Beside the road there were
daisies suspended in the delicate grass. The sun bore down, and
he pulled his visor lower.

Annie straddled his lap and hung onto the big holes in the
metal saddle. "What do you harrow the cornstalks in for,
Daddy?" she wanted to know.

"What else would you suggest we do with them? We harrow
them in and get the dirt turned over, then plant it to rye, and
then the rye grows up pretty green before the first snow and gets
a good root system and grows some more in the spring. Then
we turn it under again. With $2500 a year for fertilizer you've
got to get all the return from a field that you can." Tom bounced
up and down on the seat and went on grumbling. Running a
farm in this day and age was no business for an honest man.
Annie stopped listening. She leaned to one side and looked
back to watch the big rusty plates of the harrow turn over the
ground. One set of disks was curved one way and threw the dirt
out, the other set was curved the other way and threw it back in.
It was wonderful how nice and smooth and flat it left the ground
after churning it up. The dry weedy dusty clods came up dark
brown and clean.

Suddenly over the noise of the tractor there was a clatter and
rattle as two of the disks jammed and scrabbled at something
caught between them. Tom cursed and stopped the tractor.
Annie hopped down and looked. She got excited and clapped
her hands. "It's not a rock," she said. "It's a gun, a big gun."

"It's just a stick," said Tom, looking over his shoulder.

"No, Daddy, really, it is, it's a big old gun." Annie tugged at
it, and hurt herself. She hopped around and flapped her hand.
Tom sighed and got down to go and look. By gad, Annie was
right. It was a gun, an old flintlock, all dirt and rust. Tom stood
up and scratched his head. "Well, I'll be damned," he said.

"Just imagine!" said Annie. "An old, old gun buried in our
field like it says on the sign on the front of our house! And I

saw it first! Can I have it? *Please*, Daddy?"

Tom bent down again, and began to disentangle the gun from the harrow. "No," he said. "I'm afraid not. Unless I'm very much mistaken this gun is going to make Mr. Flower very, very happy."

The gun did indeed make Mr. Flower very happy. It filled him with joy and delight. "Leave it lay!" he chirruped into the telephone. "We'll send out the photographer and some lab men who'll know how to clean it up. Holy horsecollar, now we're getting somewhere!"

"It's not the musket?" said Homer Kelly.

"You betcher sweet life it is."

The harrow had scratched it badly, the metal parts were rusted and the wood was mildewed, but Homer recognized at once the lovely long lines of the old fowling piece Ernest Goss had handed around among his guests on the night of April 18th. Bernard Shrubsole cut notches in a couple of cardboard boxes and he and Jimmy lifted the gun into the boxes with the hooks on a pair of coathangers. Then they took it into Boston to the Department of Public Safety, and handed it over. When Mr. Campbell had worked on it, they carried it down to Lieutenant Morrissey in Ballistics. He was delighted with it. He shone a light down the barrel. "Look at that. See all that black? Wasn't cleaned after the last firing. Didn't you say Ernest Goss cleaned it after it was fired the night before?"

"We did," said Homer. "And you'll notice that the flint is missing."

"This must be the murder weapon, all right. Here, let's give her a try." Lieutenant Morrissey had made some balls from Ernest Goss's mold. He took one of them out of a drawer, along with a patch cut from a piece of linen, a can of black powder and an oilcan. "There was a backwoods rule about powder. You were supposed to put a ball in your hand and pour a cone of powder over it just enough to cover it, and that was the right charge. And then you pour it in, like this. You were supposed to use bear grease or something on the patch, but I guess 3-in-1 is good enough." He oiled the patch, set the gun stock on the floor, laid the patch across the muzzle with the ball on top of it and pressed it down a little way with his finger. Then he pulled out the ramrod mounted under the barrel and used it to push the ball and patch gently all the way down. "Okay, stand back, here she goes." He held the long gun up to his shoulder and pointed it into a barrel filled with cotton wadding. There was a great noise, and two puffs of smoke emerged from the powder pan and the muzzle. Lieutenant Morrissey grinned. He set the gun down and groped in the wadding for the ball. Then he brought it up, squinted at it and beckoned them to the other side of the room where there was a comparison microscope. He placed the ball in a holder and put it under one side of the microscope, and stared into the eyepiece for a minute, adjusting the focus and the light. "Here," he said to Homer noncommittally, "you look."

Homer looked, and Jimmy looked. "Just a lot of miscellaneous scratches on both of them," said Jimmy.

"I told you you wouldn't be able to match up the gun and the ball. You have to have rifling to do that. But, heck, you must be pretty sure this is the gun anyhow, aren't you? Goss owned a musket, his dying word was 'musket,' he was killed with a musket ball, the musket was missing afterwards and here's a musket that was obviously hidden near his house. What more do you want? And to top it off, this one has a missing flint."

"I wish that blasted Boy Scout had seen the thing," said Jimmy. "Look at the size of it. He swore up and down he didn't see it."

Mr. Campbell came in then, shaking his head. "No prints. Not a chance. If there were any there to begin with, the wet ground obliterated them all."

"So it could have been either Charley or Philip," said Jimmy. "I suppose we could confront Charley with it and look grim as if the thing were crawling with prints and stuck all over with identifying bits of hair and microbes and so on, and see if he loosens up at all."

"There's one thing we can be sure of," said Homer. "Whoever hid that gun in Tom's field had a sense of history and a feeling for the fitness of things. Tom Hand planted corn in that field every year on April 19th because old Colonel Barrett did it back in 1775. The murderer knew that, and he knew about the muskets Colonel Barrett laid down in the furrows, to hide them from the British. But that could mean either Philip or Charley."

"Or it could have been Teddy Staples," said Jimmy.

"Or Tom Hand himself, or Mary Morgan."

"If you're going to get ridiculous," said Jimmy sourly, "why don't you throw in old Mrs. Bewley for good measure?"

Chapter 45

Genius, that was it, a stroke of genius. It had occurred to
Homer that there might be some reward in going over Teddy's
journal more carefully. He had brought it with him to the Minuteman Lunchroom and he had been eating his hamburger and
working his way through the entry for April 19th again, when a
passage rose up and hit him in the face.

It wasn't in the main body of the text, it was hidden among
Teddy's marginal observations on wildlife. April 19th began
with a brief mention of the bluebird's nest. Then it went on:

> Assabbett. Saw Tom Hand &
> Finggerling pl. corn . . .

Who was Finggerling? There hadn't been anybody planting
corn with Tom except young John. Oh, of course, "Finggerling"
was Teddy's cute way of saying "one of the little Hands."

> Bl. dk nstting. 6e, spekkled.
> Gossling digging corn. Gl. ind.

Ch. Queer. Oriole's nst . . .

That was all for April 19th. And the passage was like a crypto-gram, full of abbreviations and misspellings. Homer puzzled over it and stared at the page. "Bl. dk nstting. 6e, spekkled" might mean that Teddy had seen a black duck nesting with six speckled eggs. One of the goslings had been pecking at Tom's corn. But that didn't make sense, did it? Ducks had ducklings, not goslings, and one of the ducklings wouldn't be hatched and pecking for its own food if the rest were still eggs, would it? Then Homer felt the small hairs on the back of his neck rise up. If Finngerling meant a young Hand, could not Gossling mean a young Goss? In which case the extra S was not a misspelling at all! What about "Gl. ind. Ch."? Suppose the "Ch." stood for Charley"? The "ind." could be "indicated" and the "Gl." could be "Glass," or binoculars. Teddy had looked through his binoc-ulars and seen Charley Goss digging in the cornfield. *Burying the gun!* What else could he have been doing but burying the gun? Homer slammed the book shut and looked up trium-phantly. There were no two ways about it—he was a genius! Then he frowned. Straight ahead of him was that fool who was always tagging after Mary, Goonville-Ghoulsworthy or some-body. Goonville-Ghoulsworthy gave Homer an unhealthy-look-ing bucktoothed smile. Homer grunted something, and slid out from behind his table. He paid his bill, then put his head down and charged at the door.

Mary Morgan was just coming in with Alice Herpitude, and for a minute they were all tangled up together. Miss Herpitude emerged white and shaken, groping for a chair. "Good heavens, Homer," said Mary. Granville-Galsworthy made himself promi-nent, urging them to his table, pulling out a chair for Miss Herpitude. "Oi hope yew'll join me," he said. Mary bent over and looked anxiously at Miss Herpitude.

Miss Herpitude tried to smile. "I'm all right," she said. But she looked very ill indeed. Homer grumbled his apologies, feel-ing like an oaf. Maybe he'd better join them for coffee, to make amends. Then Rowena Goss spied them through the front window, and she came in and squeezed into the wall seat beside Homer. Granville-Galsworthy transferred his wet gaze from Mary to Rowena, and licked his lips.

Rowena kissed Homer and started scattering her boarding school accent about. It was full of umlauts. "What a püfectly precious place . . ."

Mary looked away in confusion. The kiss hadn't been a warm one, that was the whole trouble with it. It was a sweetly possessive, almost wifely little peck. What did *that* mean?

"Now, Homer, I want you to just drop whatever tawdry thing you're doing and come up with me to the club for tennis. It's a püfectly gorgeous day. See? I've got my Bümuda shorts on under my sküt." She gave him a playful glimpse of a magnificent piece of tan meat. Roland Granville-Galsworthy goggled at it. Howard Swan went by on his way to the cash register, and he goggled at it, too. But Homer's attention was transfixed by the sugar bowl.

"I don't play tennis," he growled. He had to get out of here. He couldn't very well tell her he was about to go out and arrest her brother, could he? What was the matter with the girl anyway? Didn't it matter to her that her father was dead and her mother was in the looney-bin and that it was he himself, Homer Kelly, who was doing his best to clap her brother in a condemned cell? And besides, there was something strange about Rowena anyhow. She was a dish, all right, a real dish, but lately he had begun to have the queerest feeling when he was with her, as though something had been sort of pulled down over his head. She made you feel muffled or something, as though you had a scarf wrapped around you, or a gag shoved down your throat. Homer mumbled his excuses and made his escape, leaving behind him a clumsy assortment of people, crowded between the door and the cash register—one glamorous dish, one frightened old librarian, one bona fide slobbering sex maniac and one thoroughly miserable young woman.

Chapter 46

*◄§ I will come as near to lying as you can drive a
coach-and-four.*
HENRY THOREAU

Mrs. Bewley was sweeping the steps when Jimmy's official car
rolled up the drive. When she saw Homer she beamed at him
and pulled a batch of baseball cards out of her apron pocket.
(Jesus had been sending her messages about the Red Sox and
the Yankees.) "I'VE BEEN SAVING THEM JUST FOR
YOU."

Homer thanked her profusely, pressed her hand and inquired
for Mr. Goss at the top of his lungs. "IN THE BARN,"
screamed Mrs. Bewley.

The barn was back down the driveway near the road. They
walked into the cool dark square of the open door and called for
Charley, but there was no answer. Dolly, the big brown mare,
stood in her stall, looking at them with her large eyes. Jimmy
rubbed her nose and told her he wished she could talk. Dolly
bobbed her head as though she understood, and stretched her
neck and licked his face.

Homer looked at Dolly. Then he slapped his brow. "Oh, for
God's sake, Jimmy, these old-fashioned Yankees. When I said

'Goss,' Mrs. Bewley thought I said 'hoss' . . ." They walked back
to the big house and finally found Charley out in back working in
his garden. He was pulling weeds. He gave a start when their
shadows fell across the ground in front of him, and stood up.
Homer looked at the honest dirt on Charley's knees and had a
misgiving. It just didn't seem possible, there under the hot July
sun, to put together the gardener and the murderer. But then he
remembered that this gardener had been doing a different kind of
planting on April 19th, and he put away the misgiving.

Charley saw something in their faces. He started to talk before they could open their mouths. "You know," he said, standing up beside his twigged pea vines with a bunch of weeds in
his hand, "this reminds me of the times when Philip and I were
kids, and we used to have to go into Boston to the dentist. I was
always scared to death. And the worst part wasn't having your
teeth fixed, it was sitting in the waiting room, waiting for your
turn. I couldn't even read the comic books. So look here, Kelly,
make up your mind, will you? I want to get out of the waiting
room. These comic books are terrible."

Homer said nothing. Jimmy felt awful. He shifted his eyes to
Charley's garden. "What kind of a crop have you got here,
Charley?" he said.

"Oh, tomatoes, summer squash, scallions, carrots, oak-leaf
lettuce, just the usual. Those are radishes over there. We don't
bother with corn because the Hands always let us help ourselves."

"Are you sure you didn't plant any corn this year, Charley?"
said Homer.

Charley's glance turned slowly from his radishes to Homer's
grim face, and met his accusing eyes. So it was true, he was out
of the waiting room. But he made a half-hearted attempt to face
it out anyway, convinced of failure. "What do you mean?"

"I mean we've been bringing in the sheaves, Charley, and
one of them is a mighty funny-looking ear of corn. Tom Hand
ran across your father's old fowling piece when he was harrow-
ing his cornfield. We have the testimony of a witness that you
buried it there, Charley, on the nineteenth of April."

"You mean somebody saw me?"

"Somebody did."

Charley gave up then. "Okay. I hate lying. I'm no good at it anyhow. Sit down." He gestured at the grass and squatted cross-legged on it. "I suppose it was Teddy. I thought I saw him out there on the river. He had his binoculars on me, did he? Has he come back? No? Well, all right, I did bury the damn gun. Look, I'll tell you every single thing I did and thought the whole day, start to finish. You saw me make my famous ride. Well, after that was over, I rode Dolly home, put her in the barn, walked up to my room and changed clothes. It was then about 11:30. I left my Prescott outfit there on a chair, all complete, hat, boots, wig, everything. And then I found this crazy note on my pillow. 'Meet me in the gravel pit,' it said, 'between 12:30 and 1:30 . . .'"

"Meet who? Who signed it?"

"Does it matter? I destroyed it, anyway, the way it said to do, and then after lunch I spent that whole hour hanging around the gravel pit. Since nobody saw me and I saw nobody, it isn't any good as an alibi anyway."

"Was it from Mary Morgan?" said Homer. "Your brother got one, too."

"He did? From Mary?" Charley looked up at Annursnac Hill, his face vacant. "Yes, it was from Mary."

"Then what did you do?" prompted Jimmy.

"Well, I came in the house shortly after 1:30, and found my mother weeping and having hysterics. She had just hung up the telephone. Some fool had called her up and told her that her son had killed her husband with a musket at the bridge and gotten away. She rushed up to me and screamed it at me. Well, I assumed, of course, that Philip must have had a fit and done something nutty. I didn't know then that he had been wearing *my* outfit, and that he was actually trying to lay the blame on me. All I could think of was the danger he was in. I left my mother weeping in her chair and ran to the living room to see if the musket was there. It was still in its place in the cupboard. I didn't see how it could have been the murder weapon because there it was. But I knew one thing that you didn't know. You saw Philip fire the gun the night before, and then you saw my father clean the inside of the gun and wipe it all off on the outside. But I had seen Philip using that same gun that very morning. He came home from the sunrise salute in a sour mood, walked into the house, grabbed up the musket and went out again. Said he was going out to the gravel pits to whale away at a tin can. Said he had to get something out of his system."

"That would account for the missing musket balls. And the dirty barrel of the gun. Go ahead."

"Anyway, I knew he had been the last to fire the gun, and that his fingerprints were all over it again. So I decided to get rid of it."

"Why didn't you just wipe the prints off again?"

"I did. But I was sure there'd be latent prints, or something, or some way of tracing it to Philip—you people have such scientific methods now."

"You do us too much credit," said Homer wryly. "So then you buried it in Tom's plowed field."

"It was the first thing I thought of. I had seen Tom out there with the planter on my ride back home. If it had worked for the Minutemen I thought it might work for me. I ran to the barn for a spade, and then I stood in the trees along the edge of the field to see if Tom was gone. He was, so I buried the gun."

"Why didn't you dig it up again later? You must have known it would get plowed up again when the corn was ripe."

"This will sound silly to you, but I couldn't remember for the life of me where I had buried it. All I had on my mind was the idea of getting it under fast. It was out in the middle there somewhere. And I kept the line of trees along the road between me and the Hands' house. Anyway, my interest in saving Philip's neck began to fade a bit, later on."

"Then you went back to the barn and hung up the spade and came running up to Jimmy as he drove in. Right?"

"That's right."

Homer's small eyes darkened. "Isn't it a whole lot more

likely, Charley, that you were burying the gun you yourself had used to kill your father?" Homer picked up a stick and began drawing circles in the dirt and talking about Ptolemy and Copernicus. Jimmy couldn't believe his ears. What was Kelly up to now?

"Now here's another diagram, Charley. Copernicus put the sun in the middle instead of the earth, and then everything became much simpler. Instead of Ptolemy's crazy orbits with epicycles all over them, Copernicus had the planets moving in simple circles. It was simpler, you see, everything was simpler. Now suppose we do the same thing. Let's take everybody else out of the center of suspicion and put Charley Goss in there. Instantly all confusion vanishes. Isn't that right, Charley? You rode to the bridge a second time, wearing your own outfit, you killed your father and then came home and buried the murder weapon. So simple, like the system of Copernicus. But Teddy Staples saw you. *Charley, where is Teddy? What have you done with Teddy?*"

Charley got up, all color drained from his face. He threw his handful of weeds to the ground. "I swear to you, I don't know what's happened to Teddy. I swear . . . But what's the use? You don't believe me, no matter what I say. It's all gone to hell anyhow."

Homer went in the house to telephone the District Attorney. "Congratulations," said the D.A. He paused to pass the word along to Miss O'Toole. "That's great. And it just proves the rightness of holding off long enough. And I've got to hand it to you, pulling a confession with a scrappy piece of evidence like that Teddy's diary. Yes, sir, Kelly, my boy, I've got to hand it to you."

"It's not a confession. All he admits doing is burying the gun. But I'm about to detain him for a preliminary hearing. Is that all right with you?"

"Sure, it is. Hey, no it isn't either. Couldn't you just hold off till tomorrow?"

"No, I couldn't. What for?"

"Well, look here, Homer, old man. You know how the papers have been after me, you know me, 'The Do-Nothing D.A.'? Well, here's what I want those bastards to do. I want them out there on the front steps of the Goss mansion taking a picture of me, and of you and Jimmy, too, naturally, looking on while one of your boys clamps handcuffs on Charley. How about it? Let's make those bums eat crow. Besides, I sure need a little glory, this being an election year, you know how it is."

"Well, come on out here right now, and bring them with you."

"Aw, Homer, it's practically five o'clock. And you know me, I'm a family man. Besides, I bet it's going to be one of those misty nights. Do those Gosses have cows? You know how scared I am of cows. What's that, Miss O'Toole?" Homer, exasperated, could hear whimpering sounds from Miss O'Toole. Then the D.A. barked into the telephone. "You heard me, didn't you, Kelly? Who's boss around here, anyway? Put a man on Charley, and I'll be out first thing in the morning."

"But, sir," said Homer. The receiver at the other end of the line banged down, and Homer stood looking at the mouthpiece, enraged. Just because the stupid ass was petrified of the country. Homer shouted into the empty telephone line, "They haven't even got any cows, you crazy fool."

Chapter 47

How many water bugs make a quorum?
HENRY THOREAU

Howard Swan was on the line for Jimmy when they got back to the station. "Hello, Jimmy? I just want you to pass the word along to everybody there at Fire and Police to try and get to the Special Town Meeting tonight. The Armory. You know how hard it is to get a quorum in the middle of the summer, and the Water Commissioners are mighty anxious to get this motion through."

"Sure, I'll pass the word along. Tell me again what the meeting's for?"

"To vote $80,000 for resetting the pipe to Sandy Pond in Lincoln. Don't you know about the wet mess we've got there in the Milldam? All that melting snow in the spring, and the spring rains, and then so much rain on and off the last six weeks—the water table rose eighteen inches and overflowed the dam there in Lincoln, washed out the ditch, loosened up the pipe, and the water's coming down here like Noah's flood. Make all your boys turn out, and bring their wives."

"You bet," said Jimmy. Then he hung up and called up Mary

at the library to tell her about Charley Goss. It looked like everything was winding up.

Attendance at Town Meeting was not only a civic duty, it was an entertainment. Everyone who had heard about it came and nearly filled up the Armory. Mary sat near the back of the hall with Gwen and Tom and old Mrs. Hand. Charley Goss was sitting way up near the front with his two sisters. Mary saw Harold Vine, wearing his own clothes rather than a uniform, slip into the row behind them and sit a seat or two away from Charley. Philip Goss, as a member of the Finance Committee, was sitting at a long table in front of the stage with the selectmen. Alice Herpitude scurried into the empty aisle seat next to Harold Vine just as Howard Swan, the Moderator, lifted his gavel to call the meeting to order. There was a noisy pause after the opening prayer while more latecomers were seated, and Mary saw Rowena Goss turn around and radiate at Miss Herpitude. Rowena had her hand out showing Alice something. It was a ring, a giant ring on her left hand. So that was the way the land lay. Homer Kelly was handing out nice little pretty gifts in all directions. A nice spell in jail for Charley, with a pretty little electric chair at the end. A nice pretty ring for Charley's sister, Rowena. And a nice pretty stab in the back for you, my girl. Mary was horrified to discover that her eyes were filmed over with tears. Dimly she saw Homer bungle over a chair on the stage and sit down in his rumpled suit and ghastly tie with a group of other nonvoting observers. Through her head ran some bitter words of Emily's—*finally no golden fleece, Jason sham, too*. One of the other nonvoters on the stage was Roland Granville-Galsworthy. Oh, naturally. The lovely man was slumped down in his chair, his lower jaw drooping down.

Then Mary saw Mrs. Bewley, and she managed to cheer up. God bless thee, Mrs. Bewley, and thrice bless thy fur piece, Mrs. Bewley. Mrs. Bewley was sitting way up front. She was wearing her Clothe-the-Naked dress, and the sharp face of the squirrel around her neck looked clever enough to cast a vote of its own. Mrs. Bewley couldn't hear anything, but she voted both aye and nay on everything anyway.

After a few minor matters had been disposed of, the main article of the evening was moved and seconded. The topic at issue was not very controversial, but a few ex-commissioners of Public Works had objections to make or brilliant alternative solutions, and a few citizens opposed to any rise in the tax rate attempted to fog the issue, suggesting that the cost of the new pipe be laid at the town of Lincoln's door, since it was their dam which was at fault. There were speeches, amendments, motions and countermotions. Howard Swan untangled smoothly all the parliamentary snarls as they came along and moved adroitly toward a vote on the main motion. But then at the last minute there was an emotional speech from a member of the Save Walden Committee. If, he said, the town of Concord was gong to spend all that money anyway, why not use it to turn Walden Pond into a water supply, appeal to the State of Massachusetts to remove the shameful public bathing beach there, and vote at the same time to take away the trailer park and the town dump, thus restoring Walden to its original quiet beauty and creating not only an adequate water supply for the town of Concord but a true shrine to the memory of Henry Thoreau? There was a silence as the justice of this double-barreled appeal was taken in, then a burst of applause. A couple of citizens sprang to their feet to turn the idea into a motion. But the Moderator ignored them and swiftly recognized Philip Goss, who had merely nodded his head and raised an eyebrow. Philip rose and turned to address the town.

Mary had heard him speak before. But she had forgotten (she had forgotten!) how good he was at it. Dreamily she stopped listening to him and let his voice flow over her. It was a wonderful voice, liquid and smooth. Philip spoke in long polished sentences, with that aristocratic accent that stopped just short of Rowena's boarding-school affectations. "Aristoplatitudinous uppercrassmanship," that was what Homer had called it. Typical Kelly sour grapes.

Philip's melodious voice flowed on and on. He spoke of the generous offer of the town of Lincoln to lower the height of its dam, he mentioned the lengthy history of mutual benefit and good will between the two towns, he described the long and thoughtful consideration given to the matter by the boards of both towns, and explained the relatively inexpensive cost of the laying of the new pipe compared to the cost of any other solution, excellent as those solutions might be (gently laying aside alternatives). He praised the diligence and integrity of the members of the Concord Department of Public Works. He never said "I" or even "we." His verbs were always in the passive voice, and everything was "in the best interests of the Town as a whole." HIs audience was persuaded by his high tone, his logic, his sober thoughtfulness, his lack of obvious emotion, his role as an impersonal and perfect instrument of the legal arm of the Commonwealth of Massachusetts, incapable of wrong opinion, utterly to be depended upon. Mary found herself staring at Philip in fascination, barely listening. This man had proposed marriage to her once. She had turned him down, then, without hesitation. But look at him! He could certainly weave a spell. That was all it was, of course, a spell. Mary felt sure that she could snap out of it whenever she wanted to. But not now. . .

The motion passed. Howard Swan called immediately for a motion to adjourn, and the meeting was over. Afterwards in the confusion of standing up and shuffling out there were the usual expressions of satisfaction with the results of the meeting and praise for the competence of the Moderator, whose efficiency had become legendary. If there were one or two who grumbled that their points of view had been overridden, their complaints were lost in the buzz of general approval. "Best darn moderator we ever had. Look at that—we got through the whole warrant by 9:30."

Mary found Alice Herpitude clinging to her arm. "Mary," she said, "what about Charley Goss? Do you really think the police are going to arrest him?"

Mary mumbled that she was afraid so. Miss Herpitude tightened her hold on her arm. And then her next remark suddenly rang out loud and clear across the entire hall. There had been a sudden rap of Howard Swan's gavel to bring order to the hall again, so that he could ask the knot of people blocking the entrances to move on out. But Alice, her frightened eyes on Mary's, her hands tightening on Mary's sleeves, failed to hear, and it was her voice instead of the Moderator's that carried across the room. "I've got to tell you something, Mary, I've got to . . ." Everyone turned to stare at her, and she stopped, her hand going to her trembling lips. Then Grandmaw Hand put her arm around her friend's waist and drew her away. Howard Swan made his announcement, and Mary looked around for Gwen. But instead of Gwen she found Philip Goss at her side. She turned hot and red. Had Philip seen something different in her face as she had sat listening to him? He took her hand and pressed it. He was offering to drive her home. Out of the corner of her eye Mary could see Homer with Rowena. Charley was sloping off towards the stage exit. Had Harold Vine seen him? Yes, he was ambling out that way, too.

"I-I thought I might go home with Alice . . ."

But Alice Herpitude was there, staring up at Philip, her eyes blinking rapidly. Then she looked at Mary. "Oh, no. No, dear. I just—I just think I'll go back to the library and do a little work there."

"Let me go with you," said Mary.

But Miss Herpitude was adamant. She plucked at Mary's sleeve and whispered in her hear. "Never mind. You young people run along. I'm going to write it all down, and then I'll give it to you in the morning. That's much the best way."

But after Philip had driven Mary home and stood in the starlight with her at her front door and gallantly refrained from attempting to kiss her good night (was she disappointed?) and after he had driven off again, Mary walked into the house and announced to Grandmaw that she was going back to the library to see what was troubling Alice.

"I'll come, too," said Grandmaw.

"All right, fine," said Mary. "That's fine."

They found Alice at Mary's desk in Mary's office. She started up violently when she heard Mary's key in the door and stared at them with a whitewashed face. Then she put her hand on her heart. Grandmaw Hand took her in her arms and patted her back. "Whatever is the matter, Alice?"

"Oh, Florence, I'm so afraid. What *should* I do? I just don't know what to do."

Mary turned on the desk lamp in the main hall, and looked around. The rest of the great room was shadowy, with the dark doorways of the other rooms opening off it, and the deep channel of the stack wing a hollow black tunnel. Emerson's high seated figure was a white mass in the darkness, and down from the dim balcony looked the marble effigies of Concord's nineteenth century worthies. Were their eyes still open? Did they never sleep?

Grandmaw began to walk Miss Herpitude up and down. Then Miss Herpitude blew her nose and drew herself up. "Now, now," she said. "I won't be foolish any more. I'm going to tell you the whole story, right from the beginning, and I'll go right on to the end." She waved her arms with the enthusiastic little gesture both of them knew so well and started to walk briskly up and down in the little alcove of locked glass cases dedicated to Henry Thoreau. Then she stopped, and cleared her throat. "You see, I knew it wasn't true, what she claimed. So I couldn't let . . ."

Her sentence was never finished. Down from the balcony above her plummeted interrupting death—a white object, toppling forward and downward, turning over in its descent and striking Alice Herpitude on the back of the head. She fell instantly, her slight figure folded over, slipping and dropping to the floor. The white object fell beside her with a smash, shivering asunder. Mary gave a cry and threw out her hand. She dropped to her knees, looking from the broken, bleeding skull of her beloved old friend to the calamitous scattered shards that were all that was left of the plaster bust of Louisa May Alcott. Then Mary broke into racking sobs, and put her hand over her mouth. Across the huge plaster bun that had formed the back of Louisa's head, smearing the twisted, massy knot of plaster hair, was the blood of the woman she had struck down.

Grandmaw was the one who held together. She ran to the light switch and turned it on. The hall filled with light from the old-fashioned globe lamps and then from the new fluorescent fixtures under the balcony. Then Grandmaw started for the stairs. Mary jerked to her feet. "No, no," she said. "Don't go up there." She ran after her and grasped at her dress, sobbing. "No, no, please, no." But Grandmaw pulled Mary's hand away, and scrambled up the stairs, Mary stumbling after her. At the top Mary used all her tall strength to set Grandmaw aside. Then she stood shaking in front of her, staring down into the black cavern of the stacks. The little signs that announced the catalogue numbers marched into darkness along the rows of shelves. *92 Biography, 88 Travel*. Mary felt a hysterical giggle rising inside her. One of the little signs should be labelled *Murderers,* because whoever had tipped the bust of Louisa May Alcott off the balcony must have filed himself in one of those corridors. They moved slowly down the aisle, turning on the light switches at the ends of rows. It was a foolhardy thing to do. But they found nothing.

"He must have ducked downstairs and gotten out down below," said Grandmaw. She hurried down the stairs again and picked up the telephone on the main desk to call the police. Mary followed her slowly, humping her shoulders, holding the sides of her face in her hands. Oh, Alice, Alice. Charley, was it you?

Chapter 48

Their costume, of a Sunday,
Some manner of the Hair—
A prank nobody knew but them
Lost, in the Sepulchre—
EMILY DICKINSON   •

Homer Kelly came in like thunder, his face extraordinary. He saw Mary leaning, pale and drawn, against the desk and stopped short. Then he turned to the wall and struck it a great blow with his clenched fist. "My God, all the desk man said was 'one of the librarians . . .'"

Then he recovered himself and walked unsteadily over to the Thoreau alcove where Jimmy Flower had already started to work. Jimmy looked at him and shook his head, a sign of pain. There was a bright flash from the photographer's equipment. Homer knelt down and looked at Alice Herpitude. Then he got up and went to Mary and took her roughly by the arm, looking savage. "Where were you?" he said. "Were you anywhere near her?"

Mary laughed lightly. "Oh, I was up on the balcony, pushing over p-pieces of sculpture."

Homer glared at her. Then he saw that one of her eyes looked queer, with the water in it. He turned abruptly away, and started questioning Grandmaw Hand. Grandmaw was holding up heroically, being factual and terse. She was a remarkable woman.

Dr. Allen came in with his bag and bent over Miss Herpitude's body. Mary turned away. The investigation didn't interest her any more. She heard Homer tearing into Harold Vine.

"You lost him? When? How? Why in hell . . .?"

"Gee, I'm sorry."

"Gee, you're sorry," sneered Homer. "Oh, damn it, it's my own fault. There we were, assuming Charley was too much of a gentleman to do anything nasty or unsporting like run away and kill somebody. Oh, my God, why didn't I go on ahead and put him in the lockup this afternoon, in spite of the D.A.?" He beat the side of his head with his fist. "Well, okay, Harold, so what happened?"

"Oldest trick in the book. Charley headed up toward Main Street, just ambling along, then he wandered down the Milldam until he got to Monument Square by the Civil War Memorial (you know, where it says 'Faithful unto Death'), and then he just sat down for a while, leaning against it and looking up at the sky, like looking for airplanes, only there weren't any. I felt awful stupid, walking along about half a block behind him, pretending to be minding my own business. I had to walk past him and go around the corner there by the Middlesex Fire Insurance Company. Well, after a while he got up and went toward the Colonial Inn, where you folks were. I saw you in there, having a beer. He went in, and I went in, and then he went toward the Men's Room. So, stupid jerk that I am, I waited for him to come out. And of course he went out the window. I guess I'm not much good at tailing. He must have known I was there."

Homer turned to Jimmy Flower. "How did he get in here and out again?"

"The coalbin window. All the others were locked from the inside. There wasn't even hardly any coal in it, so he may have got away without any coal dust on him anywhere. I've got the state police out on the road, looking for his car."

But then the phone rang. It was Morey Silverson, at the Goss house. He had found Charley right at home, all tucked up in bed.

"Well, thank God for that," said Jimmy. "What did he say he was doing after he got rid of Harold Vine?"

"Oh, some story about just wanting to walk around for the last time under the stars as a free man," said Morey. "No, he didn't think anybody saw him. He says he cut down to the river behind the Department of Public Works, then worked his way back up to the Milldam, got his car and went home to bed."

"Well, he's in for it now," said Jimmy lugubriously. "And so are we. If it hadn't been for the dumb D.A. . . . Now, we're all going to be drawn and quartered."

Chapter 49

Where was I? . . . the world lay about at this angle . . .
HENRY THOREAU

Next day Mary walked into the police station and resigned her job. Homer looked at her stupidly, then back at his papers. "All right, if that's what you want," he said.

"It is," said Mary. She went back to the library and examined her desk. She looked for the letter Alice had said she was going to write for her and found no sign of it. Then she received a call from Howard Swan. He was speaking for the library trustees. Would Mary be willing to be acting head librarian for a while? Her official appointment would come through later. Mary would. Then Edith Goss came wandering into the library with a long face, seeking sympathy and comfort. She seemed genuinely distressed. Impulsively Mary offered her a job. They would be short-handed now, and she could use an extra pair of hands. Edith could paste labels in new books and put the returned ones back on the shelves. Edith was grateful. She didn't want to go home. She was restless and wanted to start right to work.

The next visitor to get by the patrolman at the door was

Philip Goss. He was leaving town. That was all right because he had been questioned the night before and given a clean bill of health. After dropping Mary off he had gone straight home to his apartment and played poker with George Jarvis and a couple of old friends. He hadn't even left the table. Now he was off to Buffalo to see a client. There were lines of care across his fine forehead. "Hard times," he said briefly. He looked at her meaningfully. "When this awful business is over, maybe we can begin again."

Roland Granville-Galsworthy was going away, too. (Be grateful for small blessings.) He caught Mary out of doors at lunchtime, and said so. Then he wrestled her behind a bush and gave her a hard time. "Oi want a little kiss," he said. Mary was still too much in a state of shock to put up much resistance. The rest of the day she found herself breaking out into convulsive shaking. It would be an enormous satisfaction never to see him again. He claimed to be going back to Oxford to the chair of American Literature. A liar to the end.

Jimmy Flower's men were there part of the day. The District Attorney himself came out, and stood around looking glum, with Miss O'Toole hovering beside him. Homer came in with them, but he hardly spoke to Mary. He merely gave her a moody look and handed her some of the morning newspapers. The headlines were very bad. One of them practically called the District Attorney a murderer of old women. Here was a clever one—LOUISA MAY ALCOTT SLAYS LIBRARIAN.

Mary had had enough of the whole thing. She felt tired and ill. Stiffly she reached up to the shelf labelled *Summer Reading* and started to take out the books on the High School reading list for the fall. Harden over, that will stop the shaking. Tighten up. Her fingers picked tensely at the books. She dropped one. It was *The Poems of Emily Dickinson*. That belonged on the list. She picked it up and put it on the cart. Then she took it off the cart again and looked at it. It was the new copy of Volume I, to replace the copy Elizabeth Goss had stolen from the library. What was the page that had been torn out? Page 123, wasn't it? Mary found the page and glanced at the poem printed on it. "If

the foolish, call them *'flowers'* ..." For once Emily's private
language and crabbed mannerisms irritated her. She flipped the
page over and began reading the poem on the other side—

> In Ebon Box, when years have flown
> To reverently peer,
> Wiping away the velvet dust
> Summers have sprinkled there!
>
> To hold a letter to the light—
> Grown Tawny now, with time—
> To con the faded syllables
> That quickened us like Wine!
>
> Perhaps a Flower's shrivelled cheek
> Among its stores to find—
> Plucked far away, some morning—
> By gallant—mouldering hand!
>
> A curl, perhaps, from foreheads
> Our Constancy forgot—
> Perhaps, an Antique trinket—
> In vanished fashions set!
>
> And then to lay them quiet back—
> And go about its care—
> As if the little Ebon Box
> Were none of our affair!

Suddenly Mary could bear no more. She didn't want to think
about Elizabeth Goss, who had gone mad, or about Ernest
Goss, who had been shot to death, or about Charley Goss, who
was under arrest, or about Alice Herpitude, who had been——
No, no, don't think about it at all! Mary shook herself, snapped
the book shut and thrust it back on the cart. Then she walked
stiffly to Alice's office, shut the door softly and burst into tears.

Chapter 50

✑ *Essential Oils are wrung—*
The Attar from the Rose
Is not expressed by Suns—alone—
It is the gift of Screws—
EMILY DICKINSON

Because of the violent nature of her death, Alice Herpitude's funeral was a little delayed. Mary didn't want to go to it. She didn't know how she could go through with it. If she hadn't had to sing the *Ave Verum* with the rest of the choir she might have begged off. But she had to. So she sat in the balcony of the big white church, facing sideways to the pulpit behind one of the tenors, twisting her handkerchief in her hands. Shrinking back behind the tenor, she looked past the wooden box that held the body of Alice Herpitude to the tiny face of the minister, perched on the tip of the tenor's large nose. Mr. Patterson's words flowed like honey, filling up the empty interstices of her mind, blocking and dulling her awareness. But they must not. Prick up, prick up like thorns the hairs of your attention! Mary glanced over the congregation and remembered the Sunday morning when she had looked down and seen for the first time the look of terror on Alice's face. She had seen it there often after that. Of what had Alice been afraid? The choirmistress lifted her hand, and the choir rose.

"Ave, ave verum Corpus . . ."

In the rainbow coma at the edge of Mary's swimming vision the heads of the mourning friends of Alice Herpitude were distributed in rows like round balls strung on a string, shimmering like decorations from a Christmas tree, glistening with bright glorious lights.

The ceremony at the graveside was over. She stumbled over the dry grass, turning away with the others. She shook her head at Gwen and Tom, and straggled off by herself. But there was someone standing beside her car. It was Homer Kelly. He motioned at the car door. "Get in," he said.

He was saying goodby, too. He would be assisting the County Prosecutor and the District Attorney in the preparation of the case against Charley Goss, working out of the County Court House in East Cambridge, living in his own rooms off Brattle Street. Then, he said, maybe he could get back to his book on Henry Thoreau. Homer stirred uneasily behind the wheel and glanced sideways at Mary. "Concord is too rich for my blood, anyway," he said. "I can't seem to think sensibly about Thoreau or Emerson or any of the rest of them unless I'm far away from here, in Kalamazoo or somewhere."

"You mean you've lost your critical viewpoint? You surely weren't getting fond of them?"

"What do you mean, fond? I don't believe in being fond of the subject of a biography. You lose your objectivity. You've got to be strictly impersonal, strictly impersonal. And all the stuff I've written while I've been here seems to have lost something I used to have. I don't know . . ."

"That cutting edge, perhaps?"

Homer frowned and was silent. He drove out Barrett's Mill Road to her house and slowed down. Then he speeded up again. "Come on. Let's go rent a canoe at the South Bridge Boat House."

Mary wondered dully where Rowena was, but she tried to cooperate. Jump, Mary—jump just a little longer. "Shall we have another fight?" she said.

Homer smiled at her. There was a funny expression on his craggy face. "You know I like to fight with you."

It was a heavy, humid day. Over the river the trees piled up like thunderheads. The duckweed lay in a light green scum along the shore. There were tall spikes of cardinal flower and loosestrife along the edges of the water. They drifted silently. Mary leaned her head back and folded her arms, trying to let her mind go blank. Just listen to the birds, don't think about anything. She turned her head and looked in the pickerel weed for the two that were singing, splitting hairs.

Homer looked at her and started to speak. Then he stopped, cleared his throat and started again. "Charley Goss means a lot to you, doesn't he?"

"Charley? Of course he does."

"I mean—what I means is, how much?"

"Well, he's a friend of mine in a whole lot of trouble, that's how much."

Homer digested this, and seemed satisfied. "What about this Ghoolsworthy fellow? How long have you known him?"

"Just since this spring."

There was a pause. "He seems to think a lot of you," said Homer, looking carefully along his paddle blade. He dipped it clumsily in the water and pulled hard.

"Oh, that's just me," said Mary. "I always seem to attract the goofy, adam's-appley ones."

There was another pause. "I guess they think you're nice," said Homer. His voice was thick.

"Well, I'm not," said Mary. "Not to them. After a while I start snapping at them and saying waspish things. But they just droop their tongues out and look pathetic and hangdog around again. He left today, thank heavens, to go back home."

There was another silence. Then Homer changed the subject. He looked around happily. "Look at that muskrat going along over there," he said. "Look at all those ducks!"

By the time they got back to Mary's house it was dark. At the door Homer pulled her back and started talking huskily, quoting

Emerson. "Mary, Mary," he said, "a link was wanting between two craving parts of Nature. Oh, Mary, come on. Aw, Mary . . ."

Mary had been kissed before, but mostly by men shorter than she was. It made her feel maternal. (Run along to bed now, there's a good boy.) Being kissed by Charley or Philip-was a nose-to-nose affair, like confronted elephants whose long proboscises were always in the way. But this, now, this was different—Mary struggled against it, then gave in, dissolving altogether. Then she struggled again and broke away. The crazy dope was engaged to Rowena Goss. "Oh, go on home," said Mary unsteadily. She pulled at the knob of the screen door. It stuck and she had to kick at it. It wobbled open, and Mary went inside and slammed it, and spoke through the bulge of the screen. "You give me a great big enormous pain in the *neck*," she said. What a stupid thing to say.

Homer stood in the dusk, his white shirt heaving up and down. His necktie was the one that glowed in the dark. "You're like the rest of them," he said bitterly. "Like your precious Emily Dickinson and Ralph Waldo Witherspoon and all the rest. Cold as ice. Well, go ahead. Wear a white dress, why don't you, and hide in your room and write poetry. Go ahead. It doesn't make any difference to me. I'm going to find me a girl with some blood in her veins." He turned on his heel and started walking down the road, breathing hard, his white shirt bobbing up and down. Mary went upstairs, lay down on her bed and cried hard. Then she suddenly remembered that they had come home in her car. "Oh, damn," she said. She got up and went downstairs and out of doors, climbed into her car and drove after him. She leaned over and opened the door on his side. "Here," she said.

He looked at her stiffly, then climbed in. "Holy smoke, turn on your lights," he said. Mary said nothing, struggling to control herself. When she drew up beside his car, he got out. "Thanks," he said.

"It's quite all right. Good night," said Mary. She sobbed all the way home.

Chapter 51

≈§ *Can't you extract any advantage out of that depression of spirits you refer to? It suggests to me cider-mills, wine-presses, Qc., Qd. All kinds of pressure or power should be used and made to turn some kind of machinery.*
HENRY THOREAU

Next day Homer was gone. Charley Goss was held in custody for the preliminary hearing in the Concord District Court. The judge found probable cause to bind him over for the Grand Jury, and he was moved to the jail in Charlestown. Mary forced herself to go and see him. Charley was calm, resolutely cheerful. He had been assigned a lawyer. He felt himself the victim of large forces. "I've always been unlucky, that's all. Some people are born lucky, some aren't."

"But, Charley, you might as well believe in original sin."

"Like Jonathan Edwards? Newborn babies hanging over the fiery pit? Well, maybe some of us are."

He didn't particularly want to talk about his plight. So Mary went back and forth now and then, and passed the time of day. Edith came, too, but her visits irritated her brother, her tongue was so loose and foolish. Rowena stayed home. She was struggling to maintain the dignity and glamor of her position as one of Boston's most ravishing young engaged debutantes. It was difficult, but if anyone could do it with her brother in jail for murdering her father, Rowena could. Mary had discovered with mixed feelings that Rowena's fiancé was not Homer Kelly but Peter Coopering, scion of another of Concord's ancient families, an attractive fellow who could be trusted to keep a well-balanced portfolio, play a good game of tennis and wear sensible, conservative ties. Thinking it over, Mary decided that Homer's love-making the other night had been just the result of his being on the rebound from Rowena. She was wrong, but her whole thinking apparatus was upset and running in strange grooves. She was a little bit crazy that fall, there was no getting away from it. Gwen worried about her. "She was out in the orchard last night, wandering around in her pajamas with her bathrobe on inside out and her hair every-which-way, singing."

"Singing?" said Tom.

"Yes, that Mozart thing they sang at Alice's funeral."

"Look," said Tom, "I can only worry about one of the Morgan girls at a time, and you're the one I've got my eye on. How do you feel, honey?"

"Oh, for heaven's sake, don't be ridiculous. I'm fine. But I don't want my lovely Mary to go getting spinsterish and eccentric. Another thing. Isabelle Flower told me that she saw Mary on the subway the other day, you know, the day she went to the dentist, and after the train started up Mary started to laugh, and after a minute she was doubled up, she was laughing so hard, and everybody was looking at her. Isabelle went up to her and asked her what was funny, and she said she was on the wrong train."

"What's the matter with that? Struck her funny."

"Well, it's just part of the whole picture. I think she needs a vacation. She's at the library all day trying to do everything Alice used to do and everything she used to do, too, and then at night and Saturday and Sunday she's working on those lady Transcendentalists of hers. Sometimes I hear her typewriter thudding away up there in the middle of the night. And when she's not doing any of those things, she's off to East Cambridge to cheer up Charley. And that's guaranteed to bring on the glooms."

"Look, stop brooding. I'm going to get the cider press going and surprise John. He's been nagging at me all summer. Do you feel up to washing some bottles?"

"Don't be silly, of course I do. Grandmaw'll help me after she and Freddy are through with their naps. Where's that long bristly brush we used to have?"

Gwen loved the look of the roadside stand in the fall. There was bittersweet hanging from the top of it, and on the counter there were chrysanthemums in a blue granite kettle and purple eggplants, green acorn squash, white and purple turnips, half-bushel baskets of Tom's apples, so far just the Cortlands and the Macs. Much of the produce was grown by Harvey Finn, but not the apples, of course, nor the cider. The squash and pumpkins were Harvey Finn's, piled up along the road—the Hubbard squash, so graceless in its shape, so delicate in color, like the lichen on the stone walls that bordered Tom's fields, and next to it the humble screaming orange of the pimpled squash and the mellow yellow color of the pumpkins.

Gwen scrubbed out the old washing machine that stood outside the cider shed, and got it ready to wash the burlap cloths. Then she ran the hose over the cheese-frames that would separate the layers of ground-up apple pomace. Tom unloaded the boxes of drops he had brought down from Harvard and carted them into the shed. He dumped some of them into the feeder bin. Then he connected up the hose that ran to the big wooden keg, and adjusted the belts on the little motor that pumped the squeezings into the keg. He oiled the grater-motor. He looked around for the 18-ton truck-jack that was supposed to go between the top cheese-frame and the press, and finally found it in the back of the pickup. It was rusty and dusty, so he blew on it, and wiped it off. Gwen trundled John's old metal wagon across the road with two cartons of clean gallon bottles on it, unloaded them and picked up some dusty ones. "All set?" said Gwen.

"Yup," said Tom. He turned on the switch of the pump, then flipped the toggle on the grater and turned to dump a box of apples in the feeder. There was a most tremendous terrible noise.

"Jesus X. Christ," said Tom, and he grabbed at the switch on the grater. The racket ceased.

"Some of those dern kids must have put rocks in it," said Tom. He stepped up on the edge of the press where the words American Harrow Company were painted on and looked into the grater.

"Oh, fer. . ."He stepped down again.

"Well, what is it?" said Gwen, standing still with the handle of the wagon in her hand.

Tom, as though he couldn't believe what he had seen, climbed back up again. Then he got down again and turned to Gwen. "I'm sick and tired of it," he said. "I'm just plain sick and tired of having muskets and pistols and machine guns and various odd pieces of artillery showing up on this place and stripping the gears of my machinery. Next thing you know we'll find a howitzer in the raspberry patch and it'll blow us all to blue blazes. I hope it does. I'm sick and tired of it. Those blades have got big bites taken out of 'em. Look at 'em."

He helped his wife up and she looked into the grater. "For goodness' sake, Tom, it's another old gun."

"That's what I said, didn't I? I said it's another old gun."

"But they looked around in here, the police, they looked all over."

"Yes, but don't forget they were looking for a gun about the size of a canoe. They never would have thought of looking in the grater. It's only eight or nine inches across."

"Tom!" Remember I told you Freddy saw someone on a horse, he called it a funny lady, someone who broke his balloon—that day, April 19th? Well, suppose it *was* the murderer, the way we thought—"

"Suppose it was? We kept our mouths shut to keep Freddy out of it."

"Yes. but the point is, he was right here, right outside the cider shed. And he broke Freddy's balloon. It's almost as though he wanted to draw attention to his being there—because of the gun—so that the gun would be found right away." Gwen climbed up on the press again and looked at the gun. "Look how big the hole is. That's plenty big enough to have fired a musket ball. Oh, golly, Tom, I'll bet that's the gun that killed Mr. Goss, not the other one. And the murderer *wanted* it found. Why?"

"Say," said Tom, "remember those boxes of apples that turned up in the spring, way last May or June? I'll bet somebody brought them to get us to make cider so we'd find the gun right away." He brooded darkly. "Unless somebody's just plain got it in for this farm and all my blankety blank machinery."

Chapter 52

≈ Let him not quit his belief that a popgun is a popgun,
though the ancient and honorable of the earth affirm it to
be the crack of doom.
RALPH WALDO EMERSON

"So what do you think of that?" said Jimmy. "And Charley's
fingerprints on it as pretty as can be? I'll tell you how I feel,
and that's a whole lot more comfortable. The pistol's so small
Charley could have stuck it right in his pocket. So the problem
we had with Arthur Furry not seeing any weapon is solved.
Good boy, for sticking to his guns. Ha, ha, no pun intended."

The D.A.'s voice sounded tired and buzzy over the phone.
"Was it one of Goss's old guns, too?"

"Sure. It was one of a pair of flintlock duelling pistols he had
in that highboy." Jimmy looked at his notes. "Engraved Wog-
don and Barton, made in London around 1800. That kind
usually came in a case, so they tell me, a fancy case fitted up
for two pistols. But Ernie didn't have a case, so they just lay
loose in the drawer. So nobody noticed that one was gone.
Charley should have spoken up that it was missing. So should
his brother, for that matter. And Kelly cussed himself out for
not having noticed it. You should've heard him."

"What about the flint?"

"Well, of course, this one still has a flint. Which is annoying. The only flintlock without a flint in the whole collection was the musket. But this thing has Charley's prints on it, and the ball fits it perfectly, and it's been fired. The prints were well preserved. That shed's nice and dry, but not too hot."

"But the musket? What about that? Why did Charley bury that?"

"Well, that's one of the things we've got to work out yet. We grilled Charley and he said, yes, he'd killed his father twice, once with the musket and once with the pistol. Then he denied knowing anything about the pistol. Said he must have handled it, putting it away the night before, but he hadn't seen it since."

The District Attorney rocked gently in his chair with the phone tucked against his ear and looked at the beer can he was holding on his stomach. "What about Charley's lawyer? Has he requested a delay in the trial?"

"No. He wanted to, but Charley wouldn't hear of it. So all we've got is ninety days."

"Hmm," said the D.A. sleepily. "Don't forget this is an election year. Let's hurry it along faster than that. I'd like to try this case myself, and get a fat conviction before November 4th."

Miss O'Toole, listening humbly in the corner, raised her eyebrows and looked worried. The last time her boss had tried a court case her elaborate system of communication by notes had proved impossibly cumbersome, and the D.A. had fumbled badly. She would have to think up something else. What about a set of hand-signals? If she touched her hair it would mean, "No further questioning." Putting her glasses on would mean, "Make an objection." Yes, perhaps that could be worked . . .

Chapter 53

✑§ *Politics is, as it were, the gizzard of society, full of grit and gravel.*
HENRY THOREAU

The Governor of Massachusetts had called Homer into the State House for a confidential chat. It was a nice day, and Bulfinch's gold dome rose glorious over Beacon Hill. Far below it in his handsome office in the west wing, the Governor was lending his prestige to an inglorious proposal by a certain powerful member of the State Legislature.

"Look here, Kelly," said the member of the legislature, "I've had my eye on you for a long time. Now I suppose you know how your county leaders feel about that chowderhead, the present incumbent of the District Attorney's office? With this last disaster of his all over the front pages he hasn't got a chance at the polls in November. Now it's my understanding by way of the grapevine that this blunder wouldn't have happened at all if the dumb boob had taken your advice. Now here's what I propose. I want you to resign from the case and oppose him in the party primary. You're a shoo-in. You can't lose. We'll back you to the hilt, all the way."

Homer refused point-blank, but the Governor poured on oil
and refused to take a final no. "Just think it over for a while. If
ever anybody was destined for high office in this Commonwealth it's you, Kelly. You've got the right kind of name and at
the same time you're a natural for the Brahmins. I don't know
how you're going to get anywhere if you refuse the help of your
political advisors. Think it over. That's all we ask."

Homer found his way back to his apartment gloomily. It was
a set of furnished rooms on the top floor of one of those large
wooden purplish-brown houses seen nowhere in the world but
in the vicinity of Brattle Street in Cambridge, Massachusetts.
The furniture was a scrappy mixture of Grand Rapids Baroque
and Rooming House Mission. Homer walked over to the window of the room his landlady referred to genteelly as his "sitting
room," and looked out. Beyond Longfellow Park he could just
see some of the sycamore trees along Memorial Drive and a
glint of the Charles River. Harvard boys and Radcliffe girls
would be soaking up the sun's warmth on the riverbank, more
aware of each other than of the books they had brought along to
study.

Damn them all anyway. Homer turned away suddenly and sat
down at his desk. It was a skimpy affair with peeling striped
veneer. There was an open notebook on it, but he ignored the
notebook and stared absently at the wall. Then, abruptly, he
wiped his hand across his eyes. It was a new gesture he had
adopted in an attempt to sweep away the interior vision of a
face, a vision so constant that it was like some celestial phe-
nomenon or ring around the sun. He could shake his head and
turn away from the sun, but then the face would rise silently
again from the opposite horizon, shining like a sun-dog or
bright flaring spot in the sky.

Oh, the hell with it. Homer took his glasses out of his
pocket, balanced the bow that was held on with adhesive tape
on his right ear and frowned at the open page of his notebook.
Half of the page had been written last winter, before he had had
the bad fortune to go out to Concord at all. He read it over.

The sage himself admitted his inadequacies as a husband, and Henry Thoreau continually shrank from his friends. The indriven ego, the denial of sexual drives, the glorification of asceticism and the sublimation of emotional frustrations into vague spiritual strivings—it is clear that the transcendental movement in Concord was the febrile outpouring of sick natures as surely as the ravings of a De Sade were diseased at the other extreme.

Under this firmly written, neat paragraph there was another, scrawled in a larger, looser hand. It was a non sequitur, written barely two weeks ago.

From Nine Acre Corner to Walden Pond, from the Great Meadows to the Mill Brook, these men and women knew their Concord. They knew it in all seasons and all weathers. And upon these hardy descendants of the Puritans the New England landscape with its white winters, its honeyed springs, its languorous summers, its riotous falls wrought a curious spell. Concord became for them a hallowed place, encrusted with tradition, heavy with meaning, cathedral-like with symbolism. They very nearly invented Nature for themselves, ripping it bodily from the banks of the Sudbury River or plucking it like wild flowers in the fields, and letting it grow from the pages of their journals. Beside Thoreau's woodchuck, what price Shelley's skylark? Who would exchange Emerson's rhodora for Wordsworth's daffodils?

Homer stared at the second paragraph, then slammed the notebook shut and reached for a cardboard file labelled "Goss case." His phone rang.

It was Letitia Jellicoe. "Letitia who?"

"Jellicoe. Miss Letitia Jellicoe. I've been away. I was visiting my sister-in-law. Oh, isn't it terrible. My best friend. Alice was my best friend. I said to my landlady, isn't it terrible. And she said, didn't you read it in the paper. And I said, no, it wasn't until I got home this morning that I heard about it on TV. I was eating breakfast at the time. Mercy, if I didn't choke. There was Cheerios all over my robe."

"Are you referring to Alice Herpitude's death?"

"You are correct. And I can tell you something about her that nobody knows but me. She knew something about Elizabeth Goss. Some secret from when they were girls in Amherst!"

"Alice Herpitude knew a secret about Elizabeth Goss? How do you know?"

There was a pause while Miss Jellicoe looked for a dignified way to express herself. "Well, I used to be a telephone operator in Concord, back in the old days before automatic dialing, and I sometimes heard things. Without intending to, naturally. Sometimes you just can't help—"

"No, of course you can't," said Homer, lying comfortably. "Do you know what the secret was, Miss Jellicoe?"

"No. I just know there was some secret Elizabeth claimed to have, and Alice didn't believe it."

"Don't you suppose it was just some gossip that was going around?"

"No, I distinctly remember Alice's saying, 'Don't worry, Elizabeth. I'll keep your family secret because I don't believe it anyway.'"

"That was all she said? A family secret?"

"Yes. Then Elizabeth said something very rude. She said, 'I can hear someone breathing' (as if I had been listening on purpose!) and I switched off."

"Hmmm. Well. Thank you, Miss Jellicoe, thank you very much for calling. Let's see—Elizabeth Goss came from Amherst, Massachusetts and Alice Herpitude did, too. I believe you're right about that."

"Yes, they'd known each other all their lives. So Alice knew this awful secret!"

Homer hung up as soon as he decently could. Then he stood staring at the telephone. Old Mrs. Hand had told him Alice Herpitude's last words. How did they go? "I knew that what she claimed wasn't true," or something like that. Had Alice been talking about Elizabeth Goss? At the back of Homer's head there began to arise the dimmest, ghostliest wisp of an idea. He took a railroad schedule out of his pocket and consulted it. Absent-mindedly, then, he picked up his briefcase and fumbled in a drawer for a clean shirt. There was a train from Back Bay at 2:30 . . .

Chapter 54

Fill in all the background, first. Homer Kelly lay at his ease on
a settee, ignoring the handsome homelike atmosphere of Amherst's Jones Library, leafing idly through old local papers.
Elizabeth Goss had been Elizabeth Matthews before her marriage. When would she have announced her engagement? He
started with the fall season of the year before and studied the
society pages, examining solemnly the yellowed photographs of
dewy young brides in bobbed hair. Most of them were dogs.
Their shapeless finery didn't help, and they had these tiaras that
they wore low down on their foreheads, like Indian maidens.

But, say, here was one with class. *Post-deb announces en-*
gagement to Harvard man of Concord, Massachusetts. Well, by
jeeminy, here she was. It was Elizabeth Goss, nee Matthews.
"Mr. and Mrs. Edmund Matthews announced the engagement
of their daughter Elizabeth at a supper party yesterday evening
at the Lord Jeffery Inn . . ." Homer's eyes ran on, then did a
doubletake and started over. Could this be the right Elizabeth
Matthews? She wasn't engaged to Ernest Goss, she was en-

gaged to . . . but that was impossible. Homer looked at the photograph again. No, there was no mistake. It was Elizabeth Matthews, all right. So she had had another romance . . . here was a
can of worms with a mightly peculiar smell . . .

Sniffing the new scent, Homer reared up off the settee and
nosed around among the bookshelves. After a while he went to
the desk and inquired the way to the Town Hall.

"Turn left, then right to Main Street, then left on Main across
the green. It's just a block or two this side of Emily Dickinson's
old homestead. You can't miss it."

Homer picked up his briefcase and did as he was bid. The
Town Hall turned out to be a grandly ugly Romanesque struc-
ture so glowering and heavy that Homer pictured the earth beneath it densely compacted all the way to China. The Town
Clerk's office was down the hall to the right. The Town Clerk
was out to lunch, but the girl behind the counter took some of
the big canvas-covered folios of Births, Marriages and Deaths
from the vault where they were stored and let Homer pore over
them. When the Town Clerk came back from lunch, he found
Homer crouched over one of the big volumes, his enormous
forefinger moving along a line like that of a child just learning
to read, his lips mumbling the words over and over.

The Town Clerk examined him with sharp analytic eyes.
Making instant character analyses was his specialty. Take this
chap, now. Odd-looking fellow. Giant. Obviously illiterate.
Stringy brown hair cut in big scraps. Horrible tie. And say, look
at that forefinger. Spatulate. He should have guessed. A crimi-
nal type if ever there was one. "What do you want, mister?"
said the Town Clerk nervously.

Homer lifted his eyes and bored holes that went all the way
through to the back of the Town Clerk's head with the keenest
glance seen in Massachusetts since Daniel Webster's. "Tell me,"
he said, "how long is the normal gestation period for human
beings?"

Thrilling voice the fellow had. Come to think of it, he had
very large prefrontal lobes. Obviously a fellow with plenty on
the ball, a professor or something. Funny question though. "I

dunno. Nine months, isn't it? Nine and a half?"

Homer stared at the Town Clerk. His lips moved. Then he picked up his briefcase and whirled it around in the Town Clerk's office in a huge circle. "*Wahoo!*" he said. "Me plenty heap awful smart!" The Town Clerk had to rectify his character analysis all over again. The man was a dangerous maniac, he should have seen it right away.

But Homer was going down the front steps three at a time. He was out on the street, charging back to the library, his mind alive with a wild idea. He tossed his briefcase on a library table and started assaulting the card catalogue and snatching books off the shelves. After two hours of tearing the meat out of them, he left their scattered carcasses on the table and ran down the street to the College Drug Store. He found the phone booth in the corner and wedged himself into it by a technique he had worked out years before. (You backed in, squeezed yourself into the seat, lifted your right leg and planted it on the farther wall, and then, ever so gently, you shut the door.) He began to make a series of long-distance calls.

Chapter 55

I am perfectly sad at parting from you. I could better have the earth taken away from under my feet, than the thought of you from my mind.
HENRY THOREAU

Everyone was asleep except Mary. She had been up since four o'clock, working on her transcendental women. Now she was feeling sleepy again. She propped her head on her hand and looked out her bedroom window to where the elm tree branches made an armpit. In it the morning star hung dazzling. There were red puddles in the hollows of the pavement, like pieces of morning sky let into the road. It was time for some breakfast. Mary got up from her desk, watching the star. It followed her shuffling footsteps with a wobbling retrograde motion. All she had to do was set the pattern and the star fell in with the plan . . . Pattern again! Why must she be so obsessed with pattern?

But *they* had all been obsessed with pattern, too, those Transcendentalists. They had all leaped from the particular to the general, looking for the pattern in the daily jumble. Why? What was the matter with the particular anyhow? Why couldn't she just be-there-and-how-do-you-do? Why did the bare bones of a simple act like walking to the stove with a pan of water have to flesh out into something alive and complicated, with skin and hair growing on it? (How many other women had carried water, in what vessels, from what source? Oh, forget it. This is *my* water, *my* pan with the nicked porcelain, *my* soft-boiled egg, and shut up to you. It's not part of any pattern, it's my breakfast.)

The trouble with the layers of meanings that grew like a fungus all over the little pieces of the particular was that the symbol might grow too huge, the stratification of meaning piled on meaning might become too ponderous, too heavy, too thick. One might start wandering in a forest from which there was no escaping; where every simple act and every trivial object became so much more that itself that one went mad. Mary shook her head and stared out the window. On this side of the house she could see the transparent moon. It was setting into a red horizon, looking angry and mottled, like a lump of amber with a dead fly caught in it. Red sky at morning, sailor take warning. That's right, there was supposed to be a storm brewing. But now there was no wind at all. Even Freddy's diapers hanging on the line hung limp and still, as stiff and orderly as dentil blocks on an architectural molding—a pure pattern, rosy in the dawnlight.

. . . But if you went mad, then you wouldn't be a pattern any more, would you? You would be one-of-a-kind, unique, all alone by yourself, yourself-in-yourself, crying in the forest. Look at Mrs. Goss. She had been more patterned and stylized that anybody—until she had forgotten the pattern altogether and gone crazy. Now she was, indeed, one-of-a-kind, crying in the forest . . .

Mary sat down and looked at her breakfast. The dishes matched. She wanted to break them. She got up and found a bottle of ketchup and shook it on her egg. It tasted terrible, but at least it wasn't old patterned ceremonial salt and pepper. The blue willow plate had a crack in it. Mary looked at the crack and blessed it. Among the apples in the bowl on the table there was one with a spot on it. She reached for it suddenly and bit into the spot.

There was that letter from Philip, leaning against the sugar bowl. Mary didn't want to read it. She knew what it would say. It would be Philip's pattern, nothing surprising. Philip didn't have any spots, that was the trouble with him. There was poor Charley in jail, all covered over with spots like a bad apple. He had fallen away from the pattern. He had run away from the template. He didn't fit the jig, so the jig was up. The letter looked at her. Read, Mary, read. Jump, Mary, jump. No, thank you, I don't want to jump today.

Of course, that was her transcendental ladies all over. They couldn't jump. Emily Dickinson had refused to jump. Margaret Fuller had wanted to jump badly, but she didn't know how, and she kept blundering clumsily all over the rope. There were the Parcae, those grim women in the Grecian robes, turning and turning the rope, setting a pattern for you to leap and jump to, chanting it for you—

> *Teddy bear, teddy bear, turn out the light;*
> *Teddy bear, teddy bear, say good night.*

Then *snip*, with their big scissors, and *out go you*. And sometimes it was Double Dutch they swung for you, and you had to hop and leap, frantically, between two ropes at once.

But you didn't have to jump. The little girl who was leaning in, getting ready, could just turn away and run, with her arms over her face. That was what Emily had done. She had run away. And that was what Henry Thoreau had done, too, after all, when he went to live in the woods. He had refused to jump.

Mary went upstairs and lay down on her bed and closed her eyes. The jumping rope disappeared. Instead there was that procession again, with the barrel-vaulted triumphal arch and the sublime figures and the glorious flags. She could see it clearly now, she could see it all so clearly! Now at last she could see what it was all about. It was a funeral, such a pretty funeral! Alice's? Teddy's? Ernest Goss's? No. There was the glass box, like Snow White's, with the little girl inside. It was herself, little Mary, the little girl who had refused to jump. She was asleep in there, she was dead in there—that's what the procession was all about.

Mary opened her eyes again, with the tears clinging top and bottom. Between the edge of the bed and the wall there was something wedged. It was Freddy's teddy bear. Mary picked it up and laid it against her face. Teddy bear, teddy bear, say good night.

Chapter 56

≈⟩ *There was displayed a Titanic force, some of that force
which made and can unmake the world.*
HENRY THOREAU

The wind was rising. "Oh, boy," said John, "we're going to
have one after all."

"Well, I suppose it could have been a whole lot worse," said
Tom. "We've got all the Macs and Cortlands picked. The Bald-
wins are what will get it."

"Maybe it will go out to sea," said Gwen.

The weather bureau had given everyone plenty of warning. At
Vanderhoof's Hardware Store there were kerosene lanterns in the
window and big bags of charcoal. Woolworth's did a land-office
business in candles. People with pump-driven wells started filling
bathtubs and gallon jugs and washtubs with water. Tom routed his
whole family out to pick the apples that were ripe. Harvey Finn
drove over with his sons to help. There was no school, and the
children ran up and down between the trees with bushel baskets,
shouting with excitement, glorying in the holiday. "Silly kids,"
grumbled Tom, ramming his ladder into the top of a tree, "it's their
college educations that are going to get blown all to hell." Grandmaw was out in the orchard, too. She walked around the trees

picking all she could reach from ground-level, her grey hair blowing out from her hairpins. Gwen stayed in the house fixing lunch and worrying a little. She had a suspicious backache, and the feel of her burden was different. Her center of gravity seemed lower, and she waddled around, leaning backwards to make up for it. How tiresome if she should have to be a pest just at this time. As if Tom didn't have enough on his mind. Tom came in to snatch a sandwich, and looked at her closely.

"How are you feeling?"

"Oh, fine, fine."

Mary kept the library open until noon, then sent her staff home. Edith Goss lingered in the doorway. "Don't worry," said Mary. "Go on home. That brick house of yours is solid as a rock." When Edith was gone, Mary wandered back to her new office and stood looking out at the storm. The high winds were only beginning to rise, and the brushing of the branches against Alice's window was fumbling and ineffectual, like the hand of a wandering spirit desperate to get in. Mary turned away abruptly and went to the desk. The desk had been Alice's, too, and it had cost Mary some pain to transfer her belongings to it. There was one large drawer she had left untouched. It contained Alice's hat, the eruption of pink feathers she had worn so often in church. Mary looked at the drawer. Then she reached down and pulled it open, and looked at the hat. She took it out and put it on the desk-top. Alice had left all her worldly goods to Mary, and so she supposed the hat was hers, now. So was Alice's house, down on Fairhaven Bay. So was the little rowboat tied at Alice's landing. So were the wooden swing-seats in her front yard. Heavens, what would the storm do to them? There was no one there to pull the boat up and check the house against the strong winds that were coming. Mary pulled on her coat. She must go and take care of things herself, not because they were her possessions but because they had been Alice's. She locked up the library and drove her car out Route 2 and down the mile-long dirt road that led to Fairhaven Bay. There was the fork where the road led to Teddy Staples' place. So that was two houses down by the river that had no occupants any more. And Charley Goss was gone, too, to sit out the hurricane in jail. Jails don't blow away. But lives do—they blow out. A mighty wind had picked up Charley and it was whirling him to destruction.

The tops of the pine trees were swaying as Mary got out of her car. The water of the river was almost black, and small waves crowded its surface. She stared at the river. There was something odd about it. The waves were going the wrong way. The wind was coming from the wrong direction, that was why, and wrinkling up little white crests all over it. She turned and looked at the swings. They were rocking gently in the wind. She wouldn't be able to move the frame, but perhaps she could loosen the swinging seats and drag them under the high front porch. But there was the rowboat, too. Better tend to that first. She walked down to the boat-landing and looked at the small grey-painted rowboat. It was bobbing up and down, tied to the dock with a sort of bowknot. Alice had tied that knot herself. Mary loosened the knot and looked out across the water. The river was high, there had been so much rain. The island was a real island again, the way it had been in the spring, with the water surrounding it even on its landward side, hiding all but the tops of the buttonbushes. Mary stopped still with the rope in her hand. Wasn't that someone moving about on the island? Something had come between her and the sun, which was shining out now and then under the streaking clouds. She shaded her eyes. Yes, there was a figure there at the edge of the trees. Now it was gone.

Someone must be camping there. There was no boat that she could see, but whoever it was must have come by boat. Was someone in trouble there? If they had been camping for more than twenty-four hours they wouldn't know about the hurricane. Even if they knew, there was very little time for them to come away. Perhaps it was children, camping out. With a sudden movement, Mary pulled off her shoes and stockings, left them on the landing and waded out, pushing the little rowboat before her. If there should really be a high wind it would be the trees along the shore of the island that would be dangerous. They were partially submerged, and their roots probably all leaned one way, clutching the spongy soil for support against the southwesterly prevailing breeze. With the wind coming from the other side they would go over like candle-pins. She climbed into the boat, lifted out the oars one by one and inserted them into the oarlocks. Looking over her shoulder she started to pull. Keep abreast of the waves, now, and a little pointed into the wind. Don't broach them sideways, or you'll be swamped. Choppy going. Pull *hard*, *hard*. Overhead the clouds were in clots, surging like pulses, pulsing like throbs. There was no rain and no thunder, only the ever-rising wind, but the white birch trees in the dark woods were like forked lightning. The wind in her face began to be laden with torn leaves and pieces of twigs.

And there was that sweet smell. Mary had forgotten that heavenly smell. With the dismemberment of the trees, the breaking off of branches, the sundering of leaf-stems, the snapping of the living wood there went a wonderful smell. Was it the bleeding sap from millions of open wounds? Mary drank it in—it was so sweet, so fresh. One might not mind dying if from one's broken body there arose so good a thing.

Pull. Pull. Mary glanced over her shoulder again and adjusted her stroke until the boat was headed for the small sloping landing place there on the bay side of the island. The trees on this side were rooted on high ground. Their trunks swayed and their boughs pumped strongly up and down. The sound of the storm had risen to a roar, and above the roar there was the occasional snapping sound of slender branches breaking loose. Mary got out and pulled the boat up on shore and turned it over to let out the water that had slapped in over the gunwales. The noise of the wind was so steady and so loud that her own movements seemed soundless. Her bare feet were cold. She turned and hurried to the clearing where the giant pine tree stood. This was low ground, and the pine stood in water. There was no one here. Perhaps she had been mistaken, and there was no one on the island at all. A fool's errand. Mary pushed through the blueberry bushes and sumac on the other side of the clearing. Then she fell.

Chapter 57

With Midnight to the North of Her—
And Midnight to the South of Her—
And Maelstrom—in the Sky—
EMILY DICKINSON

It was a deep hole. She hadn't seen it because it was covered over with a broken branch. But her foot had gone right to the bottom, and down she went, falling awkwardly on top of something that lay in the hole. Her foot twisted viciously in the crevice, and she had a tussle getting it out again. There was something very wrong with it. Could it be broken? Perhaps it was only a bad sprain. Now she was in a fix, for sure.

She must pull herself up and try to hobble. Mary reached one arm forward to lean on the great round boulder that filled the hole. But it wasn't a boulder—it was something that felt like leather. Leather and metal. She brushed aside the hemlock branch that lay across it and looked at it.

It was a chest. There had been the black box on Elizabeth Goss's dresser, and the bait box with the letters in it, and now this—an old-fashioned round-topped trunk. It looked like the kind that Long John Silver would dig up on Treasure Island, all filled with pieces of eight and jewels and pearls. And this was an island, too. She was in a dream of Treasure Island. Mary leaned on one thigh on the edge of the hole, with the storm raging about her, the wind clawing and tearing at her hair, her wounded foot lying at an ugly angle beside her, swelling and throbbing *broken, broken*—and opened the chest.

There were no jewels inside it. Just notebooks, ordinary three-ring school notebooks. Mary lifted them out, one by one, and glanced at them, wrenching her body around so that the rattling pages would be protected from the wind. How funny— someone was a student of Emily Dickinson. Familiar lines jumped out at her. The thickest notebook had a title, *Rowing in Eden*. That was Dickinson, too. *(Rowing in Eden, Ah, the sea! Could I but moor tonight in thee!)* There was a subtitle, too, written in by hand. Mary squinted at it. The light was bad and she had lost her glasses . . .

The True Story of Emily Dickinson's
Romantic Attachment

Oh, for heaven's sake, another one of those things. It was probably another of Ernest Goss's crazy fake documents, hidden like his letters beside the river.

But then she read a little more and changed her mind. This document was very different. It was no clever mimicry or burlesque of the real thing—it *was* the real thing, a work of profound and careful scholarship. And the suggested lover was none other than Henry David Thoreau. Mary's adventurous mind reeled and rejoiced, and she read on, hardly noticing the pitch and terror of the storm, brushing aside in annoyance the leaves that smacked against the page, heedless of the flailing fall of a tall pine tree behind her, although the dirt that was shaken from the snapped roots leaped upon her back! She neither saw nor felt nor heard . . .

The paired symbols were so daring, yet so sound. Henry had had a dream of a mountain that was his life—and Emily was the daisy at the mountain's foot. They had gone boating on the river *(Rowing in Eden)*—so Emily was the little boat, the little brook, and Henry was the mighty sea . . . it was enchanting.

And to her flower he was the drunken, fainting bee . . .

What other revelations were there? Mary reached for another notebook and opened the cover.

Facing her was Elizabeth Goss. It was an old photograph, but it was Elizabeth without a doubt, as she had looked twenty or thirty years ago. And under it, in the same handwriting (Mary bowed over it, peering at it)—"a direct descendant of the union of Emily Dickinson and Henry Thoreau"—good God.

But that was impossible. That Emily and Henry might have met one another was plausible—she would love to believe it—but this was going pretty far—Elizabeth Goss *a direct descendant of the union of.* . . . (Mary shifted her weight, and the hurt in her foot became a spasm of pain.) But, wait—wait! There was the black box in Elizabeth's room, with the coil of red hair—*Great-grandmother's!* Was it Emily's? Could it be Emily Dickinson's, that wealth of auburn hair, that was "bold, like the chestnut burr"?

Revelation beyond revelation—then the box, the black box could itself be the Ebon Box in the poem, on the page that Elizabeth had torn out of the book because it came so close to her secret truth. Elizabeth's box was black because it was ebony, and it had contained the "curl" and the "flower" and the "trinket"!

But the poem had mentioned something else. Mary mumbled the words over, closing her eyes to the wind and the storm and the pain—

> To hold a letter to the light—
> Grown Tawny now, with time—
> To con the faded syllables
> That quickened us like Wine!

Where was it then? Where was the letter?

What, what? Someone was shouting at her. Mary looked up. There on the other side of the hole stood Howard Swan. Howard? What was Howard doing here? Then she remembered. She had come to take him away. But it was too late now. They must find shelter from the storm, from the falling trees. She struggled to her feet, shaking her head over her wounded foot, smiling at Howard, apologizing. She clutched the two notebooks under her arm. She couldn't leave them behind.

Howard had a shovel in his hands. He didn't make a move to help her. He just stood with his mouth open, staring at her, his light hair streaming upwards around his bald head like a ghostly crown. Then he lifted the shovel over his head, as if he were going to smash something. He took a step forward. His lips were moving. Mary couldn't hear. "What did you say?" she shouted at him. But she could read his lips. He was saying the same thing over and over, "I'm sorry, Mary. I'm sorry, Mary..."

He must mean, about her foot. But she could manage. She showed him, hopping a little way, holding on to a tree. It would be all right.

Then suddenly she understood, and she faltered backwards. Howard jumped across the hole, and made a rush at her. The shovel—it was for her. He meant to kill her. He was sorry! Mary turned and scrambled into the clearing, running on both feet, hardly favoring her lame leg, ignoring the hideous broken pain. A livid scream arose in her throat. I'm sorry, Howard, I'm sorry, too. But I don't want to die. I'm sorry, too. She rushed at the landing place.

Oh, fool, fool. She hadn't pulled her boat high enough from the water, and the boiling waves had caught it up again and claimed it. It lay rocking six yards from shore, upside-down. And Howard was at her heels. Mary turned clumsily and dodged along the shore. She heard a mighty snap, as a tree fell on the other side of the island. Run, run. But you have no chance, not now. In the end you'll be caught! You are trapped. Trapped like a mouse some child has put into a cage with an owl. Run, mouse, run. Skitter on your small paws from side to side, dash in and out, let your small heart beat, beat, and your sides heave fear. You have no chance, you know, no chance at all...

Chapter 58

It needs a wild steersman when we voyage through chaos!
The anchor is up, —farewell!
NATHANIEL HAWTHORNE

It was a crazy time to get back. Homer drove up Walden Street, listening to the latest hurricane bulletin on his radio. The police station parking lot was full of cars. The police force was all there, a nerve center in crisis. The members of the fire department were bustling around on the other side of the building, ready for anything. Homer pushed open the door and went in. Bernard Shrubsole greeted him gaily. There was excitement in the air. All at once the Goss Murder Case seemed old hat.

"Looks like you're going to have some fun around here," said Homer.

"You bet we are. The eye of the storm is supposed to go right over us."

"No news?" said Homer.

"News? Oh, you mean—no, nary a sign of him. He was at home this morning, but nobody's seen him since. And he's not at his office. Don't worry. He'll turn up."

"Everybody's all right, I suppose? Nobody else has turned up stabbed or throttled, nobody's tipped any more statues on anybody?"

"Nope."

That was a relief. But he'd just make sure. Homer got back in his car. His fingers had to grip the wheel. It needed all his strength just to keep the car on the street. Along Barrett's Mill Road the wind tried to blow it off into the Assabet. Homer decided that once he got to Mary's house he might as well hole up and ride out the storm with the family. He bit his lip, struggling with the steering wheel. What would she say to him?

He saw Tom first. Tom was dragging bushel baskets of apples off the truck and heaving them into the barn. He had sent the children into the house. Homer pulled up beside him. For some reason the question about Mary came out first. He had to yell to make Tom hear.

"What?" said Tom. "Mary? I dunno. Is she up at the house?"

But she wasn't. And Gwen seemed preoccupied, when Homer appeared suddenly in the kitchen, with a great windy slamming of doors. Her mind was somewhere else. She supposed that Mary was still at the library. "Tell her to come home, will you? It won't be safe out on the road much longer. Or else both of you just stay there."

Homer climbed grimly back in his car, and hurtled back down the road toward town. A big branch had fallen across Lowell Road at one place, and a bunch of men from the lumber company by the Red Bridge were tugging at it. Homer fumed. He got out of the car and helped. Nothing to it. What had they been stalling around for? He got back in his car and made a jackrabbit start. One of the men from the lumber company looked at the other and flexed his biceps. "Muscleman," he yelled.

The library looked shut up tight. Damnation. Mary's car was nowhere in sight. Just to be sure, Homer got out and dodged around to the back. He had to climb up on the wall beside the delivery ramp to look in the office window. There was no one in the office. What was that pink thing on Mary's desk? Like a hat? It was a hat. It was that crazy hat Alice Herpitude used to wear.

There was a cracking sound above the roar of the wind, and the feathery top of an elm tree went sailing past, sliding and bounding up the street. Where in the hell was Mary?

Homer teetered on the top of the wall and looked again at Alice's hat. Mary wouldn't have gone down to Alice's place, would she? Yes, she might very well have gone to Alice's, to ready it for the storm, because it was her own house now. There would be things a property owner would want to lash down, to take care of. Homer made a run for his car. His was the only one on the road now, the wind was so high. It was behind him as he flew along Sudbury Road, turned on Fairhaven and crossed the turnpike. It was a mad business, charging down a narrow wood road with trees tossing right and left. Twice he had to stop his car and drag branches out of the way. At last he came down the steep descent at the edge of the river and pulled up at Alice's house. There was Mary's car. Thank God. He would find her in the house, and in a moment she would be safe again, safe in his arms. Leaning forward against the wind, Homer struggled up the steps and banged on the door. No one answered. He peered inside. All dark, the door locked. Where in God's name was she? Homer turned wildly and looked out at the river. There was no little boat at the landing, but there was something else. Homer's heart jumped into his throat. He ran to the landing. There were her shoes, in the lee of a big rock. One of her stockings was fluttering in a tree, the other had blown away.

The river had gone wild. The wind stormed over the black bay, hurling up quick frightened waves, with white spume threshing from their tops, rushing away from him. There was no sign of Mary, not anywhere. But there was something there in the water, way out in the middle of the bay near the island. It was—oh, God—it was a boat, overturned, upside-down. It must be hers, it could only be hers. Homer stumbled along the shore, looking for something to go out in, a rowboat or canoe, or something, anything. He shouted "Mary," but he couldn't even hear his own voice. Then he cursed himself for a fool, and turned and struggled in the other direction. Teddy's house was on the other side, and there would be some sort of canoe in his boathouse, if the police had only left it there.

They had. There were two of them, a canoe and a rowboat, resting upside-down on sawhorses. Homer hauled on the canoe clumsily and dragged it to the water's edge, righted it, stepped into the boggy ground, shoved off and climbed in. He was instantaneously swamped. The waves twisted the canoe sideways and washed over it. It tipped over, dumping him into the river. He grabbed at the paddle and doggedly sloshed out of the river again. Turn the canoe over, dump out the water and try again, only you've got to do some fast work with the paddle.

This time it was better. Homer dug choppily with his paddle, and managed to keep headed across the wind-torn waves. The spume streaked past him. The sun had gone out, and it was raining. Before he knew it the gale and the gale-driven water had carried him as far as the middle of the bay. Chop, chop, quick now, the other side, chop, chop. Nearly had him that time. Homer blinked the deluge out of his eyelashes and tried to see ahead. It was impossible to do anything but try to keep abreast of the waves. Any other kind of steering was out of the question. He was being carried to the east side of the island. The little boat was nowhere in sight. Homer glanced to right and left, fearfully, half expecting to see Mary's poor drowned face floating above the water. Why had she come out in this, the crazy fool girl? Then something caught Homer a terrible blow across the left shoulder, and he cried out and nearly lost control. A giant object hurtled past him, turning end over end, and foundered in the river a few yards away. It was the wooden slat-backed swing from Miss Herpitude's place, torn from the ground by the savage strength of the tempest. Branches went scudding past him. On the island the cracking trees sounded like tiny snaps of a scissors above the locomotive roar of the storm.

Suddenly the water quieted a little. He was in the lee of the island, and he could stop plowing at the water for a minute and look around. Water streamed from his hair down across his face. His shirt clung to him. His lap was full of water. If he didn't bail the water out of the bottom of the canoe it would sink. There was nothing to bail with. He had better try to land. Homer looked over his shoulder at the island.

There she was! She was running along the shore of the island, bowed over, stooping, racing, looking like a child, her hair loose and blowing in front of her, her feet bare. Oh, thank God, thank God. What was the matter with her foot? Homer shouted at her, but his words were blown back in his mouth. He lifted his paddle and tried to turn the canoe, but it wouldn't budge. It was those buttonbushes, damn them. The water between the island and the mainland was thick with them, and what had looked like a clear channel was a sunken morass of bushes. Homer looked for Mary again. Where was she? *And who was that?* Someone with a great heavy spade in his hand was struggling from one tree to another, moving in pouncing rushes, ducking across the point to cut her off. It was Howard! Oh, God, it was Howard! Homer clawed with his hands at the bushes, tearing at them, inching forward. Too slow, too slow! Why in the name of God didn't he have a gun?

The storm had passed its height, and the force of the wind was abating slightly. For a moment the squalling winds died. But deep down in the muddy roots of the giant pine that stood in the clearing the thickened clods supporting the last clinging root-strands began to be waterlogged by the rising watertable, and slowly—slowly—the old tree began to tremble loose. It leaned a little way toward the clearing, where there was nothing to stay its fall, and began to topple.

Mary stopped in the clearing. She dropped the notebooks and put her face in her hands, breathing in great sobs. In snatches between her indrawn breaths she began to mumble and pray...

Homer saw her. He stood up in his canoe and roared at her, with a shriek that tore his throat—*"Jump, Mary, jump!"*

She heard it, and looked at him, her white face blank. Then she looked up and stood frozen for a second. Then she jumped. The pine tree caught her a glancing, scraping blow, and she fell. But it caught something else, too, and destroyed it . . .

And the thing that it killed had once been worthy and good (one of those dependable people that everyone turns to and relies on)—the best fellow in all the world.

Chapter 59

❧ *...And we went on to heaven the long way round.*
HENRY THOREAU

"Hoy there." It was a tiny sound. Homer, dazed, turned toward it. Someone was pulling strongly across the water, looking back over his shoulder at him, pulling with his oars and heading his prow firmly across the churning waters of the bay. It was Teddy Staples. He was nearly at the island.

Homer stared at him vaguely and started scrabbling at the bushes again. But then Teddy maneuvered carefully among them and pulled Homer's canoe free by stretching an oar to him. Then they landed together on the shore. Homer, his knees weak and nearly folding under him, struggled to the place where Mary lay. Teddy strained at the limbs of the tree, and Homer lifted her tenderly. She was unconscious. "I think she'll be all right," said Teddy. "The trunk just missed her."

The triumphal arch was founded on the sea, and through it, looking far away, Mary could see her distant blue peninsula. There was someone standing on it, and her eyes were so miraculous that she could see right past the columns and the arches and the moldings and the coffered barrel vaults, way across the water, with its dolphin-drawn shells and seagods, to the very texture of the cloth on the person's sleeve. There were long telescopic feelings in her fingers, too, and she could reach out through the arch, far away, and feel the cloth. And her ears were like conch shells that amplified the sound, so that she could hear what the person was saying. He was saying her name, and cursing.

She woke up and smiled at Homer. He stopped cursing. But he went on saying, "Mary, Mary." He was kneeling beside her bed with his arms around her. How lovely, how lovely.

The nurse was touching Homer's arm. He shrank back in dismay. "Oh my God, I'm hurting you."

"No, no. Do it some more."

He did it some more very carefully, while the nurse grinned. "I thought I'd lost you. And you were the only one that would ever do. I knew that right away, the first day I saw you. You spoiled all the others that ever were or ever could be."

"I did? Oh, I'm so glad. How lovely. Oh, that's nice."

Homer leaned back and glared at her. "And, by God, you're going to marry me right away, before you slip through my fingers again. I'm not asking you, I'm telling you. Please, Mary."

Mary closed her eyes. Her head hurt. What was it she had been trying to decide? Had it been something to do with jumping? She had decided not to jump, that was it. Like the Transcendentalists . . . Then Mary put her head back on the pillow and her mind began slowly to unclench like an opening fist. She opened her eyes. "I'll tell you what," she said. "I'll marry you if we don't have to go away for a honeymoon. Could we spend it in the library? I've got a whole new idea—oh, ouch. What's the matter with my foot?"

"It's broken. Compound fracture. You had a concussion, too. You're all beat up."

"Then that's why my head hurts. Listen, Homer. You know how Henry Thoreau would jump rope? He wouldn't refuse. No sir, not Henry. He would just take the rope right away from the two little girls and swing it for himself, at his own pace, with those two strong legs of his leaping up and down. Isn't that right?"

"Oh, sure," said Homer, nodding fatuously (humor her).

"And Emily, too. Emily would have a little rope, like a whip, and she'd swing it quickly, jumping in her small white dress, with her little black shoes tripping up and down in a tight rhythm like a verse, skipping all the way to the stars and back."

"There now, my darling, you just go back to sleep, there's my good girl. And of course we don't have to go away. Libraries are my favorite for honeymoons. We'll live in Alice's house on Fairhaven Bay, and we don't ever have to go away at all."

Next morning Mary woke up feeling a little more like herself. Homer came in again after breakfast, and took a good deal of time kissing her tenderly and telling her exactly why he loved her. Then he helped her out of bed and into a wheel chair and pushed her down the hospital corridor. "There's someone upstairs who would like to see you."

"Oh, oh, it's not Gwen?"

It was Gwen. She was sitting up, eating breakfast, looking wonderfully flat. Tom stood up as they came in, and started to complain. "I wanted to call her Augusta, for Augusta Wind. I mean, how many children do you ordinarily have born in the teeth of a howling gale?"

"No," said Gwen, "that won't do. Oh my, isn't the food good? Just think I didn't cook it. Do go see the baby. She's the nicest one yet."

Homer made a literary suggestion. "What about calling her after Prospero's daughter, in The Tempest? What was his daughter's name? Miranda."

"Oh, good for you. That's it. Miranda. Miranda Hand. I hope you like it, Tom, because that's what it's going to be. You do like it, don't you?"

"Oh, I do, I do."

Homer wanted to know what it had been like, getting Gwen

to Emerson Hospital in the middle of the storm. Had they had any trouble?

"Oh, no trouble at all," said Tom. "You don't call driving seventy miles an hour in a hundred-mile-an-hour gale *trouble?* The only little mishap we had with the pickup, which was all that was running at the moment, was picking up some broken window glass and puncturing a tube. But we didn't even stop. We bumped all the way to the hospital and got here on three wheels and a bent rim."

"Say," said Homer, "that gives me a good idea. Why don't you call the baby Tube-blows Begonia? All these Morgan girls look like flowers."

Mary felt dizzy and silly. "Flat-tirey will get you nowhere," she said.

"Oh, please don't make me laugh," said Gwen. "It hurts."

Homer pushed Mary down the hall and they looked in the window at the baby, which didn't look like anything much yet, and then they went back to Mary's room. Out of the window they could see the Sudbury River, glittering in the morning sun. Down below in the garden someone was tidying up, sawing a fallen aspen into small lengths of firewood.

"It was the worst hurricane around here since '38," said Homer. "Trees are down all over, especially the old diseased elms. There's a little foreign car wedged between the columns in front of the Middlesex Savings Bank, and a tree fell on the roof of the Rod and Gun Club. One good thing, though: you know that awful fake Colonial Woolworth false-front? It tore off and blew away, like a sail before the wind. It's probably over Connecticut by now." Homer looked up. There was someone standing shyly in the doorway. "Oh, Teddy, come on in. I guess we don't need to tell you how glad we are you came along."

There was a big bunch of ugly-looking flowers in Teddy's arms. Mary smiled at him and reached out her hand. "Teddy, you look wonderful. Where have you been? Are you going to try to tell us you didn't know everyone was looking for you?"

"I sure am. Homer told me the police were after me. But I guess the only way I'd have heard about it was if they'd written it in the sky over Moosehead Lake. I've been down in Maine."

"In Maine? But why? I mean, what made you go off so suddenly, without saying goodby or anything? If you knew how worried we've been about you . . ."

"Well, I told Homer how it was. I had this crazy notion I only had a few more days to live. Did he tell you? And there was something I had to get done first."

"I know. There was someone you had to meet . . ."

"Someone?" Teddy looked puzzled. "No, not someone. There was something I had to see—my whiteheaded eagle."

"Your whiteheaded——?"

"My whiteheaded eagle. You know, our national bird. It was the only bird Henry Thoreau saw that I didn't have on my lifetime list. I just had to see it. So I went up Annursnac Hill one day, feeling pretty poorly . . ."

"Yes, I remember. Tom saw you that day."

"That's right. And I saw it."

"You saw it?" said Homer. "What, you mean you saw your eagle?"

"That's right. He came dropping out of the sky far, far away, just as the sky cleared. I knew it was him as soon as I saw the speck. I hardly even needed my glasses. He just hung there in the sky, banking in a circle over my head. Then you know what he did? He veered off and headed in a straight line to the northeast, like an arrow flying to its target. Heading straight for Maine. And it seemed to me like it was Henry himself, beckoning to me, telling me where to go. It was like he said that Maine was where *he'd* like to have died, not in a stuffy room somewhere, but out in the open woods, in the forest, with nothing but Indians and the wild creatures of the woods around him. S-so I ran down the hill, climbed in my flivver and took off up north. Didn't even stop to pack my clothes."

"And then you didn't die, after all."

"No, I began to feel revived as soon as I got up past Bangor. I bought some provisions and a little equipment and headed for the wildest part of the woods. And you know what happened? It occurred to me that, now I'd seen all the birds Henry saw, I might as well tackle the plant life. And I got so busy doing that, I forgot what day it was, and before long May 6th was gone by without my even thinking about it. And I got a darned good list. I saw spotted touch-me-not, and spikenard and several kinds of orchis and the hog-peanut. And I made me some lily soup, the way Henry did when he was there."

Teddy's clothes were green with rough usage, but he had just mended them and here and there a bright new staple flashed. Homer remembered the staples he had found on the monument at the bridge, and he asked Teddy about it point-blank.

"Was I at the bridge that day? Yes, as a matter of fact, I was. I was paddling around waiting to see if the bluebird would come back to make one more try for her hole, when I saw Ernie there at the bridge, and went over to speak to him, to put in another word for throwing out those golblasted letters. I pulled my canoe up and went up to him. But I never got a chance to say anything. He was huffy, wanted to know if I was the one who had sent him a note making an appointment to meet him there. Seems he'd gotten an anon-anonymous note, offering him a lot of money for the letters, and he was mighty suspicious, thinking it might be one of the members of the Alcott Association trying to put one over on him. You know, get him there with the letters and then get them away by force. But he was too cagey for us, he said. He'd hidden the letters where nobody'd find 'em, and there they'd stay until someone came along with a real offer or a genuine promise of publication. I said, heck, it wasn't me sent him the note. And then I left, and got back to my birds and forgot all about Ernie."

"Didn't you hear the shot?" said Homer.

"Yes, and I paddled up close enough to use my glasses and see a lot of folks and a p-policeman standing around Ernie Goss, who was lying on the ground. And I knew I'd be better off out of sight, since I must have been the last one except the murderer to have seen him alive."

Teddy looked down at his bouquet of swamp nettle, and turned to Mary bashfully. "Here," he said. "This is for you."

Homer decided reluctantly that he had better tell Teddy what the situation was, so he broke the news gently, and asked for his congratulations. Teddy looked a little crestfallen and stuttered badly trying to say something nice. But then Mary exclaimed over the swamp nettle, and Teddy got quite enthusiastic telling her its botanical name and how the Indians had used it to swat flies. After a while he left, looking cheerful. After all, he had all the flora in Concord to find and catalogue, and it might take him years.

Mary smelled her flowers and wished she hadn't. She made a face and laughed. "Did you notice? Teddy's stuttering is better."

Homer looked at her sentimentally. "And your color's coming back. You know what? Your cheeks are like red roses."

"Oh, for heaven's sake, Homer. . ."

"Look, if a person's cheeks happen to be like red roses it's merely a fact of scientific observation to point it out. I've tried a whole lot of other flowers from time to time, and none of them was right. It's red roses they're like."

> *Down by the river where the green grass grows,*
> *There sat———, as pretty as a rose.*
> *Along came———and kissed her on the cheek.*
> *How many kisses did she get that week?*
> *One, two, three, four, five, six, seven . . .*

Chapter 60

He is moderate. I am impetuous. He is modest and humble. I am forward and arbitrary. He is poor but we both are industrious. Why may we not be happy?
MRS. AMOS BRONSON ALCOTT

Tom, Homer and Grandmaw were colliding with each other in the kitchen, clearing away Sunday dinner. It was Mary's first day home. Struggling awkwardly with her crutches she got the tablecloth off the table and stumped to the front door and shook it out. Then she stood and smelled the fresh air. The ragged leaves that were left on the old elm by the road were turning a rusty yellow. There were leaves growing even from the trunk and along the lower reaches of the limbs, like hairs in an old man's ears. Miraculously the storm had spared it, although it had taken nine young apple trees behind the house. Mary folded the tablecloth again and made her way laboriously to the kitchen to put it in the drawer.

"If you ask me," said old Mrs. Hand, "I could get along a whole lot better all by myself. What did you people all have to grow so big for? You're all over the place. Why don't you all get out of my way and go off somewhere?"

"Can I come?" said Annie.

"Me, too!" said John.

"No, not you children. Freddy has to go to bed and I need the rest of you to wipe."

"Okay," said Homer. "But don't you let that John lick the dishes clean."

Tom, who didn't want to sell his apples on a flooded market, went off to truck them up to the town of Harvard, where there was a big storage warehouse. Homer helped Mary out to his car and lifted her into the front seat. "We'll take an old-fashioned Sunday afternoon buggy ride," he said.

First they drove down Fairhaven Road to Alice Herpitude's house, and looked possessively out of the car window at its modest white clapboards. "Maybe Teddy will build us a nice birdbath for a wedding present," said Homer.

"He'll make a charming neighbor, anyway," said Mary.

Then they headed back across Route 2 to the center of town, and up into Sleepy Hollow cemetery to Authors' Ridge. "Do you think Henry would mind a couple of quiet neckers on a Sunday afternoon?" said Homer.

"Not as long as they kept things pretty transcendental," said Mary.

"Don't forget, if Howard Swan was right, Henry was no slouch himself when it came to romance."

"It's a lovely story. It pleases me, somehow, that those two might have found each other. But, Homer, there are still some things I don't understand. How could Howard Swan have killed Ernest Goss? He was supposed to have been in New York on the nineteenth——"

"It's Longfellow's fault, that's whose it is. That old cornball poem of his. What immortal lines does every man, woman and child in the country have engraved across his memory in letters of gold?

> Listen, my children, and you shall hear
> Of the midnight ride of Paul Revere,
> On the eighteenth of April, in Seventy-five . . .

The *eighteenth* of April. Howard went to New York on the *eighteenth*, not the nineteenth, and then made a big point with his lunchtable companions about its being Patriot's Day in Massachusetts. 'You remember, boys, Paul Revere and all that kind of thing—on the *eighteenth of April in 'Seventy-five*. They're having a big parade back home today—' It wasn't until I discovered there in the Amherst library that Elizabeth Goss had once been engaged to Howard Swan, that Howard came back somewhat forcefully to my attention. And then I remembered an extremely small fact Jimmy had told me. He said that Howard's business friends had all agreed Howard was with them on Patriot's Day—remember?—'*just the way he said they would*.' Howard must have said to Jimmy, 'Ask them where I was on Patriot's Day,' so Jimmy, the obedient little fellow, did just that. Well—by nearly asphyxiating myself in a phone booth for an hour and a half I got hold of all of them. And sure enough, one by one, they all told me that Patriot's Day was the eighteenth of April. 'Don't you remember?' they would say condescendingly, and I could hear the words coming out of the telephone in red, white and blue, *'On the eighteenth of April in 'Seventy-five?'* Then I would hang up and salute the flag. So you see what happened—Howard flew to New York on the eighteenth, got back in time for the dinner party, left early, then came back again when everyone was gone, to set things up. The only person still in the house would have been Mrs. Bewley, and he didn't have to worry about her as long as he kept out of her sight. Now—the first thing he had to do was prepare the weapons. One of the duelling pistols was to be fixed up as the official 'murder weapon.' It was the one that Charley had handled, putting it away. The *other* pistol would be the true murder weapon, but it would be cleaned out afterwards, wiped off and returned to the drawer so that it would not seem to have been touched. At this point he never touched the musket, because it didn't enter into his plans at all. The next thing was the manufacturing of the notes that were to lead Charley and Philip and Ernie to the right places at the right times the next day. For these he used Charley's typewriter in Charley's room, tracing your name for the notes that were to be sent to Charley and Philip from a letter of yours he found in a drawer. Then his preparations were about done. All he had to do was drive off somewhere far away from houses and fire the 'official murder weapon' into the woods so that it would be blackened inside. That was tricky because he didn't want to disturb Charley's prints. He must have used tools to do it with, clamps or something."

"But next morning he had to look as if he were going to New York."

"That's right. He headed off toward Boston, then just circled around wide and came back the back way and parked in some inconspicuous place like, say, the little road that leads in to Annursnac Hill. Then he snuck over to the Goss place and just hung around there, ducking in when he could to leave his notes. He watched Charley come back from his ride on Dolly and enter the house in his Prescott outfit. Then he saw him come out again in his own clothes and head lickety-split for the gravel pit, hell-bent on high romance. So then Howard just went in the house, snatched up the outfit, took it to the barn, changed clothes, leaving his own behind the hay somewhere, and galloped off through the woods on Dolly, keeping away from the road. It was all right to be seen, in fact that was the whole point, but not up close. He galloped up to the bridge, killed Goss, galloped back, giving Arthur Furry a good rear view, deposited the 'official murder weapon' in the cider press, leaving behind him his horse's hoofprints and a lost balloon to point the way, changed clothes in the barn and slunk into the house once more to leave the real murder weapon, all polished and cleaned up, back in the drawer. But then he struck his first snag."

"It had something to do with the flint, didn't it?"

"Good girl. That's right. It was only then, I'm convinced, that Howard noticed that the flint had dropped out of his gun—the real one, the true murder weapon. Crisis. What to do? He didn't dare now to go back and take the flint out of the gun he had deposited in the cider press. But *this* gun mustn't be found

without a flint. Because then its twin in the cider press would be
betrayed as a put-up job. So he took the flint from the musket.
Up until then he must have been working with gloves on, careful not to leave any prints. With his gloves still on he opened
the door of the cabinet where the musket was kept, took it out,
and then I'll bet he took off his gloves to work the small screw
that holds the flint in place. He took the flint out, transferred it
to the murder weapon and put both guns away again, wiping
everything off carefully. But he forgot one thing. While his
glove was off he left a thumbprint on the inside of the cabinet
door. Campbell saw it there, but there were so many others on
the door anyway it didn't help us much. Well, anyway, then he
was all done. He just had to duck back to his car, swing around
by back roads again, bide his time, and then drive home to
Concord from Boston around five o'clock as though he had just
come back from New York."

"All right. I understand all that. But now will you please
explain what it was all for? Why did Howard Swan, of all the
people in the world, think he had to kill Ernest Goss? And then
why did he kill poor Alice? And why did he almost——"

"Oh, God, don't say it——"

There was a car coming. It contained Rowena Goss, out for a
spin with her fiancé. She started to slow down as she recognized Homer's car, but when she saw how he was behaving
with that Morgan girl she frowned and speeded up again, with a
disapproving crescendo from her exhaust.

"Well, where were we?" said Mary, sitting up and straightening her hair.

The nosepiece of Homer's glasses was resting on his ear. He
put it back where it belonged. "You were asking about Howard's motive. I suppose you want me to tell you what it is that
will turn an apparently just, honest and respected citizen,
scholar and gentleman into a murderer—right? Well, my darling, what are the usual reasons why people murder other people? Revenge? Self-defense? Jealousy, greed, lunacy, hatred,
sudden passion?"

"Oh, Homer, you know it wasn't any of those. The only

motive he could possibly have had was the suppression of those letters. But that just doesn't seem a strong enough reason to me. Not for Howard."

"Just think about it." Homer leaned back, put his arms behind his head and closed his eyes. "First, let's go back a long way. A long, long way. All the way back to an engagement between a young Harvard senior named Howard Swan, who was majoring in literature, and a pretty young debutante at Miss Winsor's school named Elizabeth Matthews. Now Elizabeth had something she felt she ought to confide to her husband-to-be—something that was a romantic family secret. She thought it was her duty to let him in on the story of her sublime origin, the royal bar-sinister in her ancestral past. So she did. She whispered it tenderly in his ear. Then Howard, to her astonishment, far from being merely suitably impressed, urged her not to keep it a secret any longer. He recognized it for the bombshell it was, and he yearned to be the agent for the explosion. But Elizabeth wouldn't let him. No sir. I don't know whether she felt protective about the reputations of her great-grandmother and grandfather or whether she just didn't want her name bandied about as the descendant of any kind of illicit union, no matter how august. Anyway, my guess is that this was why they broke up. Elizabeth forbade Howard to use her secret and Howard was good and mad. 'Oh,' says Elizabeth, 'you nasty, nosy man!' 'Why,' says Howard, 'you selfish little stupid bitch!' So the engagement was off. And the next thing you knew the selfish little bitch had rushed into the arms of Howard's classmate from Concord, Ernest Goss. And you can be sure of one thing—Elizabeth never mentioned her glorious ancestry to Ernie when she was confiding to him her intimate little girlish secrets. Okay, then—all right so far? Well then. Take another look at Howard. Here he was, left alone with his conscience and this tantalizing delicious tidbit of historical gravy. So what did he do? He did what any well-trained student would do. He began searching for evidence to back up Elizabeth's bald statement of fact. Over the next twenty years he sought and studied and researched, poring over the journals and poems and letters of Thoreau and the

letters and poems of Emily Dickinson, everything he could find
that would give him a lead. It took him that long partly because
he was thorough and partly because he didn't have much spare
time, what with all the committees he was on and the organiza-
tions he was chairman of. But he stuck to it. And what he
finally came up with in those notebooks you found is pretty
solid-sounding stuff. Howard was darn clever. And his theory
took care of some of the Dickinson mysteries pretty neatly. For
example—you know how everyone who has looked into
Emily's life agrees that somewhere around 1860 or '61 or '62
she must have gone through some sort of crisis of love and
renunciation, and nobody is sure what it was . . ."

"Yes, and it was supposed to have started her writing a flood
of poetry and it was also supposed to have made her begin to
withdraw from the world and shy away from visitors. What
about the theory that it was that Reverend Wadsworth in Philadelphia that she was supposed to be in love with? That's what
most people say. And when he moved to California it was more
than she could bear, it was almost like dying."

"But why? There she was in Amherst, and in those days
Philadelphia would have seemed as far away as the moon already. What difference could it have made to her that Wadsworth left Philadelphia for California? Well, anyway—that's
the way Howard reasoned. Emily's lover was not Wadsworth at
all—it was Henry Thoreau. Of course, first of all he had to
explain how they met. That was easy. Emily must have come to
Concord to visit her cousins there, the Norcross girls, and she
might very well have stayed in Henry's mother's boarding
house, the way Ellen Sewall did, the girl he had loved before.
And so, naturally, he took her out boating on the river, just the
way he took Ellen, just the way he took Margaret Fuller."

"I love it. I can't help it, I love it. Oh, Homer, just think of
the two of them (Henry Thoreau and Emily Dickinson!) out in
the sunshine on Fairhaven Bay, just like us. I'll never look out
from our front porch without seeing them there. And I've just
thought of something else. Both of them were small. They were
little people. Little homely people. Forgive me for saying it, but

I think they must have made a charming pair."

"I know. It's pretty, it's all mighty pretty. There they were, the two of them, small in stature only, giants in every other way. And each of them beginning to recognize in the other an extraordinary and unique person, an opposite-sexed but true counterpart. After all, each of them was perhaps the one most worthy audience for the other then alive."

"So they fell in love. But do you think they could really have gone so far as to——"

"Well, read what Howard says. He makes it sound pretty plausible. He goes on and on about the powerful loving responses in Henry's journal, his appeals of affection to his friends, the depth of his reaction to the natural world around him. And all of this convinces him that Henry had a nature capable of passionate attachment. In spite of the coldness his friends accuse him of."

"Oh, that," said Mary scornfully. "That was just his New England mask for the strong feelings underneath."

"Listen. I wrote down some of it." Homer took a small notebook out of his pocket and opened it up. *"All that a man has to say or do that can possibly concern mankind, is in some shape or other to tell the story of his love,—to sing; and if he is fortunate and keeps alive, he will be forever in love . . ."* Homer put the notebook back in his pocket. "And as for Emily, do you remember how she scandalized her sister-in-law, even after years of retirement, by being discovered in the arms of a man? It was probably that old judge who loved her at the end of her life. Oh, it's reasonable, all right, the whole thing. And therefore, says Howard, the marriage of Henry Thoreau and Emily Dickinson in the flesh was a true marriage of the exalted spirit. Okay, let's say we accept that. Afterwards Emily went home again, gushing poetry, her true poetic self aroused and awakened, writing a masterpiece a day from then on. So half of the Dickinson mystery is solved—the reason for the spout of poetry. But what about the other half? Why did she begin to act like a female hermit, retiring to her room, refusing to see anybody?"

"Naturally," said Mary softly, "it was to bear Henry's child . . ."

"To do what? My dear, you scandalize me. Squire Dickinson's daughter? Bear an illegitimate child? Impossible! The affair must be hushed up. Emily must renounce her mysterious lover. The child must be carried in secret and delivered in secret and then turned over to the faithful stableman to be brought up as his own. And here's where the Matthews family comes into the picture. Richard Matthews and his wife had sixteen kids. The addition of one more would hardly cause a stir. And the fact that the child grew up with a mop of auburn hair like its mother's, and eyes, maybe, like 'the sherry in the glass that the guest leaves' wouldn't have bothered anyone. I caught on myself, finally, there at Amherst, to what Elizabeth's dark secret was. If you trace the Matthews name back far enough you come to the Richard Matthews who worked for Squire Dickinson and sired seventeen kids, one of whom, a son named (of all things) Henry, was born only four months after his elder brother Frederick. Four months? There's a precocious embryo for you. So I made a wild stab in the dark and guessed that Elizabeth Goss regarded herself as the great-granddaughter of Emily Dickinson, which explained why she was mooning around in McLean Hospital in a white gown and wouldn't come out to see anybody. What I didn't guess then was that she also had grandiose ideas about who her great-grandfather was."

"What I love most about Howard's idea," said Mary, "is the fun he had with internal evidence—the symbolism and the images in Emily's poetry and letters. The way she called herself 'wife,' and the obvious Freudian interpretation of her poems about bees and flowers. Some of it was pretty strong stuff for a spinster, don't you think? Remember 'Wild night, wild nights'? And what about 'the wrestlers in the holy chamber' and her 'unique burden' that she wrote about—do you think she was really talking about pregnancy and childbirth?"

"Well, you've got to admit that it's all very ingenious. Poor old Emily. If all this happened in 1860 it was only two years before Henry was dead. So she lost him twice, once by renunciation and a second time by death. And thus, Howard says, began her preoccupation with her 'flood subject'—love seen through the barrier of death, the lovers reunited only in immortality."

"I believe it. I believe it all," said Mary. "It only puts me even more in awe of them. I'd like to think it was all true, and that they had each other, even if it was only for a little while."

"Oh, hogwash."

"What did you say?"

"My dear, there isn't a scrap of truth in it. It's all the purest, most delectable bunk."

"Oh, no, it isn't, it isn't. I refuse to give it up. Homer, please——"

"Look, my darling, in the first place those Norcross cousins of Emily's didn't even move out of Cambridge to Concord until after Henry was dead."

"They didn't?" Mary's voice shook with disappointment. "But what about Elizabeth's secret? Where would she have got the notion that she was descended from the two of them? I mean if there was no truth in it at all? And what about the stableboy, Richard Matthews? How did he get an extra child? That one that was born only four months after one of the others? And the red hair! Did you see that, in the black box in Elizabeth's room, in the envelope that was marked *Great-grandmother's?* How can you explain that away?"

"Oh, the hair. Do you honestly think Emily Dickinson was the only redheaded woman in her generation? And as for the stableboy's too many babies—damned if I know. Maybe his wife was wet-nursing it along with her own for some feckless relative, and then got stuck with it. And don't bother your head about Elizabeth's secret. May I remind you that she is now confined in an institution for the insane? Pure and simple old-fashioned delusions of grandeur. She was a nut. If you don't believe me, listen to this. I looked into what I could find out about her parents and grandparents, and I discovered that her father went to his grave claiming to be the Stuart pretender to the British throne. And her grandfather, the original Henry Matthews, you know what he did? Well, first he made a fortune in carriages and buggies, and then he died. But before he died he built himself a fancy Moorish mausoleum on which were inscribed these words:

> HERE LIES ALLAH BEN BUDDHA,
> THE TRUE MESSIAH,
> KNOWN TO THIS WORLD AS
> HENRY RICHARD MATTHEWS.

You can read it yourself in the cemetery there in Amherst."

Mary shook her head, covered her face with her hands and laughed. "Oh, no, no. All that lovely romantic story going up in smoke."

"Look, all you have to do is examine Henry's journal for the last few years of his life, when this great passion was supposed to have possessed him. Does he moon in his secret heart about love and longing? Well, does he?"

"No, no, I know. He goes on and on about tree rings and skunk cabbage and the height of the rivers after a rain. Oh, I know."

"Well, I call that pretty dry stuff for a man who was supposed to have met his Fate. And look—you talk about internal evidence—do you honestly think that any of Emily's poetry expresses the experience of giving birth to and then giving up a child? It expresses some other colossal experience, sure—one can't deny her some sort of excruciating personal knowledge of both love and death. But *motherhood?* No. And what about *guilt?* Don't you think a sensitive soul like Emily would have felt some sort of complicated kind of shame if she had been forced to drop the fruit of her love for Henry Thoreau into the lap of someone else? No, no, there's nothing like that in her poetry. And another thing—if Emily Dickinson was anything, she was honest, you agree? And don't you remember that she said somewhere, 'My life has been too simple and stern to embarrass any'? What does her white dress mean, anyway, if not purity, the bride of Christ, and all that? And anyhow, all things considered, I still can't see Henry Thoreau, that stiff and rustic gentleman, dallying with Edward Dickinson's daughter among the daisies. Those times were different, after all."

But that sounded familiar. Mary looked at Homer, unbelieving. It was what she had said herself, hadn't she? She had been talking to Charley Goss, a long time ago. (How long ago!) Men and women didn't have to be lovers, she had said. In those days the restraints were so universally accepted, the two sexes could be friends with each other. And then Charley had scoffed at her. "Listen, girly, men and women have only one relation to each other, and that's all they've ever had. Don't kid yourself." But now even Homer was saying that Charley was wrong . . .

"Well, all right. I give up. But I'm terribly disillusioned. It would have been so beautiful. And you know you still haven't told me how a man like Howard Swan could be a murderer."

"I'm getting to that. In my own mind it goes back to Henry Thoreau again, and to the fact that a sign of his greatness is the diversity of his influence. Look at Rousseau, for instance. You might call him the father of collectivism as well as the father of democracy. For every disciple Henry Thoreau has, you'll find a different image of the man. On the one hand we've got Teddy Staples, re-creating Thoreau the harmless naturalist and village eccentric. And on the other hand you've got Howard Swan. Remember what Howard was saying that night in Sleepy Hollow Cemetery when we thought for a minute he was Henry's ghost?"

"Yes, of course I do. It was something from *Civil Disobedience,* that part about any man more right than his neighbors being a majority of one already. I think I'm beginning to see what you mean."

"*Civil Disobedience!* There's another Henry Thoreau for you! The Henry Thoreau who wrote that glorious essay, that incendiary document, that ringing call to the just citizen to refuse to obey unjust laws, setting the individual conscience above rules and decrees—that Henry Thoreau is a far cry from the one Teddy knows. If God is on your side, that's all the majority you need. Shades of Robespierre!"

"But he was writing against slavery, wasn't he? God was certainly on his side there."

"Of course. I'm not denying it. But it's like all glorious ideas: it's dangerous when perverted. What it comes down to is, *who says* God in on your side? Howard liked to have things his way. 'Any man more right than his neighbors constitutes a majority of one already.' That's what Howard was, all his life, a majority of one. He was influenced by the least attractive side of Thoreau's personality—the scornful side, what Walt Whitman found so disagreeable in him, his disdain for men. Henry disdained men by withdrawing from them. Howard disdained them by exerting power over them. God was on his side, naturally. If he couldn't get things his way by simply running them, as chairman, or president or moderator, he did it by bending the rules somewhat. You saw him make a sort of personal juggernaut out of that town meeting. And God was still on his side, even when the only tactic left was murder. And so he murdered Ernie to protect his child."

"His what?"

"His child. His manuscript. His masterpiece. His thesis. His life's work, his heart's darling, his bid for immortality, his great discovery. Here it was, almost finished at last, nearly done. He could see his picture in *The New York Times,* he could imagine the excitement, the controversy, the praise of the scholar, the delight of the student, the enthusiasm of the popular press—all so near. And then what happened? Along came Ernie Goss, the great booby, with a screwy set of nutty letters that he swore he was going to hit the market with, right then and there."

"But what difference would that have made? Anyone could tell that Ernie's letters were forgeries. No one would have believed in them."

"That's right. No one would believe in them. Nor would anyone believe in *another* crackpot theory appearing on the heels of the first, invented by a close friend and colleague of the screwball—a theory attempting to establish the truth of precisely the same kind of scandal, involving some of the *same parties*—and with its chief evidence stemming from a statement by the wife of the donkey with the forged documents. A statement the wife would deny and disown."

"Oh, oh. Of course. Yes, I see."

"So Howard begged and pleaded with Ernie. He tried bribery. He even threatened violence. That was what you overheard the night of the dinner party. Then, when everything else failed, he thought he had no alternative but to silence Ernie by killing him. Howard was a clever fellow and he sat down and figured out an intelligent and daring crime, as intelligent and as daring in its way as the arguments in his manuscript. And then look how everything played into his hands. First of all Ernie himself misbehaved dreadfully, providing both his sons publicly with apparent motives for murder. And next morning, although Howard didn't hear about it until afterward, Philip practically killed his father himself in full view of half the town. And even the mixup about the flintlocks turned out to work in Howard's favor. There *we* were, too stupid to find the planted gun in the cider press, and there was Tom Hand, too stubborn to make cider with the apples Howard spirited onto the place in May. But then Charley, the poor fool, had to go and bury that musket, and Ernie himself led us all astray by gurgling 'musket' as he died."

"All right. I can see why Howard thought he had to kill Ernie. But what about Alice? Why Alice, Homer, why, why?"

"Because she knew, that's why. In the first place she knew the same 'secret' about Elizabeth Goss that he did, because she was an old and intimate friend of Elizabeth's. But *she* was too sane and sensible to believe it. And then Howard confided in her, too, this same secret, not knowing she already knew it. He told her, I suppose, because she was the closest thing to a fellow Thoreau scholar he had to talk to, and because as chief librarian she was guardian of all his precious sources. And of course Alice must have been appalled. Here was this good man dedicating his life to something she regarded as a false notion. Then along came Ernie with his cuckoo letters, and she must have seen as clearly as Howard did that they were a threat to Howard's theories. So then when Ernie was killed she couldn't help suspecting. I think she must have come right out with it, and accused Howard of it. That would have been like her."

"Yes, and I know when it was. It was that day in church, way last spring. That was the first time I saw her looking frightened. Howard was an usher that morning and I'll bet when he met her in the vestry she looked straight at him with that honest clear look of hers and said, 'Howard, it was you, wasn't it?'"

"Yes, and then he threatened her, no doubt, and made her swear to shut up about his book, or she'd get it, too. So she did shut up, until it became more and more clear to her that Charley Goss was going to lose his life if she didn't speak up. Poor old Howard. By the time he was so entangled in his own web that he had to kill Alice Herpitude, he was no longer defending his beloved manuscript, he was saving his own skin. Of course when Elizabeth Goss went out of her mind he must already have begun to lose hope that his theories about her glorious ancestry would ever hold water. And it must have become more and more evident to him that this very document would itself incriminate him by attaching to his name his own true and powerful motive for murder. He had killed for nothing, after all, and now he had to go on killing in order to keep from being suspected. Crime, they say, never pays. 'I am in so far in blood that sin will pluck on sin.'"

"Tell me one more thing," said Mary. "What in heaven's name was he doing on the island in the middle of the storm? Oh, I suppose he was afraid the water might rise and reach his manuscript and ruin it."

"I suppose so. And of course it was still very dear to him. I know I'd rush into a burning house to save the stuff I've written on Henry Thoreau. Some of it, anyhow. I'm going to have to throw out a lot of it, but the new stuff is pretty good . . ."

"You know, Homer, if I hadn't stumbled all over Howard's manuscript like a great clumsy ass he might still have gotten away with it. No wonder he thought he had to . . ."

"Oh, Mary—"

Rowena Goss was driving past again, on her way out along the winding drives of Sleepy Hollow Cemetery. Good heavens,

Homer was *still* necking. It was disgraceful, right there in broad daylight and in a cemetery, too, right beside the grave of Louisa May *Alcott*. Rowena's beloved, peeking through the chinks in his bushel basket, agreed with her completely.

"I'd better get home and mind the children so Grandmaw can take a rest," said Mary.

In Monument Square the autumn color of the ravaged trees was at its height. The elm leaves that had not been torn off by the storm were a shopworn yellow, but the abandoned maples raged in red and orange fire. There was someone standing on the sidewalk in front of the Town Hall, looking around wildly.

"It's the D.A.," said Homer. "For Christ's sake, he must have seen a cow." He slowed down and waved his arm and shouted.

The District Attorney ran up to them, his face pale and perspiring. "Homer," he said, "help me. I can't find my car. Where's my car?"

"It's all right," said Homer. "There it is right over there." He got out and helped the D.A. into it, and slammed the door. "How's the campaign coming?"

The District Attorney mopped his face with his handkerchief and wound the window down two inches. "Fine, just fine. Didn't you hear? My opponent just got caught in a raid on a private club across the state line in the company of his gorgeous blonde secretary. I'm sitting pretty."

"Say, that's great. His secretary, well, well. You watch out for that Miss O'Toole of yours, now. These secretaries are murder."

Chapter 61

⌇ *Romans, countrymen and lovers by the banks of the*
Musketaquid . . .
HENRY THOREAU

Mrs. Bewley was walking down Walden Street, swinging her
pocketbook on its long chain strap. It was a big black patent-
leather pocketbook that had once belonged to Isabelle Flower.
She marched up to the door of the police station and walked in.
Jimmy Flower was tapping away at a typewriter in the outer
office.

"HELLO, THERE, MRS. BEWLEY," he bellowed, "COME
IN AND SIT DOWN. WHAT CAN I DO FOR YOU?"

Mrs. Bewley pushed open the swinging gate and sat down
beside the desk. She put her pocketbook in her lap. Jimmy
recognized it instantly. Only Isabelle would buy a fright like
that. It had been missing since Town Meeting. "WHY, MRS.
BEWLEY, WHAT A GOOD-LOOKING BAG. SAY, THAT'S
JUST THE KIND MY WIFE LIKES, THAT SHINY BLACK
STUFF THERE."

"REALLY?" screamed Mrs. Bewley, highly flattered. She
picked up the pocketbook by its long chain and thumped it on
the desk. "TAKE IT, TAKE IT."

"OH, I COULDN'T."

But Mrs. Bewley's generosity soon overwhelmed Jimmy's modest scruples, and he gave her a paper bag to empty the contents into and put the pocketbook in the desk drawer. "NOW, WHAT CAN I DO FOR YOU, MRS. BEWLEY?"

It was Priscilla, that was the trouble. Her hen Priscilla was missing. "MY BEST LAYER, AND SUCH A DEAR GIRL. NAUGHTY? I HOPE TO TELL YOU. BUT NICE. NAUGHTY BUT NICE. THAT'S PRISCILLA."

"SURELY SHE'S JUST SITTING ON SOME EGGS OUT-DOORS, MRS. BEWLEY? NO? WELL, EXCUSE ME A MINUTE. I'LL HAVE SERGEANT SHRUBSOLE FILL OUT A CARD."

Jimmy got up and went out. Mrs. Bewley smiled seraphically and sat quietly in her chair, looking vaguely around the room. Her gaze fell dreamily on something that was lying on Jimmy Flower's desk. Why, it was that Jesus-message with the pretty flower. Mrs. Bewley remembered it very well. She had known it was meant for her the first time she had seen it, there in that box in Mrs. Goss's bedroom. So she had tucked it in her apron pocket. But then (she was so generous) she had left it as a present for Mr. Goss in exchange for that sweet letter-opener on his desk. And then the next time she had dusted his room she had seen the message again, right there in his desk drawer, and she just hadn't been able to resist it. So pretty! (Mrs. Bewley loved flowers.)

Sergeant Shrubsole came in then and patiently filled out a file-card on Priscilla. He wrote down a description of her appearance and her habits, and at Mrs. Bewley's shrill insistence, a transcription of her very distinctive soprano cluck. Then Mrs. Bewley went home, where she found Priscilla roosting naughtily on the rubber plant. She shrieked with relief and proceeded to give Priscilla a severe screaming-to and a whole bowlful of crushed graham crackers. Then she took her in her lap and scratched Priscilla's pinfeathers affectionately. Naughty she was, Priscilla, but nice.

Back at the police station, Jimmy Flower was entertaining

Charley and Philip Goss. Released from captivity, Charley was as amiable as ever and he meant to show that he harbored no hard feelings. It was apparent that the brothers were enjoying one another's company. The revelation of the truth had freed them of a burden of mutual suspicion that had been heavier, even, than the fear of death. But Jimmy looked at them and wondered if things could ever be altogether the same. After all, Charley had jumped to take the blame, and Philip had not. But perhaps Philip's reluctance could be explained away—he must have known from his legal experience that lies on his part wouldn't help a guilty Charley, and that only a good trial lawyer could be of any use at all.

They were putting a good face on it, however it was. Charley had come to say goodby. He was on his way to school. "I've got a few credits to finish up and then (don't laugh) I'm going to take a crack at law school. I can't think why the legal profession should suddenly interest me so much. It's not as if I'd ever had any contact with it or anything."

"We're saving Charley a blank space on our shingle," said Philip. "Some day it will be Goss, Jarvis and Goss."

"Say, that's great," said Jimmy. "Oh, by the way, Charley, look here. That fingerprint expert, Mr. Campbell, has sent back that other letter you wrote. You know, the one Thoreau was supposed to have written to Emily Whatsername. I had it right here. I was just about to look over his report on it. You want the letter back? (Where in heck did I put it?)"

"For sentimental reasons? Good God, no. Which letter did you say it was?"

"You know, the one that turned up in Mrs. Bewley's trash collection. Or didn't you know about that? It's the one Thoreau was supposed to have written to Emily Dickinson. It was right here on this desk a minute ago."

"You must be wrong there. I never wrote one like that."

Charley and Philip said goodby, then, and Jimmy got down on his hands and knees and looked under the desk. The letter wasn't there either. Shaking his head, Jimmy got up again and unfolded Campbell's report. He read it to himself. "Well, I'll be damned. Hey, Shrubsole, come here. Look at this. Campbell says that last letter we sent him had a couple sets of old prints on it. They turned up when he tried this ninhydrin test. He thinks they're very old prints indeed. And the lab says it's old paper and old ink."

"Well, say, then, it must be real. A real letter from Henry Thoreau to that lady poet. Where is it?"

"That's just the trouble. I can't find it. It was right here on my desk. Of course there weren't any last names on it, it was just 'Emily' and 'Henry,' so who knows if it was really.... Still, holy horsecollar, the thing could be worth thousands of dollars. Come on, let's turn this place upside-down."

Together they stirred through the wastebasket and looked all over the office and then all over the building. Jimmy ransacked his drawers, scrabbled through the files, went through his pockets and bawled out three sergeants. But they couldn't find the precious letter anywhere.

Jimmy had a doleful conversation about it on the phone with the D.A. "How'll we tell Kelly?" he said. "He was awful interested in things like that."

"Look, Flower, take my advice. Don't tell him nothing. The first thing I learned at my blessed mother's knee was when to shut my trap. Say, I'm glad you called. Did you ever run across a loony kind of pervert out there in Concord, called himself Granville-Galsworthy? He turned up in the jail the other night here in Cambridge for attacking a schoolteacher. Turns out he's wanted all over the map from London to L.A. for crummy offenses like that. The scholarly type. Specializes in librarians and schoolteachers. His last stop must have been out in your territory. You had any complaints out there? I mean he's got four stranglings on his record, not to mention rape and——"

"Kee-rist, no kidding? No, thank the Lord, no complaints that I've heard of. But it's a mercy that Morgan girl is all in one piece though. He took a real shine to her. Say, that's something else Kelly better not hear about, or he'll tear us all limb from limb, himself included. He's sweet on Mary himself."

"Attaboy, Flower, you're learning fast. Plenty of times the

only thing to do is clam up. Keeps you out of all kinds of hot water."

The letter never did turn up. Its disappearance continued to bother Jimmy, and for weeks he kept poking absentmindedly around his office for it. After all, a thing like that must be worth thousands of dollars . . . It was a shame they couldn't find it and give it back to Mrs. Bewley, so she could get the cash. Of course, she had probably swiped it from Ernie in the first place, but what the heck, the Gosses didn't need the money. And there it had been, that letter, right in Mrs. Bewley's paper bag.

But Jimmy was wrong about Mrs. Bewley. She didn't need the money either. She had gone back to a primordial system of exchange that predated all forms of currency, a system that had been invented long before gold standards and stock markets and chancellors of the exchequer. Mrs. Bewley's system was as old as trade and barter. Swap or swipe. She could get along very well without cold hard cash.

—— *Was it all transcendentalism? Magic-lantern pictures on mist? As you will. Those, then, were just what we wanted.*
JAMES RUSSELL LOWELL